The
Legend

a Kate Tyler novel

The
Legend

a Kate Tyler novel

Nancy Wakeley

Light Messages
Torchflame Books

Durham, NC

Published 2022, by Torchflame Books
an Imprint of Light Messages
www.lightmessages.com
Durham, NC 27713 USA
SAN: 920-9298

Paperback 978-1-61153-461-0
E-book ISBN: 978-1-61153-462-7
Library of Congress Control Number: 2022902350
-

To my amazing grandsons
Brendon and Jacob.
Your music and words are beautiful
expressions of your souls!
Keep dreaming
Keep creating
Leap boldly into your futures.

With haunted fevers and passions
that invade our dreams
with doubts and disquiet,
the past grabs hold of the present,
desiring to set it on a new course.

1

The Calloway House and Gardens
East Stalton, England

KATE TYLER MOVED BETWEEN the purple stalks of betony and the blue spikes of clary sage, carefully choosing which bits of green to pull from the rich soil of the herb garden, and which to leave behind. She knew how to tell the difference now, after months of caring for her own gardens at Howard's Walk. Trial and error had taught her discernment, in gardens and in life—or so she thought. In the garden, she was sure of herself. Life was an entirely different matter.

Mr. McGregor, the head gardener at the Calloway House & Gardens—where Kate found herself that afternoon—had offered her gloves, but she had declined. It didn't matter that her fingernails were broken and knuckles scratched. It was good to have her hands working in the soil again, conjuring up scents of lemon, dill, and lavender as she brushed her hand over the leafy tops of the herbs.

A fragrant sigh skated over the flower beds on a soft breeze, and she turned her head in vague recognition of the aroma. But it was an elusive, distant memory, and evaded her grasp. She refocused on the task at hand as she moved along the row of herbs. The loose soil responded to her touch, settling back into itself like a breathing thing. There was a rhythm here in the garden and in the distant trill of birds, and Kate began to center her thoughts around why she had left her home at Howard's Walk so abruptly and fled to England almost two weeks before.

Fled was the right word, although it had seemed too dramatic at the time. Running away was how the old Kate handled difficult situations—not the new, more confident Kate that she had tried to become since moving to Howard's Walk. But a panic attack—the first she had experienced in over a year—had rocked her to her core. A frightening sense of suffocation had engulfed her at the time, and even now, the mere thought of it stopped her in her tracks.

Her life at Howard's Walk with Ben, her boyfriend, was everything she had thought she wanted—security, fulfillment, love, a sense of belonging. She still struggled with the reason for the attack. Maybe it was the magnitude of the work they had taken on by opening the public gardens at Howard's Walk that was worrying her. Maybe it was that her travel blog, *The Wayfarer*, had taken a back seat in her life, and the old feelings of wanderlust still tugged at her.

Before coming to Howard's Walk, she had never understood roots or how anyone could live their whole life in one place. But now, that was what she seemed destined to do. Was it the price she had to pay for the good life that she had found there?

So she fled to Rye, England, hastily booking her flight and hotel room, and throwing together an itinerary on the plane, consisting of the places she wanted to highlight in her blog.

Rye and the surrounding countryside were a tourist's paradise, filled with fascinating history and character—the perfect backdrop for enticing her readers to visit there. But it was also a place she remembered visiting as a young girl with her family when they had lived in London, a location she associated with a time of freedom and reveling in the fascination of new places—a place of good memories.

It had not been part of that itinerary to be on her knees in one of the most famous gardens in East Sussex. Nor did she expect to be involved in a mystery—one that had quickly become very personal to her. A book, a legend, and a young woman whose destiny, and the choices she was faced with three hundred years before, now seemed intertwined with Kate's decisions about her own future.

And there were the dreams. Like a retreating tide, the dreams she had been having were pulling her—to what, she could not have said at the time. Kate had never been one for finding meaning in dreams, and would not ordinarily be looking for significance in flocks of ravens, or in recurring symbols of the sun, moon, and stars. But those things were close now. The dreams that had started at Howard's Walk, had now physically manifested themselves here in England. Ravens flew too close for comfort, and she was seeing the cosmic symbols everywhere. Or so it seemed.

The truth was here somewhere. Somewhere in the Calloway Manor, Kate believed she would find the link to the past that would answer all of her questions.

2

I JUST HAD THAT DREAM AGAIN.

Kate texted the words, then quickly backspaced until they were gone.

She glanced at the time. Three o'clock in the morning. She couldn't seem to orient herself and laid back down on the pillow. A damp chill settled around her, and she pulled the comforter up close to her chin. She closed her eyes to recapture the dream before it slipped away.

The vision, as always, was in the dead of night. She was standing at the edge of a towering cliff, overlooking an expanse of water that stretched far out to a hazy horizon. At the bottom of the cliff, a roiling confusion of waves broke over black boulders on a thin strip of beach. The light of a pale moon sifted through the clouds as they raced across the sky.

In the distance, wild surf battered a large vessel, its sails taut against the wind, straining mightily against the mainmast. She watched from the height of the cliff as the ship rose and fell with the waves, but at the same time, she felt her own balance shift and correct itself as if she were standing on the wet boards of the deck, the salty sting of the surf slapping her face.

⁂

She blinked her eyes open. The room was now bathed in the dim glow of the moon, coloring the walls with formless, shifting shadows. The air felt heavy with a musty smell, somehow familiar, but she couldn't put a precise memory to it.

She turned her head toward the door at the sudden sounds of laughter in the hallway—the deep-throated guffawing of drunken men—distant but clear, followed by the thud of boots tramping on a hardwood floor. The life of a travel journalist had landed her in hotels, inns, hostels, motels, and even campgrounds, all around the world, and she could recite plenty of horror stories about the noises and smells she'd encountered. But what she was experiencing here was somehow different—real, yet ghostly. Physical, yet dreamlike.

Kate switched on the bedside lamp and sat up on the edge of the bed, pushing the clammy rumpled sheets away from her. She gathered her hair and twisted the long auburn curls into a loose braid to pull the dampness off her neck. The practiced movements calmed her and slowed her breathing.

She searched on the bed for a light sweatshirt, one that belonged to her boyfriend, Ben, but which she had claimed as her own. She pulled it on and crawled back under the covers, unable to shake the chill that had settled around her. Somehow the mingling of the sounds in the hallway, the smell in the room, and the vivid flashes of the sea cliff and the storm that battered the ship in her dream—it was all a tangible thing to her. Once again, the dream had fused imagination and reality, but this time in a peculiar and unsettling way.

Kate was beginning to hate the dreams. Not just because they wrecked her sleep, but because they made no sense. If there was a meaning to them, she couldn't grasp it, and they refused to reveal it to her. And now, they had followed her to Rye, England.

When the dreams started at Howard's Walk, her home in Eden Springs, North Carolina, she only saw the vague outline of the ship, tossing on the waves in a violent storm. Her vision of it was from a great distance, distorted as if looking through a rain-slashed window. It wasn't particularly frightening at first, but the memory of it was always vivid and powerful. Then, with each successive dream, the ship appeared to come closer to its destination. She was no longer viewing it from a distance. And soon, she became the person on the cliff, alone as she faced the hostile elements of salted wind and rain.

Kate closed her eyes, and as she lay there, a strange connection began to make itself clear. The musty odor in the room here at the Mermaid Inn had been undeniably present after each of her dreams at Howard's Walk. At the time, Ben had convinced her that it was because the bedroom she had chosen as her own had been closed up for so long. The rural estate and gardens that she had inherited the year before had been abandoned for almost fifteen years before she moved in, and she had agreed that it might be the reason. But now, the same sensation was happening here, in England, four thousand miles away.

Kate knew she hadn't needed to delete the text message to Ben. She knew he would have understood. But he also would have been concerned, and she didn't want him to worry.

Her trip to England had been hastily planned. The past year had been a good one, but she had never gone that long without traveling overseas. She was trying to feel settled at Howard's Walk, and had been for a while. She had been busy with the house renovations, replanting the gardens, and arranging publicity to advertise, *The Gardens at Howard's Walk*, while doing some local traveling for *The Wayfarer*. But she had started to feel restless, and, for her, that was not a good thing.

She had tried to tamp the feeling down, hoping it would go away, but it had persisted. So she bought her plane tickets to London, made reservations at the historic Mermaid Inn in Rye, and set off on a thirteen-day trip. But the suddenness of her decision had also left Ben responsible for quite a few loose ends at the estate. She rationalized that it was the one-year anniversary of her twin sister Becky's death, and she was missing her adoptive parents, who had passed away several years before. Rye, England, was a place of good memories from her childhood when the family had visited there together. And it would be a great introduction of international locations for her blog. Why shouldn't she choose to go there?

Ben had said, although not very convincingly, that he understood her reasons for the trip. But what terrified Kate was that she herself didn't understand why she wanted or needed to go. Her wanderlust had damaged a previous relationship. Although, the final nail in that coffin had been because her ex was a cheating slimeball.

She knew she was putting everything that was currently good in her life at risk. She knew this, but she had come to England, anyway.

Her eyes grew heavy. She pulled the soft comfort of Ben's sweatshirt around her and soon fell into a deep sleep.

3

THE PALE, DRIZZLE-SOAKED SUNLIGHT sifted through the latticed windowpanes of the Mrs. Betts room at The Mermaid Inn and nudged Kate awake. She opened her eyes and stretched. All she could see out of her window was a square of sky, gray and wet, and it only added to her uneasiness about the dreams the night before.

She unpacked and showered, finally dismissing the vague memories of ships and storms and high cliffs. She needed to start her day before Rye was thoroughly drenched.

Kate had arrived in Rye on the 6:07 p.m. train from London's St. Pancras station the evening before. Only when the train slid away from the hectic platform had she finally been able to relax after a frantic race from the airport to the train station.

Once settled in her seat on the train, soothed with the rhythmic sounds of engines and tracks and the murmur of fellow passengers, she caught glimpses of the River Thames. It was distended but tranquil, and the sight of it reminded her of a desire to someday travel the great river from its humble source near Thames Head, Gloucestershire, to its estuary, where it met and mingled with the salty waters of the North Sea.

But that was a journey for another day. She was in Rye for both business and pleasure, her itinerary planned out day by day. She had learned, from years of experience as a travel journalist, that having a well-thought-out strategy for any overseas trip helped get the job done quickly. It was particularly important for her on this trip to see as much as possible for her blog and still fit in a few special side trips.

Kate dressed in her usual travel clothes of leggings, T-shirt, and sneakers. She put her hair into a ponytail, pulled it through the back loop of her ball cap, and finally took in the features of the Mrs. Betts room.

The room was small, but she didn't plan on spending much time in it, so it suited her needs perfectly. The single brass bed was set on one wall next to a writing desk. An antique dressing table with an attached mirror and matching dresser were placed along another wall. The contemporary features in the room worked well, even in this ancient space, and Kate was amazed at how it was even possible to have preserved so much rich history in a building that was almost six hundred years old. The past had left its mark here, and the present held onto it tightly.

Gilbert, her porter, had explained when she arrived, that each room at the inn had a unique story. Kate's room was named for Mrs. Betty Betts, who had previously owned the cottage next door. The cottage, like many of the buildings in Rye, dated back to the sixteenth century. It was eventually bought and became part of The Mermaid Inn, an iconic landmark in England in its own right, dating back even further, to the fifteenth century.

Kate stepped up to the latticed window, and from her vantage point in the second-floor room, she could see far out over the moss-covered roofs of Rye, to the dull green fields in the distance. Thin blue clouds skimmed the horizon, only slightly masked by the morning fog and a light rain. But even rain could not stop her from her plans. She grabbed a light jacket, rearranged her packable tote to carry only what she needed for the day, along with her laptop and journal, and closed the door behind her.

Kate retraced her steps from the evening before, down a narrow hallway. Several small, elaborately framed paintings were spaced out along the cream-colored walls on either side of the hall. An occasional window let the gray morning light into the space. She was beginning to feel more in tune with the inn, the history seeping into wordscapes that were already forming in her mind.

She took a steep stairway down to the first floor, each tread squeaking in protest as she took in even more of the inn's beauty. Like many of the older establishments in Rye, and throughout England, the Mermaid Inn was as much a museum as it was a place of lodging. The mixture of medieval, Roman, and modern influence collided in a cacophony of furniture, art, and statues.

The main hall was as narrow as the one on the second floor, with low ceilings and walls of wattle and daub. Hefty wooden timbers, rough and blackened, bore the weight of the building, as they had since the inn was rebuilt in 1420.

"Good morning, Miss Tyler!" Gilbert called to her from the front desk of the inn.

"Gilbert!" She approached him. "I'm surprised to see you are still here. I hope you had a quiet night."

"Oh, I'll be off in a bit. But maybe I can help you with something before I go?"

"Yes, I'm looking for a place to have breakfast. Can you recommend a café or tea shop?"

"Of course." He selected a few brochures that included maps of Rye. "We have a continental breakfast and a full English breakfast here at the inn, of course. But if you are looking for something in town, these should help. I recommend the Cobbles Tea Room on Hylands Yard. Or the Mermaid Street Café over on The Strand. It's underneath the Old Borough Arms, just down the hill from here. You can't miss it. Perhaps you could explore Rye a bit before they open. Morning is a great time to walk about."

Kate agreed and tucked the brochures into her bag. Gilbert went ahead to the entrance. As he opened the door, a sheet of rain flew in at them, and he quickly closed it.

"On second thought, I don't think you will want to go out in this quite yet," he said. "Why don't you sit a while in the lounge until it clears up. We have coffee and tea there." He pointed her toward a sitting room to his left.

Kate thanked him and stepped into a room that held furniture of a slightly more modern style. High-backed banquette seating of red and brown leathers stretched along one wall, and a grouping of small tables and chairs, all antiques, filled out the rest of the room.

She poured herself a cup of coffee from an urn on the sideboard, and found a low table to sit at where she could watch the rain as it slapped against the latticed windows. A crackling fire had already been set in the grand fireplace at the far end of the room, and it burned brightly, warming the room enough to ward off the dampness of the English morning.

A few moments later, she heard a woman's voice.

"Hello, dear. Mind if we join you?"

Kate looked up to see a man and a woman approaching. They were middle-aged. Both dressed in rain gear and had a ruddy look about them. The woman's green eyes sparkled, and the mass of red curls framing her round face gave her an impish look. Kate invited them to sit with her, and introduced herself.

The woman smiled broadly. "Oh, Leonard, listen to that accent! She's from America!"

She set two steaming cups of tea on the small table before reaching her plump, warm hand out for Kate's, and shook it vigorously.

Leonard, a man who seemed to tower over everything else in the low-ceilinged room, including his companion, folded his newspaper in half and tucked it under his arm. He squinted at Kate, then shifted a pair of glasses from atop his head to his nose and nodded.

"Welcome to England, Miss Tyler."

"I'm Isabelle, and this is my husband, Leonard. We're the Crossthwaites." The woman dragged two heavy chairs closer to the table. "Lovely morning, eh?" She laughed. "We're from up north, near Newcastle. This is our first trip to Rye. I always said to Leonard, let's go down to Rye, but we never seemed to make it happen. So this year, we decided to chuck it all and come down. Let's see..." She began counting off on her fingers the places they had visited. "We've been to Brighton, London, Cornwall, Cliffs of Dover, of course, and some other places. But Rye always called to us, didn't it Leonard?"

He was sipping his tea but managed a grunt in response. He set his cup down, refolded his paper, pulled a pencil out of a pocket in his raincoat, and began to work a puzzle.

"Are you waiting out the rain, too, dear?" Isabelle said.

"Yes," Kate replied. "Do you think it will last long? I have several places I want to see today."

"I can't be sure, but we hope it will stop soon, too. We are going to the Calloway House and Gardens this morning. Have you been there?"

Kate shook her head. "But I would be interested in seeing it. Especially the gardens. Is it far from here?"

Isabelle explained that it would be a short trip, and that they had bought their tickets at the train station, for a bus that would take them there and bring them back.

Kate made a mental note that the gardens would be a good side trip to take outside of Rye. It was one of the few she hoped to fit into her itinerary, since the original owners of Howard's Walk had loved the gardens of England and had tried to reproduce them on their property after World War II. She wondered briefly if the Howards had ever visited the Calloway Gardens, and if there would be similarities in the styles of plantings.

After a few moments of conversation, a voice bellowed from across the room, chastising the Crossthwaites.

"Isabelle, Leonard, take off those coats before you overheat!"

A woman approached and sat on the edge of an empty chair next to Kate, adding her cup of tea and a Danish to the crowded assortment of breakfast items on the table.

The woman was dressed in a shapeless, no-frills blouse over a loose-fitting pair of pants that ended at mid-calf. She wore yellow sneakers, and a light rain jacket was tied around her waist by the sleeves. A braid of gray hair lay over one shoulder, and a rain hat hung by the ties down her back. Her outfit was clearly utilitarian, from head to toe, and Kate sensed that she was a kindred spirit.

She turned to Kate. "I'm Lillian Bingham, world traveler," she proclaimed brusquely, and shook Kate's hand in one firm motion.

Kate noticed that everything about the woman was efficient, from her quick step and sparse movements to the shoulder bag she carried with pockets for every item a well-organized traveler would need. Kate knew a thing or two about efficient packing and was impressed.

"Isabelle, did you hear me?" Lillian turned back to the Crossthwaites. "You are red in the face already with those coats, and you've both likely got sweaters on underneath, too. Am I right? Dressing in layers is fine, but you must think of the weight, dears, especially when you are tromping around the countryside. One or two light layers will be called for today."

"You have a point, Lillian. Leonard," Isabelle nudged her husband, "this rain might be a while. Let's take these off."

Leonard dutifully set down his paper and removed his raincoat, revealing a high-necked sweater. His wife removed hers in turn and hung it on the back of her chair.

"That's better, right, love?" Isabelle said. "Now, where were we? Oh, the Calloway House and Gardens. Lillian, we've got our tickets. You have yours yet? We are trying to convince Kate to go."

"Yes, I've got mine, but we might need a car to get down to the train station if this rain doesn't let up soon. The gardens might be wet today, but we'll have to make do since we already have our tickets. I'll ask at the desk." Lillian scurried off.

"Now she's a real-world traveler, Kate," Isabelle said, after Lillian was out of earshot. "Well, you heard her. Oh, the places she's seen. We just met her earlier this week, but we feel like we've known her forever. Right, Leonard?"

Another grunt emanated from her husband as he flipped his pencil and erased a word from the puzzle. Isabelle counted the countries off on her fingers.

"France, Germany, Spain, South Africa, America, and," she whispered, "even Viet Nam, if you can imagine that." She shook her head. "I wouldn't want to go there, would you, Leonard? But I think it would be lovely to go to France."

"No reason to leave England, if you ask me." Leonard did not look up from his paper.

"Well, maybe Lillian and I will just have to go by ourselves, then," Isabelle retorted.

Leonard lifted his head and looked at her with tired eyes. "A lovely idea, dear."

"I mean, it's not that far." Isabelle turned to Kate. "Have you been to France, Kate?"

"Yes, I've been there several times," she said, with a pang of nostalgia. "Paris is one of my favorite cities in the world. But I'll never forget the time I spent cruising the Seine a few years ago. It was an unforgettable trip."

A flood of images suddenly came to her, as vividly as if she were standing on the ship's deck, feeling the gentle movement of the river, carrying her back in time, past magnificent cathedrals, ancient chateaus, and the quaint villages that hugged the shoreline. Kate's love of the Seine and the places along its banks was so evident in the article she had written that she had won an award. She briefly wondered where the award was now.

She shook herself out of her thoughts and took a sip of her coffee.

"Well, you are a world traveler, too, then! Lillian," Isabelle said, as the woman returned and took her seat, "Kate was just telling us that she has traveled all over the world. Oh, I envy you both."

Lillian scrutinized Kate as if assessing her with this new information.

"Yes, I can see that," Lillian said. "Not the typical tourist type. I could tell that right off. What is it you do for a living, Kate?" She took a large bite of her Danish and flicked the crumbs off her lap. "Are you here for business or pleasure?"

"A little of both, really. I visited Rye years ago when my family lived in London and I'd like to revisit some of the places we went to. And I also have a travel blog called *The Wayfarer*, and I'm here to write for that."

"A writer, too!" Isabelle said. "Dear, you are a very impressive young woman, traveling by yourself, all the way from America. With your own blog, no less. Yes, very impressive."

"I'll google your website and write a few comments," Lillian said. "We might have been to some of the same cities, had the same experiences. I'm happy to share stories any time."

Kate thanked her and pulled out two business cards to give to the women. Then she leaned in close to the small group.

"Let me ask you," she whispered. "Is it true what they say about the ghost sightings here at the Mermaid Inn?"

Kate was familiar with the tales of ghosts in Rye, and especially there at the inn. She had no fears herself, but she was curious to see what her fellow travelers thought about the rumors of spirits and apparitions.

Isabelle glanced at her husband, nodded at him and whispered back, "Well, dear, my Leonard doesn't believe the stories, but I do. Mysterious things have been known to happen all around Rye, but especially here at the Inn." She took a sip of her tea, her hand shaking slightly as she set it back down on the table. "Smugglers, murderers, all types of scallywags—the dastardliest criminals you can imagine! They've walked right here in these very halls, even partied in the bar, they say! Of course, that was hundreds of years ago. But oh yes, I believe that there are ghosts here. Those kinds of spirits don't give up a place easily. I checked my door twice before turning in last night, I can tell you."

"Ghosts aren't concerned with doors, Isabelle," Leonard intoned, looking up from behind his paper. "As I mentioned last night."

"I agree, Leonard," Kate said. "But I'm with you, Isabelle. I checked my door a few times, too, just to make sure."

Kate caught herself. She was trying to make Isabelle feel more comfortable, but suddenly realized that telling her own experiences with sounds in the hall that night, and the musty smell in the room, only would have frightened Isabelle more.

"What about you, Lillian?" said Kate. "Do you believe in the ghost stories?"

"Well, I don't believe in such things myself, but I'm here to see what I can see. And if that means facing down a ghost or two, then let's carry on! That's what I say. I've even convinced Isabelle and Leonard to do a ghost tour this week. You should join us!"

Kate quickly thought through her itinerary, and since she had already planned for a ghost tour, she agreed. Seeing the rain had stopped, she finished her coffee and assured the three they would get together again soon. Then she zipped up her jacket and stepped out of the inn, onto Mermaid Street—two steps that took her back in time.

The symbol of the Mermaid Inn, a simple black wrought-iron frame with a gold mermaid in the center, jutted out from the entryway. Thick green vines clung to the front of the black and white timber-framed building, contrasting with bright-pink hydrangeas nearby.

A narrow cobblestoned street ran up the hill to her left and careened down a steep hill to her right, to what appeared to be the business section of Rye. Looking down the hill was a disorienting sight, as if the quaint homes along the street would tumble down the precipitous passageway if they weren't so tightly huddled together.

Kate leaned down and ran her hand over the wet cobblestones. The surface of the stones felt smooth, worn down through the centuries by horse-drawn carts, the hard-soled boots of men, and by time itself. The cobbles were widely set, the spaces between them filled with sand and clumps of moss. As the morning sun began to break through the clouds and illumine the ancient pathway after the rain, the stones unexpectedly colored from a dull gray to an iridescent jewel-like sheen, as if emeralds and diamonds and sapphires had been scattered in the street.

A truck rumbled toward her, and Kate quickly retreated to the flagstone walk. She opened a map and turned it to orient herself. It directed her down Mermaid Street until she reached The Mint, a main shopping area in Rye. At that hour of the morning, delivery trucks took up a good part of the narrow streets, and other than a few pedestrians, mail carriers and shopkeepers preparing to open, the scene was rather subdued.

After a passing glance in the windows of the clothing stores, antique shops, and boutiques lining The Mint, Kate noticed a narrow stone archway on her right that opened into a shadowed alley. She stopped at the entrance and peered in. The only illumination came from a scattering of bare light bulbs suspended from braces in the stonework overhead. As her eyes adjusted to the gloom, she saw that the alley widened slightly after a short distance.

The alley was paved in cobblestones smaller than the ones on Mermaid Street, and they were still wet from the earlier rain. Wondering if the moisture ever retreated from this spot, Kate tiptoed onto the slick stones and into the alley. Several shops were tucked away along one side of the passage. A faint light diffused into the space from one of the shop windows, and she walked toward it.

A wooden sign that simply said, BOOKS, extended out over the green doorway of the shop. Mullioned windows on either side of the door were covered with faded flyers from events long past, and book posters for novels that had been released years before. The sill on the indoor side of the window was piled with stacks of paperbacks and magazines. A sidewalk sign propped up against the building announced, BOOKS BOUGHT AND SOLD.

Kate stepped up to the window, framed her eyes with her hands, and peered in. There was little visibility to the interior, but the lights were on, which led her to think that the shop was open. Tall bookshelves lined the walls of a large room, and a set of shorter shelves occupied the center. Boxes of books stacked one on top of the other were pushed into the corners, and with all of the disarray Kate thought it looked like the store was under renovation, or perhaps just not opened for business yet.

Suddenly, the door opened, setting off a shopkeeper's bell which tinkled in greeting.

A small man stood just inside the doorway, one hand on the door handle, and the other grasping the top of a simple wooden cane. He was thin and seemed frail and spent from life, his skin wafer-thin and streaked with bluish veins. A shock of long white hair swept back from his forehead, settling down on the worn collar of a dingy white shirt. Plaid suspenders held up pants that seemed too large for him, and as Kate looked down, she noticed he had only a pair of stained and tattered slippers on his feet.

The old man adjusted a pair of wireframed glasses that were set far down on his nose and leaned toward Kate as if to get a better look. A wide smile erupted on his face—a look of recognition spreading from ear to ear.

"My dear, come in, come in!" He opened the door wider and motioned her into the poorly lit room. "It is so good to see you. Are you well?"

Kate was puzzled with the elderly shopkeeper's greeting but intrigued enough to see where this chance meeting would lead.

"I'm well, thank you," she replied. "And how are you?"

"Oh, I'm very well," he said. "I must say, I wasn't expecting you this early, you know. I've been up for hours, though. Lots to do here in the shop, of course."

Kate again felt he might have confused her with someone else. Or maybe he was just referring to customers in general.

"I wasn't sure if you were open yet," she said. "There were no hours posted on the door."

"We are open whenever we want, you see."

He selected a book from a precarious stack by the door and peered over his glasses at its spine as he shuffled away. He turned back and motioned for Kate to follow.

"That is the beauty of being the proprietor of one's own little bookshop, don't you think? We are, as the sign says, BOOKS!"

He gleefully, but carefully stepped around more boxes on the floor, and a few randomly placed tables and chairs.

"Now what can I do for you today?" He set the book down on a dusty shelf.

Kate followed him to an old wood and glass display counter at the back of the shop. More books and an antique cash register sat on one end of the counter, and the rest was covered with rolls of brown wrapping paper and cartons of books in various stages of being unboxed.

"Do you have any books about Rye?" she replied. "I'm looking for something about its history and folklore."

"A book about Rye, you say? I think I might have just the thing."

He stepped behind the counter, opened the top of one of the boxes, fumbled around a bit, all the while mumbling to himself, and pulled out a book bound in rich brown leather. He leaned his cane against the cabinet and caressed the cover. It was embossed with the title of the book and what appeared to be a family crest. He then laid it on the counter, facing Kate.

"This is what you were looking for, of course?" he said. "It was written by Sir Archibald Mallard and published in 1904. Oh, he was a fine historian. One of the best, in my humble estimation. This particular book is the fascinating history of the tales and legends of Rye in the seventeenth and eighteenth centuries. You are familiar with the name, surely?"

Kate shook her head.

"Well, no matter. It is a thorough treatise on the subject." He chuckled, a wheezy attempt at laughter that soon turned into a light cough.

He pulled a threadbare handkerchief from a deep pocket in his pants and dabbed at the corners of his mouth, then returned it to his pocket.

He handed the book to Kate. "Here, my dear. You will find it very interesting. Just what you were looking for."

Kate flipped through the first few pages of the book and decided he was right.

"How much is it?"

"A mere twenty pounds, my dear."

As Kate pulled out her wallet, she noticed the man had laid his hand on his chest.

"Are you all right, sir?"

A look of confusion had spread across his face.

It seemed to clear after a few moments, and he said, "Of course. But I'm afraid I am just a bit done in." He shuffled from behind the counter, then turned and looked back at her with a puzzled expression. "Do stop by again."

With that, he stepped through a curtained doorway at the back of the shop. Kate caught a glimpse behind the curtain of what appeared to be a storeroom and a set of stairs going up to another floor. The old man disappeared from her view after the second step, and she soon heard a door close.

Kate looked around the empty shop.

"Hello?" she called out, but there was no answer.

She turned the book over and then checked inside the front cover, but did not see a price visible anywhere, and decided to take him at his word. The book seemed much more valuable than that, but she pulled twenty pounds out of her wallet and left the bills on the counter.

She tucked the book in her bag and left the bookstore. Her first morning in Rye had taken a very interesting turn already, and she decided it might be worth her time to return to BOOKS to interview the man and highlight his story in her blog. She loved writing about unique people and out-of-the way places on her travels, and thought that after meeting Lillian, the Crossthwaites, and now this strange little bookshop owner, she would have a great start for *The Wayfarer,* and perhaps be able to put her worries behind her

4

KATE MADE HER WAY out of the dark alley to the street. She backtracked on The Mint, passing a framing shop, The Standard Inn, and several charming boutiques. The Mermaid Street Café was just opening when she arrived a few minutes later, and she joined the line at the counter to place her order.

The café was cozy and cheerful, the sounds of the morning floating in from the street as the door opened and closed. The smell of freshly baked pastries and brewed coffee filled the air. Friendly banter between customers and staff in accents of all nationalities reminded her that Rye was a tourist town with visitors from all over the world. She let the rhythmic sounds settle on her brain.

Kate ordered the avocado toast with roasted mushrooms and an Americano, then made her way up a narrow staircase to the rooftop terrace of the café. The morning sun was beginning to burn through the mist and gloom from earlier, and it looked like the day would be clear after all.

Kate found a seat at a small blue wrought-iron table with a view out over the rooftops along The Strand, and a glimpse of the River Brede. The waterway soon joined with the larger River Rother, and together, according to her map, the mingling waters eventually emptied into the English Channel.

A breeze carried the smell of the river to her rooftop perch. But it was not unpleasant and brought with it images of brightly painted fishing boats unloading their catches at the quayside. This was the livelihood of generations of fishermen in Rye and the nearby Rye Harbour at the mouth of the River Rother.

As she waited for her breakfast, Kate dug into her tote and pulled out the book the old man had recommended. The leather cover was in surprisingly good condition for a book over a century old, with only a bit of wear and tear along the edges. The spine was designed with several parallel ridges running from top to bottom. She ran her hand lightly over the embossed coat of arms on the front of the book, as she had seen the old man in the bookshop do, and then carefully lifted the cover.

Inside, there was an illustration of the streets of 1800 London on the frontispiece. A tissue-thin paper, partially loosened from the binding, separated it from the title page, which read:

ANCIENT TALES OF AN ANCIENT TOWN
BY SIR ARCHIBALD MALLARD
A HISTORY OF THE LEGENDS OF RYE,
EAST SUSSEX, ENGLAND 1600–1800

Just as the old man described, she thought. But she saw something on the page that surprised her. The book was a first edition, signed by the author, Sir Archibald Mallard. And she had only paid twenty pounds for it, probably a fraction of what it was worth. She decided that, in all good conscience, she could not keep the book and would return it when she went back to interview the shopkeeper.

Kate flipped through the first few pages and noted that the book was organized into various tales. She wondered if the stories were as accurate as the old shopkeeper claimed, or—more likely—if they were legends and unverified anecdotes.

Out of curiosity, she googled the title of the book on her phone. The name appeared on the screen, but she set the phone and book aside when the server arrived with her breakfast.

She finished eating and took pictures of the quaint view from the rooftop, and then of the front of the café at street level.

She made some notes and sketches in her journal, and then headed east, across town to her second stop of the morning, the Rye Castle Museum.

Kate first followed The Mint, then High Street, and soon turned right on East Street. The sounds of traffic and the aromas from the cafés filled her senses. She had started out that morning, eagerly anticipating her first real look at Rye on this trip, but soon the short walk became a déjà vu experience. It was as if she had been transported back in time, and was once again sightseeing with her mother, father, and sister. She and Becky had skipped on ahead of their parents on this very street, and she heard their voices in her mind, chastising them for almost getting lost in the crowd. Kate closed her eyes and savored the memories.

This was the feeling she longed for, recalling that wondrous time and place from her youth—a time of innocence and goodness, of curiosity and adventure. The time in her life which had cast a spell on her, sealing her future as a wanderer, inquisitive and unencumbered.

But the memories of her family were like a pendulum, one swing bringing a smile, and the next bringing a tear. Maybe it wasn't just our hearts that held memories, she thought, but the streets themselves in all of those places that people go. And maybe the ancient buildings in Rye carried the remembrances and dreams of every person that had passed by them throughout the centuries, wafting like a mist into the walls, to be held there for times like this.

Kate was suddenly overcome with a sadness she had not felt for almost a year. She had lost everyone dear to her, and it was only through sheer determination and unwavering support from friends that she had dragged herself back to a life that had a semblance of normalcy.

The season of renovations to the house and gardens at Howard's Walk had been a time of healing. Ben's love had sustained her and made her whole again. It should have been enough, and she missed Ben terribly. But as she stood there on East Street in Rye, she knew that the lure of her old life, the sense of wanderlust she had, even as a young girl, had recently been pulling on her like quicksand. And she had, perhaps too easily, given into the temptation.

The life that she had left back in Eden Springs should have been enough. But now, she wondered if that were true.

Kate arrived at the museum and made her way through rooms filled with displays from ancient Rye and the surrounding area. But her own memories overshadowed the carefully curated exhibits, and she soon left the building. A group of tourists had been directed to Rye Castle, just a few blocks away, and she joined them. But as they reached Church Square, Kate suddenly felt pulled by a long-ago memory onto West Street. She left the group and followed the narrow cobblestone street until its curve drew her to the front of the Lamb House.

The brick exterior of the two-story house was the color of rust, made even darker by the morning rain. A simple sign beside the front door announced that it was THE LAMB HOUSE, HOME OF HENRY JAMES. The house was well-known for being the writer's home, where he had written three of his novels, from 1898 until his death in 1916.

Kate took the three steps up to the front door and stepped inside. The entryway and adjacent rooms were set up with displays from the era when James lived there, but it was a clear memory of the famed walled garden of the Lamb House—one of the largest gardens in the old town of Rye—that was tugging at her.

She walked through the house to a door at the back and stepped out into a lush expanse of lawn with red hibiscus, yellow roses, and crimson canterbury bells edging the bright-green grass like iced flowers on a cake. A grassy path led Kate to a gurgling fountain, and just past it, a wrought-iron bench tempted her to sit. Masses of pale-pink roses cascaded over the top of the brick wall behind it, their sweet aroma permeating the air. She sat alone, simply taking in the serenity and beauty of the space.

She glanced through the brochure for the house that she had picked up at the entrance, and flipped to the back of it, where earlier she had seen a quote from James.

It's time to start living the life you've imagined.

Maybe that was what drew her to this house, and to this spot in the Lamb House gardens. Was she living the life she had imagined she would? Or was she running away...again?

Kate took out her journal and began to write.

What does it mean to live the life we were meant to live? Or imagined? How do we know? Why are some people so sure of their destiny and the path they must take to fulfill it, while others struggle as if chained to their past, or to an unrealistic sense of self, or the perceptions of others? Are the glimpses of their futures the same, but one person believes in their destiny and dreams, while the other person does not? Does one person's future lie out before them like a bright path, while the other only sees a wall of no's and should nots and cannots?

A bright path can grow dim. It can fade with the things that come to us in the night. But the wall blocking our futures can also be broken down, brick by brick, until a body can fit through to the other side, a side filled with yes's. Fate can propel people forward into their futures as surely as it can turn them away.

Fate. Looking back at her life, she saw fate had wielded a considerable influence. Coincidences had brought her to places she had not expected to go, and had put people in her life that she never expected to have encountered. She had discovered heirlooms from the past in the abandoned rooms at Howard's Walk that had prompted her to take steps she would never have taken otherwise. Fate had moved her forward when she needed to be moved. But she felt, somehow, that her trip to Rye, while it was of her own doing and her own desire, was no longer completely within her control.

Maybe fate was having its way again, and she would simply have to see where it led.

5

THE DRONE OF A BEE, the trill and warble of the birds, and the low hum of traffic beyond the garden wall made up Kate's playlist for the rest of the afternoon. Other visitors to the Lamb House strolled past as if in slow motion, as she contemplated the surroundings and wrote down her thoughts.

A docent from the house approached and reminded Kate that the house and gardens would be closing soon. With only a protein bar for her lunch, Kate was more than ready to find a place to eat, and leave her musings and memories behind her in the Lamb House gardens.

She searched on her phone for a nearby restaurant and found The Smuggler's Inn & Pub on the Rye Strand Quay, overlooking the River Brede. It appeared promising and was just a short walk down the hill from the Mermaid Inn.

Kate was seated in a booth shortly after arriving at the pub, and ordered a local amber IPA.

"What can we get for you tonight luv?" the server asked, when she returned with Kate's drink.

She was dressed in what looked like a period barmaid dress from the 1700s. Kate doubted that it would have been her dress of choice since it seemed to clash with her spiked pink and blonde hair and tattooed arms.

"I'll tell you a secret, Callie," Kate said, after glancing at the woman's nametag. "I'm here to write for my travel blog, *The Wayfarer*. What would you suggest? Any specialties?"

"Well, not to brag too much about it, but we've got the best fish and chips in the country, and that's no lie. People come from all around the world, just like you, to eat our fish and chips. Our pork pies are world famous, too."

Kate hesitated for a moment.

"Well, I haven't got all night, luv. Fish and chips it is, then." The waitress made a note on her pad, then looked at Kate with skepticism. "That comes with mushy peas, you know."

"I was hoping it would," Kate replied, knowing that the side dish was a traditional accompaniment to the meal in England.

"Fish and chips and mushy peas, then, luv."

The atmosphere of the pub was cozy, with dark wood, low ceilings, and a checkerboard pattern on the floor—what Kate thought of as a quintessential English pub. But soon, the atmosphere began to change. Men and women, young and old, in all styles of dress from the 1700s, and probably centuries earlier and later, were coming through the doors, crowding past Kate's booth to get to the bar.

Her server soon returned and set down a steaming plate of freshly battered cod, fried to a perfect golden crisp, with an enormous pile of chips and the side of mushy peas.

"Callie, everyone seems to be in costume here," Kate said. "Is there a party tonight?"

"Tonight, is the Rye Gang of Sussex Night. It's all in fun. Everybody gets to dress up, including me."

Kate took an obligatory picture of her meal for the blog, then speared her fork into the crispy coating of the fish and broke away a generous piece. The chips were hot and perfectly salted, and she had to agree with the server that this was the best fish and chips she had ever eaten.

Kate was finishing her meal when she noticed a man who had taken a seat at the bar. He was in his thirties, dressed in a black trench coat over black jeans and a dark gray vest. A loosely tied white cravat peeked out from the neck of the vest, perhaps, Kate thought, a nod to the Regency era.

A diamond stud glinted through a tousled mass of jet-black hair. But it wasn't the clothes he wore that set him apart from others in the room, although, that was decidedly a factor. Kate surreptitiously studied his profile. Chiseled jaw... no, too heroic. But there was a fearless strength in his features, although she could not define exactly how it revealed itself. Self-confidence...yes. And it was the good kind, she thought. The dependable kind that could handle any circumstance. Good cheekbones...yes, definitely.

He smiled, then, at something a man sitting next to him said. But it was subtle, the corner of his mouth turning up only slightly. That small movement was all that was needed.

He shifted to lean on the bar and Kate noticed, head to toe, that he not only looked the part of a swashbuckler from days gone by, but he could have stolen the heart of every woman in the room. Many of them were already staring at him over their drinks.

Kate looked away as his eyes, intense sapphire blue, and roving, suddenly landed on her. A few seconds passed, and she chanced a look back at him. He was still staring, and then he raised his glass and nodded at her. She nodded back, trying to contain a smile.

As Kate waited for Callie to return with her check and credit card, the man approached her booth and slid into the seat across from her.

"Do you mind if I sit here for a minute? The bar is getting crowded."

Kate thought the line was not very original, but somehow, he had managed to deliver it very nicely. And it was not the first time on her travels that she had been approached by men wanting to strike up a conversation. But the party-like feel of the place and the costumed crowd was intriguing enough that she wanted to learn more, and this swashbuckler might be a good place to start.

"Sure," Kate replied.

"Miles Pixley, at your service." He extended his hand.

As she began to reach for it, Callie returned with her credit card. Kate withdrew her hand, added a tip to the check, and signed it. The man leaned against the back of the booth.

"I take it you are here for the festivities tonight?" Kate said.

He smiled again, that subtle crooked turn of his mouth.

"Just a distraction, really. Some friends, who are notorious for not showing up when and where they say they will, invited me. We'll see." He took a sip of his beer. "I didn't catch your name."

"Kate Tyler."

"You're American?"

"Yes. North Carolina."

"I thought I detected an accent. Well, Kate Tyler, are you enjoying your stay here in our ancient town?"

"I am. I'm actually here to write for my travel blog, *The Wayfarer*."

"Ah, a travel writer, then? We have our share come through Rye. Are you interested in anything in particular?"

"I think it would be great to hear more about the event here tonight."

Miles laughed out loud this time. "Oh, this? Just locals having some fun. There's nothing special about it, really. You might be familiar with the bonfire societies, though?"

Kate nodded. "I've heard of them. But the bonfires are an annual event, right?"

"Yes, they are. Many towns around here have bonfire societies with their own celebrations starting in September. The last one takes place in Hawkhurst in late November." He took a taste of his beer. "This group here, though—some belong to the societies, and some don't. But they miss the camaraderie of the official Rye Bonfire Pageant, so they get together here once a month to dress up and have some fun. They call themselves the Rye Gang of Sussex."

"And you are part of this gang, I take it?" Kate said, becoming more relaxed as they talked.

"Not really. An occasional observer, I guess you could say."

"How did the real societies get started?"

Miles finished his beer and motioned for another one as Callie walked by. When he asked Kate if she wanted another, she declined.

"Early morning," she said.

"I understand. Well, there used to be bonfires and fireworks in the area years ago, but they were stopped in the seventies. Then in 2012, a man from Hawkhurst decided they should start them up again. Are you familiar with the Hawkhurst Gang?"

"Yes. It came up in some research I've done. But what else can you tell me about it, as a local, other than what I find online. You are a local, right?"

"I guess you could call me that. I think I should mention that the societies are also very charitable in their fundraising for various causes. Completely opposite from the nefarious Hawkhurst Gang of smugglers, robbers, and murderers in the 1700s, who took and never gave back. Our society in Rye is called the Rye and District Bonfire Society, and we are very proud of it. You should see the bonfire we do here. I'm hoping to take my son, Josh, to his first pageant this fall, if I can convince my ex that it will be safe for him. Which it will be, of course," he added, at Kate's doubtful reaction.

She could not resist the temptation to glance at his left hand—an afterthought since he mentioned his wife as his *ex*. There was no ring, and she refocused on what he was saying.

"She was never a fan of the pageants. Now, in the past, they were known to burn boats as part of the bonfires."

Kate looked skeptical. "Why did they burn boats?"

"It's a tradition from medieval times, when Rye was always being attacked by the French," Miles said. "The folks in Rye would burn their boats so that they wouldn't fall into the hands of the enemy. But now they just take a stack of pallets and set it on fire. Quite the honor for the person chosen to set it aflame."

"What are you setting aflame now?" A man approached the booth and slapped Miles on the shoulder. "You know that's against the law, except for those who know what they're doing, eh?"

He laughed and sat down next to Miles, shoving him into the corner of the booth. He was heavily bearded and brawnier than Miles, with muscles that stretched his tattered white shirt. An eye patch, a tricorn hat, and red scarf finished his costume.

"Well, well, now," he said. "I must say, mate, things are looking up for you! But," he glanced at Kate with a wink, "for a man as dashing as our friend Miles here, well, I guess anything could happen."

He reached down to his side and hefted up a wooden sword and laid it across the table between the glasses of beer and dishes.

"Miss, I am disarmed by your presence. Allow me to introduce myself. Sir Lochland McFarland Warlock is what they call me." He tipped his hat, grinning widely.

Miles rolled his eyes. "Don't believe a word he says, Kate. His name is Jeffrey Dunst."

Kate laughed. "I am pleased to meet you, Mister Warlock. I'm Kate Tyler."

A shocked look came over his face. "Oh, no, no, no! The name does not do you justice, miss. You deserve a name like...

like..." he snapped his fingers, "Eleanora...Godiva...Warlock. If only you would do me the honor of becoming my wife."

At that, Miles attempted to push him out of the booth.

"Enough of that, Jeffrey." He laughed. "You'll scare her off, and we've barely met."

Jeffrey put up his hands in surrender. "Suit yourself. But a lady's got to know there are choices, even in the small town of Rye. Am I right?"

"But there are the right choices and the wrong choices," Miles said. "We were just having a nice conversation here."

"Well, no more of that." Jeffrey waved at a group of people at the bar. "Our new friend, Eleanora, needs to meet the rest of the gang."

He waved again, vigorously, and his friends, all in pirate attire, grabbed their drinks and walked over to them. Jeffrey did the introductions while Miles sat shaking his head in the corner of the booth. Two women slid into the booth next to Kate, and the men pulled up chairs.

Kate agreed to another beer when they insisted on buying her one, and as soon as it was in front of her, they joined into a bawdy tune that the band was playing.

"So tell me, Kate," Jeffrey said, when the song was over. "Have you ever met a pirate before?"

Kate thought for a moment, enjoying the banter.

"Well, Mister Warlock, no. But I know quite a bit about Edward Teach. Maybe you are related?"

They all laughed, and Jeffrey jabbed Miles in the arm.

"I like her, Miles!" He turned his attention back to Kate and ran a hand over his beard. "Well, no. Not related, but I see how you could mistake me for Blackbeard. You see, we pirates have a certain mystique. And it seems that the ladies just can't resist us."

The woman sitting next to Kate laughed. "Right, Jeffrey. And when you aren't in your pirate get-up, you wear a suit and tie like every other insurance salesman in Rye."

Jeffrey looked hurt. "At least you can't say I didn't try."

Kate glanced at Miles as the friendly conversation continued. He smiled at her and shrugged.

By eleven o'clock, Miles's friends had moved on to another part of the pub, leaving Jeffrey in deep conversation with Kate about life in North Carolina. Miles caught Jeffrey's eye and tapped his watch.

"Oh, well, guess that's my cue to move on, then. Am I right Miles?" He tipped his hat to Kate. "Miss Tyler, it's been a pleasure. I hope you enjoy your stay here in Rye. And Miles, say happy birthday to Joshy, won't you?"

"Thanks, Jeffrey. I'll be sure to do that," Miles replied.

Kate looked at her watch and slid to the edge of the booth to leave as well.

"Going so soon?" Miles said. "Things are just getting started here."

"As much as I have enjoyed this, I do need to go." She smiled. "I have to do my job now and write about my day."

She almost felt sorry for him. The disappointed look on his face told her that he might have been hoping for more than just conversation that evening. But that was not what she had in mind at all.

As she got up from the booth, Miles also stood. He was tall and fit, his broad shoulders filling out the military trench coat.

"May I walk you out, then?"

"No need, but thank you. Good night, Miles. It was nice meeting you and your friends. I honestly haven't had this much fun in a long time."

"Speak kindly of us in your blog, then, Kate. Good night." Miles gave her a deep bow.

≼◊≽

Kate was relieved when he didn't insist on walking out with her. She didn't need an awkward situation at that hour.

She left the pub and hurried across The Strand and up Mermaid Street, blending in with the late-night crowds of tourists and pub-goers, and finding it difficult to get the image of Miles Pixley out of her mind. But the evening had also reminded her that Ben was an ocean away, and she had promised to call him as often as she could.

She fumbled for her phone. It was much earlier in the day at Howard's Walk, and she dialed Ben's number.

"Hey, Kate!"

"Hi, Ben." She passed another pub and skirted out into the street to avoid the outdoor tables.

"Sounds like a party there. Are you getting a taste of the night life?"

"Actually, I'm on my way back to the inn. I just had supper at a pub. There was a party going on there, and I met some great people. I'll tell you all about it when I get back. The streets are packed this time of night, so that's what you are hearing. How is everything there?"

"Good. Some new shrubs came in today, so I'll get Billy to help me plant them tomorrow."

"That's good. Listen, Ben..."

"Yes, Kate?"

Kate wasn't sure where to begin. As much fun as the evening had been, Ben had been on her mind since earlier that day.

"I know I left in kind of a hurry. I'm sorry about that."

"That's okay," he replied, after a moment. "But I'm worried about you. That panic attack was scary. Are you sure you're okay over there?"

As always, Ben was trying to be understanding. But what he didn't understand—mostly because she couldn't explain it to herself, even—was the reason she had left like she did. She was still sorting it out. But simply hearing his voice and sharing a bit of her evening with him helped to alleviate her fears about what might be happening with their relationship.

She reached the Inn and stepped into the lounge to take a seat by the fire.

"I'm fine, really," she replied. "I miss you."

She could hear the smile in his voice.

"I miss you, too."

She heard the screen door at Howard's Walk slam in the background, and she realized it wasn't only Ben she missed. There was a rhythm to their days and nights that she was missing, too. She had experienced a year of the seasons there, of clearing land and planting in the spring, a hot dry summer and a late-October hurricane. And they had weathered it all together. All the doubts, all the hesitation and worries—she had to believe it would all work itself out.

"Ben, don't worry about me. I'm fine. It's beautiful here in Rye, and I've got lots of ideas for the blog. I'd better get to bed, though. Tomorrow's an early day, and I've got some writing to do tonight still. I love you."

"Love you, too, Kate. Have a good night."

She ended the call and took the steps up to her room.

6

THE ALARM ON KATE'S CELL PHONE BUZZED at six o'clock the next morning, muffled but persistent, until she fumbled to find it and turn it off. She had used her phone as a bookmark in Ancient Tales of an Ancient Town, right where she had stopped reading the night before, at the true story of the Hawkhurst Gang.

The gang, as her friends at the pub had briefly discussed the evening before, was a notorious group of smugglers in the area, from 1735 to 1749, and had often been found carousing right there in the Mermaid Inn. She had learned that there was even a secret tunnel between the inn and the nearby Olde Bell, which they had used for their illegal activities. The gang's existence was very real, and the legends surrounding them had become ingrained in the very fabric of Rye.

Kate reached for her journal on the bedside table and jotted a few notes about smugglers, as a reminder to ask at the front desk about their involvement with the Mermaid Inn. She propped herself up against the pillows to read the next chapter, about Rye Castle and its history as a prison, from the sixteenth to the nineteenth centuries. Sir Mallard told the legend of prisoners who had escaped their fates, some say, by creating sleeping tonics from herbs growing in the prison garden, and giving them to the guards, mixed in with tea.

Kate finished the tale, turned the page, and was stunned when she saw the next etching.

She was looking at an image of herself.

The woman in the etching was younger than Kate, possibly in her teens. But the features—the long wavy hair, the high cheekbones, piercing eyes, and determined chin—were Kate's. The precision in the lines of her dress, the details of a ribboned bonnet she held loosely down at her side, and the impression of a strong wind blowing off the ocean were perfect to the last detail. The young woman stood on a cliff. The artist captured wild clouds on the distant horizon, and monstrous waves breaking against a tall, masted ship. Not only was the likeness of this young woman astonishing it its detail, but the artist had also perfectly portrayed the turbulence of Kate's own recurring dreams of a sailing ship battling a terrible storm.

Kate slammed the book shut and threw it down on the bed. She pulled the comforter close around herself. The random way that the book had fallen into her hands, from a chance meeting with a strange little old man in a bookstore who seemed to know her, was mystifying by itself. But now? Was the book somehow meant to be in her hands for her to see this etching, to read this story?

She reached for the book, took a deep breath, and leafed through the pages to find the etching again. It was a coincidence, of course. It had to be. But the determined, fearless look in the young woman's eyes was riveting. She was, at once, rebellious and defiant, but filled with heavy sorrow and resignation. It was as if she were staring directly at Kate, challenging her.

Finally, Kate tore her eyes away from the image. She turned the page and began to read *The Legend of Arabella*. The brief but tragic story was about Arabella Courbain, the daughter of William Courbain, a notorious sea smuggler who, some said, was even more treacherous than Jeremiah Curtis and James Stanford of the Hawkhurst Gang. In 1766, at the age of sixteen, Arabella was promised in marriage to John Rogers, an acquaintance of her father. It was believed that she was promised as the settlement of a debt. Rogers was older than even her father, and just as dangerous. It was agreed that after the two men returned from sea, Arabella would be wed.

Arabella had been raised by an aunt. Her mother had died in childbirth, and her father was non-existent as a caretaker. The aunt was devoted to her, and had raised her as a loving and kind girl. The announcement of Arabella's impending marriage was devastating to them both, but they knew that to defy it would have terrible consequences. And as fate would have it, Arabella was already in love with someone else—a handsome young man from a wealthy family nearby. Soon after her father left on his voyage, she became pregnant with the young man's child.

The young man went to London to make a way for his family, and promised to return so that they could be married. But tragedy followed him, and he perished in a fire. Word of his death came to Arabella, and she fell into despondency, her heart shattered by the loss. Her only happiness was that she was carrying his child. The months passed, and with no knowledge of when her father would return from sea, Arabella became increasingly frightened for the safety of herself and her unborn baby.

Arabella gave birth to a son. She begged the aunt to take him far away and raise him, as she had done for her. Arabella would marry, as pledged by her father, and pray that someday she would be with her son again. But as time passed without the comfort of her aunt and her son, and with the loss of her lover, she could not bear the life that had been decided for her.

Sir Mallard finished the heart-wrenching tale with the young woman's fate. One moonless night, with only ravens as winged witnesses, Arabella stood on the edge of the high cliffs overlooking the ocean, stepped off into the jagged rocks and wild surf below, never to be seen again.

Sir Mallard ended by saying that, "The legend was that Arabella would return one day to finally live the life she was meant to live."

Kate turned the page back to the etching of Arabella. It was as if this daring, defiant young woman was challenging her. *There is more to this tale,* her look said. *Help me.*

Kate was entranced by Arabella's story, a legend that had been passed down through the centuries. But she was struck even more by the twin image of the young woman and herself, in the etching and the striking similarity with her dreams of a storm-tossed ship in a raging ocean.

She set the book aside. Maybe it was just a coincidence, but she could not deny her curiosity about the tale she had just read. Was it true? Or was it simply a legend?

Kate felt a pull toward Sir Mallard's account and the images of Arabella Courbain as if the young woman had taken her hand and said, "Walk with me along these cliffs, and let me tell you my story." She wanted to investigate the legend further, but it would pull her too far away from her plans for this trip.

She decided to put it out of her mind and focus on the day ahead, which was to return the book to the bookstore and to visit the Calloway House & Gardens in nearby East Stalton. After hearing the Crossthwaites mention it, Kate was eager to see the famous gardens and compare them to those at Howard's Walk, and she had adjusted her itinerary to make the side trip.

She called the front desk and asked about the details of getting to the Calloway House & Gardens. They confirmed that tickets could be purchased at the train station, and that it was only a short bus ride through the countryside from Rye. She checked her map of Rye and found that Opal's Tea Shop was not far, and she was soon stepping out, once again, onto Mermaid Street.

A few minutes later, Kate walked up the brick steps to the front door of the tea shop. It was a small place, tucked in between an antique store and a greengrocer. A paper menu was taped to the front window on the inside, and she took a moment to look it over, then stepped in.

Several small, mismatched tables and chairs were lined up against one wall, each with seating for two. Kate noticed that the entire shop seemed to be a mismatch of styles—not in a planned eclectic way, but in a jumble of tastes. There was no host that she could see, or a designated spot to order, so she waited near the door to be seated.

Just then, a young woman came through a set of swinging doors at the back of the shop, balancing a tray of teacups and small plates of food. Kate tried to catch her eye, and when she did, the tray of cups and plates crashed to the floor.

Kate started forward to help her, but the young woman held up her hand as if to say, *Stay back*, and had a strangely fearful look on her face. Kate obliged and stayed where she was.

An older woman rushed out from the kitchen. Her gaze instantly locked onto Kate's, and she grabbed the edge of the counter as if to steady herself, her red lip-sticked mouth an *oh* of surprise. A moment later, and more composed, the woman looked down and noted the broken dishes on the floor.

"Tonya, go get something to clean this up," she said to the server.

Then she turned to the other patrons, who were looking on from their seats, and waved her hand to diffuse the situation.

"Sorry for the noise, everyone. Just a little accident. We'll take care of this straight away."

She gave a weak smile and quickly disappeared into the kitchen. By this time, Kate felt everyone's eyes on her, and she quickly turned and left the tea shop, embarrassed and wondering why the two women looked as if they had just seen a ghost.

Kate hurried up the street and turned right onto The Mint. She couldn't chalk this incident up to simply another strange encounter. The book weighed too heavily in her bag for that. Maybe the two women's reactions had something to do with the etching. But their look was not just of surprise, but seemed to be mixed with fear. Kate needed to return the book to the man at the bookstore, and quickly.

The alley was just ahead of her. She stopped and pulled the book and her phone out of her bag, and took a picture of the cover, the title page, the etching, and the story. Then she turned into the alley.

The bookstore was more brightly lit than the day before, and she went in. She looked around for the man she had talked to, but he was not in the room. A woman stood behind the counter, and Kate approached her, the book in hand.

The woman was dressed all in black. Thick black hair, smoothed back on her head like feathers on a bird, was gathered into a tight bun at the nape of her neck. A black scarf embellished with a fine silver stitching was tied over one shoulder and secured with a large silver brooch. The only other color on her was a thin swath of blood-red lipstick.

As the woman tracked Kate's movements, she raised her hand to touch the brooch at her shoulder. It was an intricate design of three stars and the moon, and two birds engaged in a struggle, and she fingered it nervously. Her only other movement was a widening of her eyes.

"May I help you?"

Kate laid the book on the counter. "Yes. I am returning this book."

The woman began to reach out to touch the book, but then pulled it back when she saw the cover. Several moments passed before she spoke.

"I see. Do you have a receipt?"

Kate explained how she came to have the book. "So you see, the gentleman who was here yesterday sold it to me. But when I saw that it was a signed first edition, I didn't feel right about keeping it. It must be worth much more than the twenty pounds I paid for it. Is he around? I am sure he will confirm what I am saying."

"There is no one else working here, so I am sure I don't know who you are talking about." Then the woman seemed to consider Kate's story for a moment. "Perhaps you could describe this man?"

Kate gave her a description of him, emphasizing how pleasant and friendly he had been to her.

The woman shook her head. "You are mistaken. In fact, there are no men working here at all. At any rate, you couldn't possibly have spoken to anyone if I were not here. The door would have been locked." She peered over her glasses at Kate. "I simply can't imagine how you came to get this book."

"No, I can assure you, this is your book. A man here in this shop sold it to me yesterday, and I am returning it. I left the twenty pounds on the counter, which is what he said it cost. You must have seen it. But he left and went into the back before giving me a receipt. Really, ma'am, I don't mean to cause any trouble. You can keep the money...and the book." She turned to leave.

"Wait," the woman called to Kate, as she reached the door.

Kate turned back to face her.

"Did you read the book? Did you study it at all?"

Kate wondered if the question had anything to do with the etching of Arabella. There were questions she would have asked the old man, but she could see that this woman would not be receptive to her. She considered her words carefully.

"Very little, actually," she replied.

The woman nodded. "Very well, then."

Kate left the bookstore, glad to have the book out of her hands, but still wondering about the significance of it, the presence of the old man in the bookstore the day before, and the strange reactions she had been getting from people in Rye.

7

MYRLIE SHAW-WINDHAM FOLLOWED the young woman to the door and flipped the plastic sign on the window ledge to CLOSED. She felt around in the deep pocket of her dress and grasped the largest key on a steel ring. She locked the door to the shop, then hurried to the back and pushed aside the curtained divider. She went up the stairs to her flat, the book in hand.

The flat was small, even for the two of them—her stepfather, Edward, and herself. There was only one bedroom, and he was kept there. Myrlie slept on the sofa bed in the living room and cooked—if soups and sausages could be called cooking—on an unpredictable two-burner stove in the kitchenette.

There were two windows over the sofa, and she kept them closed and curtained. Closed because of a ghastly dank smell that seeped in from the wet stone wall on the next building. And curtained because the sun rarely found its way there. The only other windows were in the bedroom. They looked out onto the alley in front of the bookstore—another dismal view. Edward never showed any interest in looking out the windows, anyway, so they, too, were kept curtained.

Myrlie had lived in the flat since buying the bookstore two years earlier, with the help of a small inheritance from her father. She had just retired from her job as a librarian. Loaning out books at the library was fine, but she always preferred to own them. She believed that people should be able to mark the words and passages that had struck a chord with them so that they could return whenever they wanted to feel that emotion again, to revel in the prose, and to be surprised, again and again, at the imagery created by a masterful storyteller. A person should be able to turn down the corners of the pages and make notes in the margins—deeds that would be intolerable in a loaned book, but quite gratifying in one's own.

Myrlie found solace in books from the moment she could put significance to words on a page. The transformation of typeset letters into words with meanings, and then to images in her mind, was a phenomenon that she thought was not fully appreciated by most.

Some of her cherished books were factual, some were fantasy, and she loved them all. But she was especially fond of adventures of strong and honest men, and the women caught up in romances with them. As a young girl, these romantic figures and the books they lived in were tucked away in a secret box so that her disapproving mother could not find them.

A marriage at a young age to a man that she had believed to be strong and honest quickly proved to Myrlie that real life was not at all like what was found in books. Yes, there was often heartbreak in fiction, but her favorite stories always ended happily ever after. Myrlie's husband had betrayed their vows by having an affair with another woman, and the marriage had ended in hate and despair.

Myrlie's life took another turn when her mother died shortly after Myrlie bought the bookstore. Her stepfather, Edward, began to show signs of dementia after that loss. Perhaps it was Alzheimer's. Perhaps not. But the downward spiral of his abilities meant that he could no longer live by himself. He had no one else, so she brought him to her little flat over the bookstore and gave him her bedroom. And with that, her dreams of a successful business, and living life on her own terms in a cozy flat in Rye, had begun to crumble.

The door to the bedroom was ajar, and she stood there for a moment, the book still in her hand. She knew she had taken one box of books out of the storage room in the cellar for a brief time. She had just left the bookstore for a quick appointment. And now she realized that in that time, in a bizarre moment of clarity, Edward must have made his way down to the shop, found the book, and sold it to a complete stranger. It was incomprehensible. But there was no other explanation. She had been puzzled by the twenty pounds on the counter when she returned, but never dreamed it had anything to do with this book. She knew that she must be more careful. This could not happen again. Ever. The thoughts of what might have resulted from that one lapse made her angry and afraid. He had put everything at risk.

Myrlie pushed the door open. Edward was sitting on the edge of his bed. He looked up at her with vacant eyes. She wondered if he even knew who she was anymore.

"What were you doing downstairs yesterday?" she shouted, just as much in anger as to make herself heard. "A woman said you were talking to her." She shook the book at him. "How did you find this book?"

Edward simply tipped his head quizzically, infuriatingly silent.

Myrlie went to the bathroom and returned with a bottle of pills and a glass of water. She shook out a pill, pressed it into his thin, dry hand, and ordered him to take it. She watched as he slowly put it into his mouth, drank from the glass of water, and swallowed.

"I'm not playing games, Edward. The next stop for you is the nursing home. Mark my words." She turned to go, but stopped at the door. "You are never to go downstairs again." She looked back at him. "Do you understand me?"

Edward lifted his legs stiffly onto the bed, and drew a threadbare cover over himself. Myrlie shook her head and slammed the door behind her. Then, at the outer door to the flat, she clicked the deadbolt into place.

8

AFTER LEAVING THE BOOKSTORE and reaching The Mint again, Kate got her bearings and walked the five minutes to the railway station. She was glad to get away from the bookstore. She'd had two strange encounters already that morning and hadn't even had her breakfast yet.

She found the ticket counter and purchased a round trip ticket for the 10:20 a.m. bus and entry tickets for the Calloway House & Gardens. At a small kiosk, she purchased a Danish and a cup of tea.

The bus arrived, and she settled into a window seat. Once they were outside the village of Rye, the countryside began to reveal itself.

The bus trundled past small villages clustered at every crossroad—a mix of old mossy-roofed cottages and new apartment buildings. Large stone churches stood guard over the people of the town, both living and dead. Simple homes, some centuries old, crowded together on the narrow streets, their boundaries marked by hedges and weather-worn picket fences. Kate envisioned herself taking a bicycle ride along the same route, maybe stopping to pick wildflowers, and to get a pint at a pub and chat with the locals. She pulled out her journal and phone and began taking notes and pictures.

The bus continued farther out into the country, making several turns, then the final one at a road sign announcing Blackbird Lane. Another larger sign set in the corner of a stone wall showed that it would lead to the Calloway House & Gardens.

The lane began to narrow, and soon became no more than a tunnel of trees, their branches arched so tightly overhead that only a few glimpses of the sun could be seen. Occasionally, a break in the tree line along the side of the road exposed the rushing water of a rocky brook, and a hint of the vast rolling fields that lay far off in the distance, where sheep grazed, scattered like white tufts on a green quilt.

A few moments later, the trees parted above them, and the Calloway House was revealed. It was a hulking structure with a massive tiled roofline, towering brick chimneys and a timbered front. The main house, which looked to be the oldest section, was easily accessible from the parking lot, while two additional levels terraced down a gradual slope to the left.

The driver announced their arrival at the Calloway House & Gardens and instructed everyone to exit the bus and follow the signs to the entrance, reminding the group that the bus would be leaving at one o'clock sharp. Kate shouldered her bag, and along with the other tourists, stepped out into the parking lot.

They were directed to a flagstone path that curved from the parking lot, up to the house. A riot of flowers hugged the walls on either side of the entrance, the late morning sun glinting off the water-sprinkled blooms. Deep plum and lavender delphinium, and a mingling of crimson and buttery-yellow hollyhocks, stood tall against the walls, framing a handsomely carved entrance. Dark-green vines scaled up the ancient timbers, to the roofline and around the chimneys high overhead. An ambitious sapphire-blue morning glory trailed the vines up to the top of the window ledges. On the ground, ruffled petunias snuggled in with the greenery and leggy black-eyed Susans swayed in the breeze.

Off to the right, a meandering grass pathway beckoned the guests to come into the gardens and experience the beauty that awaited them. Some of the tour group blithely walked past the colorful displays and went on into the house. Perhaps, to them, they were simply a jumble of pretty flowers, if they noticed them at all. But Kate knew from experience that meticulous planning had gone into each and every planting, into every garden. Nothing was random to a serious gardener. In spite of the haphazard appearance of the border garden here, each flower had been carefully chosen and timed for best blooming effect. She knew she could not leave before following that pathway.

She presented her ticket at the door and followed the tour group inside, but then lingered behind until she was at the end of the line. Soon, she stepped over the rough threshold, into the massive Great Hall, its beamed ceilings soaring overhead. The guide informed them that this was the oldest part of the house, dating back to the 1400s.

Kate stepped off to the side and closed her eyes. She envisioned the room without the modern touches and roped-off areas. Instead, she saw dirt floors and an open fire burning in the center of the room, around a brick base. Smoke curled up through gaps in the roof, the timbers blackened by centuries of fires for cooking and warmth. Perhaps there were thick tapestries depicting victorious battles covering the walls for decoration, and to protect against the cold winds off the coast. Colorful banners with symbols of lions or dragons hung on crosspieces at the head of a vast, crudely hewn table. Servants carried trays of meat and fish to noblemen and their families, or to travelers passing through their lands. The lord of the manor would signal for the musicians to begin the entertainment, and the goblets would be filled again and again with ale and wine.

Kate opened her eyes, stored the vision away in her memory, and hurried to reach the rest of the group, which had moved on to the next section of the house. She stepped down into the second level, which, according to the tour guide, was added in 1595. Again, the rooms had been modernized to some degree over the years, but she could tell that the family had preserved the original medieval structure. The woodwork in the newer rooms showed the skill of the artisans from that era, with intricate carvings in the furniture and beams.

"The final and lowest level was added very recently," their guide joked. "In 1620."

The tour continued through what would have been the family dining room, kitchen and pantry, and servants' quarters, all with a mixture of displays dating from the 1200s to the latest time when the house had served as the Calloway family's home, in the 1950s. The house and gardens had survived civil wars and had served in both World Wars as a hospital for wounded soldiers and civilians alike. There were photographs from those eras to show the sacrifices that the Calloway family, and the country, had made during that time.

At the end of the tour, the guide noted that Virginia Calloway, a direct descendant of the original Calloway family that built the house, lived in the modern manor behind the older medieval buildings, and that it was not open to visitors.

The group finally exited through a pantry doorway at the end of the house, and followed the guide around to the front again, where they could pick up the birdwatching tour or take a walk through the gardens. Kate chose the grass pathway that had called to her earlier. It soon became a gravel path, and she skimmed her hand over the tops of the lavender that bordered it. The motion sent a flight of butterflies, and the sweet scent of the herb, into the air. She breathed in the calming fragrance and made a mental note to include lavender in future plantings at Howard's Walk.

After a few moments, Kate heard the sound of water rippling over rocks in the distance. She followed the path down a slight hill, and soon came upon the source. A wide, shallow stream bubbled gently, following the curve of the landscape around a copse of majestic weeping willows. Their branches draped over the water, the fine filaments of leaves murmuring in the gentle breeze.

A wooden bench had been placed near the stream, and Kate sat down. The scene around her was just the way she envisioned an English country garden to be, with natural landscapes, winding pathways, and wide lawns, the bubbling brook and natural growth of shrubs and trees. A group of birders with binoculars were huddled farther up the stream, and if even low tones of conversation erupted, they were quickly hushed by the rest of the group.

Kate was startled out of her thoughts by a dog that bounded up and jumped onto the bench beside her. She heard the owner whistling and chastising the dog from a distance, and she petted him until the man arrived.

"I'm so sorry, miss. He shouldna' run off like that."

The man ordered the dog off the bench and motioned him to sit. After several false starts, the beagle finally obeyed and sat at the man's side, nudging his hand for a pet.

"He's young, and I'm still workin' with him. I hope he was no bother to ya."

"No bother at all," Kate said. "What's his name?"

"This is Alfie, miss." The man removed a gardener's hat, revealing a full head of gray hair.

He ran his hand through it and settled the hat back on his head. His clothes were simple khaki work clothes—the knees of his pant legs permanently darkened, no doubt, from years of working in the gardens. His large, calloused hands looked to be hardened from a young age by farm work, and his tanned face wrinkled from the sun, in spite of the large, brimmed hat he wore. His eyes were soft gray-green, like the dusty millers that Kate planted along the walks of her own gardens.

"My name is Kate. Kate Tyler." She offered her hand, and the man shook it.

"Graham McGregor, miss." He tipped his hat. "Have you seen the house yet?"

"Yes, it was wonderful. I love history, so it was fascinating to me. But I must admit, I am partial to the gardens. I have gardens at my home in North Carolina. I'm a bit envious of what you have here."

"Ach, 'tis nothing, miss. I've worked on many of the larger estates near here over the years, but I've been happy working for the Calloways. They've been good to this McGregor, so I can't complain."

Alfie began to sniff around, forgetting his orders to sit and stay, and the gardener let him go.

"I think this one is going to be stubborn to learnin', but he's the last of the pups, and I'm too old to be very strict with him." McGregor took a step forward. "Do you mind if I set a bit, miss? My arthritis..."

"Yes, of course." Kate moved over to give him room on the bench.

He sat down with some effort and gazed out over the stream. Then she felt him take a sideways glance at her.

"Excuse me, miss, my eyesight ain't what it used to be. But I coulda' sworn from a distance...well, you just looked a wee bit familiar, that's all."

Kate sighed loudly.

"I'm sorry. I shouldna' said anything. It's just that—"

"Mister McGregor, I'm the one who should apologize. But you are not the first person today that seemed to know me. In fact, it's been rather unsettling."

She decided not to share what had happened at the bookstore, or at the café, since they could not possibly have been related to the musings of an elderly gardener at an estate miles away from Rye.

"Maybe I just have one of those faces."

"Sure, miss. That's what it is," he said, although, he didn't sound very convinced. He stood. "Well, I best be getting back to my work now." He whistled for Alfie, and the dog bounded up to him. "It was nice to meet you. You have a good day now, Kate Tyler from North Carolina." He tipped his hat again and walked away, Alfie nipping at his heels.

Kate suddenly had the urge to call after him.

"Mister McGregor."

He turned and looked back at her.

"Have you ever heard of the legend of Arabella?"

Mr. McGregor pulled himself up as straight as his arthritic back would allow, and gave a slight nod.

"But if you're askin' that question, miss, maybe you should be talkin' to the lady of the house. I canna' help you."

Kate watched as he disappeared behind the willows and around the bend of the stream. A strange feeling continued to tug at her, stronger than ever. Her dreams, the book, *The Legend of Arabella*...this was not a coincidence. But what possible connection could there be between Arabella and the Calloway House & Gardens? And how could the lady of the Calloway House, assuming he was speaking of Virginia Calloway, possibly help her?

"Who are you, Arabella?"

There was no answer, except for the murmur of the leaves on the trees, and the whispering high grasses along the banks of the stream.

A few moments later, a young man approached, letting her know that the house and gardens would be closing in fifteen minutes. Kate began the walk back to the parking lot, thinking about all that had happened to her that day. Her time at the Lamb House gardens yesterday, and walking the still-familiar streets of Rye, were both comforting and unsettling to her, and had in many ways set the tone for her trip so far. And seeing her image in the book of legends, and reading the sad story of Arabella, only added to her disquiet.

Kate needed more answers about the legend of Arabella. It had all started at the bookstore.

And that was where she needed to return.

9

AT 4:50 P.M., MYRLIE ARRIVED at the Calloway House & Gardens. The guard house was empty. A slight breeze moved across the flower beds and into the trees, whispering through the leaves. The afternoon sun was lowering to the horizon, drawing shadows across the front of the old house.

Four other cars were parked in a neat row near the front of the building. Myrlie stopped her Fiat a few spaces away and turned off the ignition. Two women were just disappearing around the far corner of the building. Myrlie knew that they would be continuing along a narrow path that led to the secret meeting place of the Corvos Sisterhood.

Myrlie's habit was to arrive at the meetings exactly on time. More than once, she had witnessed Virginia Calloway vent her displeasure with sisters who arrived late, and Myrlie vowed she would never give her that same opportunity.

A month after arriving in Rye, Myrlie had been first introduced to Virginia Calloway. Opal Godwin, the owner of a nearby tea shop in Rye, had invited her to a luncheon at Virginia's private home, the Calloway Manor. Virginia was giving a talk on herbal remedies, an area where she had much expertise, and Myrlie had eagerly accepted the invitation. The subject proved to be fascinating, and Myrlie was flattered that after the talk, Virginia seemed very interested in learning more about her. Their conversation touched on various philosophies, and soon turned to spiritualism, subjects that Myrlie was widely read in. She had dabbled in séances and the occult, and for reasons she herself could not explain, opened up to Virginia about her curiosity to further explore these topics.

To Myrlie's surprise, Virginia had invited her back to the manor, and that was when she had learned that Virginia, Opal, and others were part of the Corvos Sisterhood, a small group of women led by Virginia herself—all of whom held the same interests as Myrlie. When Virginia asked her to join the Sisterhood, she readily accepted. Myrlie began to take part in their séances, and that was when she learned that Mathilde Calloway, Virginia's grandmother, had started the Corvos Sisterhood with a singular goal: to reach out to the spirit of Arabella Courbain, and to await her return, as foretold in *The Legend of Arabella*.

Myrlie had been fascinated with the story of Arabella. It became a solace to her, and indeed a romantic thought: the prediction in the legend was one of hope, that a tragic life could be made whole again, that a woman could finally have the life she was meant to live, no matter the circumstances.

Others might have thought it a silly notion that Arabella would return in some form, at some time, to recapture the life she should have had. But Virginia's absolute belief in the legend convinced Myrlie that it could happen.

Myrlie loved the early days of belonging to the Sisterhood—the secrecy, the ritual of the séance, the sense of belonging to something that might expand beyond space and time. But her circumstances changed, and the allure of the Sisterhood, and indeed Virginia Calloway herself, began to fade. Over the past few months, she began to wonder if the Sisterhood had become nothing more than a pointless exercise, anticipating the return of a woman dead for almost three hundred years.

And there was a change in Virginia Calloway. The more time passed without any sign of Arabella's return, it seemed the more desperate she became, the more frequent the séances, the more despair she seemed to feel that the legend would never come true in her lifetime, as she had hoped.

Then, just hours earlier, an American tourist with an uncanny resemblance to Arabella herself had appeared in the bookstore, with the book of legends itself—*Ancient Tales of an Ancient Town*. The fact that she'd had the book in her possession for even a brief time was alarming.

Myrlie had originally come to be the owner of the book purely by chance. Soon after buying the bookstore, she began organizing the storeroom, which was really just a damp cellar beneath the store. One day, in the midst of cataloguing a stack of books there, a rat darted between her legs. She screamed and threw the books at the dirty rodent. He escaped unharmed, but her ammunition had slammed into a bookshelf, breaking the rotting shelves and sending their contents crashing to the floor. After gathering her wits, she saw that the destruction had revealed a hidden door behind the shelves. She pulled away the broken pieces of wood and found that the door opened into a large closet which held even more crates of books. It had been an exceptionally long day, and her nerves were already frayed by the encounter with the rat, but she was curious and pulled one of the boxes out into the larger, lighted room.

What she discovered were dozens of rare books, hidden away and unaccounted for in the inventory of the previous owner's estate. The books were in near perfect condition, even after many years in storage. Many of them were first editions, and most were signed by the authors. She estimated them to be worth thousands of pounds, maybe more.

Myrlie was cheered beyond her wildest dreams. Finally, after all of the struggling, she owned something of great value. Something that could secure her future. She did wonder how the previous owners had collected such a wealth of books, and why they had hidden them in a secret room. But then it came to her that it was possibly for the same reason that she had hidden books from her mother as a young girl. They simply didn't want anyone to know about them.

She searched the Internet then for any information she could find about the books. Her initial delight in finding the cache was short lived. Seventy out of the eighty-five books were listed as stolen, including the book by Sir Mallard.

Having valuable books that she could not sell was maddening. Myrlie briefly thought of turning them into the police. But if they were stolen, she reasoned that the owners were probably reimbursed by insurance already. It was really no loss to them. She had tried to think of a way to sell the books, but knew nothing about how to fence books. She certainly didn't move in those circles. So she had kept them hidden away in the secret room.

Now the book of legends was back in her hands. It was possibly the most valuable book in the entire collection, not just because of its provenance, the quality of the etchings, and the famous artists who had produced them, although those things increased its value significantly. But it was a first printing of the book, signed by Sir Archibald Mallard, and it held the legends of Rye, and most importantly, the original description of an earlier oral legend of Arabella Courbain.

Virginia Calloway did not know that Myrlie had the book in her possession. If she knew, she would demand that it be turned over to her. And Myrlie could not allow that to happen, even if it meant going against Virginia and the entire Sisterhood. And if Virginia found out that Myrlie had seen, with her own eyes, a woman who looked like Arabella in her bookstore...it would change everything. And most frightening of all, what if the young woman had actually seen the etching of Arabella in the book and recognized herself on the page? That would set everything on a new course.

The alarm on her phone buzzed, startling Myrlie out of her thoughts. It was 4:59. She got out of her car, locked it behind her, and resolutely headed to the meeting.

The path that led around the back of the Calloway House curved suddenly and became five stone steps, well-disguised in the tall grass. She stepped carefully down the wet and mossy stones to a heavy wooden door situated beneath the ancient house. This entrance was known only to a few people: Virginia, her staff, and the members of the Corvos Sisterhood.

Myrlie had received the summons to come to the meeting just hours before, as she imagined the others had.

"Arrive promptly at five o'clock," Virginia had instructed. *As if I would ever be late for anything,* Myrlie had groused to herself. The Sisterhood was expected to accept Virginia's invitations without question. In truth, Myrlie had better things to do, and her encounter with Kate Tyler earlier had been distressing enough. But she accepted that she must attend. She didn't want to draw any more unwanted attention to herself.

She approached the door and checked her surroundings, as she always did, for anyone who might be watching. But there was no one. She drew back a curtain of ivy that completely hid the door, and lifted the latch. The door opened, and she stepped into a long, dimly lit tunnel. She continued on to a second door, which then opened into a large room. She checked her watch. It was exactly five o'clock.

Eight women were already seated in a half-circle of chairs. Myrlie suddenly realized that they were all dressed in red robes and gloves, the uniform of the Sisterhood. Her heart sank. She had left hers in the car. It was too late now to go back to retrieve them. She quickly sat down, knowing that she would have to endure whatever chastisement Virginia chose to deliver.

A tall pillar candle was the only light in the room. Shadows flickered against the stone walls and created peculiar angles on Virginia's tall, thin form as the woman took her place in front of the group.

"Sisters, I have called you here for an urgent matter. It has come to my attention that a young woman visited the gardens today who bore a striking resemblance to our own Arabella."

A low murmur of surprise rippled through the group. Myrlie stiffened at the announcement. Virginia's eyes gleamed with anticipation in the candlelight.

"The legend says that Arabella will one day return to live the life she was meant to live. We have seen others through the years that raised our hopes, but none that looked so much like our Arabella as it seems this young woman does. I must ask you all now: have any of you also seen this young woman?"

Opal immediately raised her hand, and Tonya slowly followed.

"Yes, Sister Virginia! I have. That is, Tonya and I. We saw a woman this morning that looked just like Arabella, right in our shop! Scared us half to death, I don't mind telling you. Looked exactly like the portrait and the etching of her that you showed us."

"I see." Virginia took a step toward her. "And did you speak to her?"

"Oh no, she left right away." Opal turned to Tonya. "I told you it was her."

Virginia scanned the group of women. "Has anyone else seen her?"

They all shook their heads in turn.

"Sister Myrlie, you have a shop in Rye. Have you seen her?"

Myrlie cleared her throat and bolstered herself to tell the lie, even as she reached for a tissue in her pocket to dab at the moisture collecting on her upper lip and forehead.

"No, Sister Virginia, I certainly have not. I mean, what are the chances of that?"

"Very good chances, indeed, Sister Myrlie!" Virginia retorted. "This young woman might frequent a bookshop such as yours. And she was seen not far from your establishment."

It was as if Virginia just noticed Myrlie then without the proper robe and gloves required for the meeting. Virginia said nothing, but she didn't need to. Her disapproval was evident, and it rankled Myrlie. She hadn't joined this society for judgement. One little slip up didn't deserve a reprimand. She regretted that she had brought this on herself because of ruminating on the past instead of focusing on the dress protocol for the meeting.

She pressed her lips together, willing herself to stay silent, be calm, and let the interrogations move on to someone else.

Virginia finally moved to a table that had been set in the middle of the room. Myrlie's transgression seemed to dissipate, and she breathed a sigh of relief.

"Opal, Serena, and Myrlie, please set the table for the séance."

Myrlie hesitated, surprised that Virginia had chosen her to take part in the séance, especially without the required attire. Virginia noticed her hesitation.

"Sister Myrlie, is there a problem?"

"No, of course not."

She made her way to the table, her mind racing with the implications of what would be required of her—total concentration, a clear mind, focused attention. None of which she was feeling at the moment.

Opal lit tapers of incense and waved the scent into the room, her round form swaying in a dance as she performed her part of the ritual. Myrlie did not care for Opal's theatrics, but she said nothing. Serena set four chairs around the table. Myrlie found the three candles that were central to the séance and set them into the holders on the table.

"Sister Myrlie, the candles are wrong." Virginia's voice cut through the silence. "The violet candle faces north, always. The others are at the corners of the triangle—blue to the left, and grey to the right. Please correct it."

"Yes, of course, Sister Virginia." Myrlie reset the candles and took a seat at the table with Opal and Serena.

Virginia approached, lit each of the candles and sat down.

"Close your eyes, clear your minds, and focus as we try to reach the spirit of Arabella."

For several minutes, Myrlie could hear nothing but the sounds of breathing—in and out, in and out. Finally, Virginia instructed the three women to join hands, and Myrlie reached out to clasp Opal's soft, clammy hand on one side, and then Serena's vice-like grip on the other.

Still, there was silence. Maybe this would be the last séance she would attend, Myrlie thought. The last meeting of the Corvos Sisterhood. She could be honest with herself now. Her future plans did not include the sisterhood, or her stepfather, or even the bookstore. Her mind wandered to a picture she had seen in a magazine, of a cozy house on a beach in Spain. The advertisement said it was only a short walk to shops and restaurants, and museums. The picture was now taped to her refrigerator, and she often mused that it would be a lovely place to live.

Virginia's voice finally broke the silence.

"Arabella, we are awaiting you here in this circle. If you are near, please make your presence known."

Myrlie was quickly brought out of her daydreaming. The séance had officially begun.

A minute passed, and Virginia repeated the incantation, her voice louder this time as she raised it up to the heights of the room. Twice more, the incantation was spoken.

Myrlie felt Opal's hand begin to tremble in hers. And there were sounds in the room now—whimpers from Serena beside her, the low hum of an icy wind as it blew through, wrapping itself around them, nipping at the candle flames.

Opal stood, shaking off the hands that just moments ago had completed the circle. Her chair fell back, and she stood still, hands covering her face.

Everyone's eyes were on her. Nothing like this had ever happened in a séance before. It could have been explained away as a natural occurrence, and nothing to do with the spirits. Nothing to do with the impending arrival of Arabella. But then Opal began to cry.

Virginia stood and called out, "Sister Opal!"

But there was no response. Myrlie got up from her chair, took Opal by the shoulders and led her away from the table to the other women waiting to comfort her.

Myrlie turned to face Virginia, thinking she might see a look of surprise or concern on her face, or hear some explanation of what had just happened. But there was nothing. It was a mask that she could not read.

"Sister Virginia," said one of the women. "We'll take Sister Opal home now."

Virginia dismissed them with a wave of her hand. Myrlie turned to follow them, but Virginia placed a bony hand on her arm.

"Do you know what happened here, Sister Myrlie?"

"I'm not sure that I do. I hope Opal is all right." She looked at the door.

"Arabella was here," Virginia said. "She was closer than she has ever been. She was trying to communicate with us."

Myrlie looked back at her. "But we can't be sure, can we?"

Virginia stiffened. "Oh, I am very sure. And I am surprised that you are doubting it. But the circle was broken."

"Yes, Sister Opal broke—"

"No," Virginia whispered. "It was not Sister Opal." Her mouth was set in a hard line, and her eyes glinted in the half-light of the candles. "It was you that broke the circle, long before Sister Opal. I could feel it. There is something you are not revealing to me. What might that be?"

"I-I have no idea w-what you are talking about," Myrlie said, willing herself to stay in control and not obey an urge to run from the room.

"I will find out. I can assure you of that."

Myrlie backed away from Virginia and hurried after the others.

10

THE NEXT MORNING, KATE TURNED the brass door handle at BOOKS, triggering the tinkle of the doorbell, and went inside. There were a few customers in the store, perusing the sales racks. The room appeared more orderly—the counter at the back of the store had been cleared off, the shelves had been dusted, and the table and chairs arranged more comfortably for the customers. In general, the room had a brighter look. But that did not apply to the woman working there. She was as severe as Kate remembered her. In fact, it appeared that what she was wearing the day before was her uniform: black dress, scarf, silver brooch, and red lipstick.

Kate browsed through the book displays, the woman watching her every move. When the customers left, Kate approached her.

"Good morning. Do you remember me from yesterday?"

The woman nodded. "Of course."

She straightened a stack of books on the counter, then picked up a stamper and pressed it on the inside cover of the top book, avoiding Kate's eyes.

"I haven't introduced myself. My name is Kate Tyler."

"Myrlie Shaw-Windham," she said, with a slight hesitation as she looked up.

"Miss Shaw-Windham, I'll get right to the point, then. Yesterday, I said that I had read little of the legends book, which was true. But the part I did read has been bothering me."

Myrlie continued stamping the books, the sound now echoing through the shop.

"And what part was that?" she replied.

Kate took out her phone and tapped on the photo icon. She selected the picture of the etching of Arabella, and showed it to her.

"I read *The Legend of Arabella*. And I saw this etching of her."

Myrlie slammed down the cover of the last book and pushed the stack off to one side. But she said nothing.

"This looks like me, right?" Kate said. "I know it must be a coincidence. But you are not the first person who seemed shocked to see me here in Rye, as if you knew about this etching and this story, and somehow made a connection. Is that what it is?"

Myrlie carried the stacks of books to a nearby table, and Kate followed.

"Please, ma'am. I need to know what this is all about. If it is just a coincidence, I am feeling extremely uncomfortable about it. And it looks like I'm making others uncomfortable, too, including you, which is not what I want."

Myrlie composed herself and smoothed back a wisp of hair that had come loose from the bun at her neck.

"You are right, of course," she replied. "It is all just a coincidence. There is a slight resemblance, I guess. But there is nothing to it. Nothing to it at all. You should not give it another thought. My apologies for any discomfort you might have felt."

The shop door opened, and a man and woman entered.

"Now, if you will excuse me, I have work to do." Myrlie walked away to greet the customers.

Kate debated whether she should try to get any more information out of Ms. Shaw-Windham. Nothing that had been said so far gave her any comfort. If anything, she continued to be surprised by people's reactions to her. She had no more answers now, than when she walked in minutes before. She decided that pursuing it any further with her would be pointless.

For the rest of the day, Kate did whatever she could to distract herself from the legend, her dreams, and the strange interactions with people in Rye and at the Calloway House. By late afternoon, she was satisfied that she was back on track. She would order room service for her supper, work on her blog all evening in her pajamas, and get a good night's sleep.

As she passed the front desk of the Mermaid Inn, Gilbert caught her attention.

"I have a message for you, Miss Tyler."

He handed her an envelope the color of buttercups and embossed with an elaborate monogram of raised lavender lettering that Kate finally interpreted as VMC. Inside was a note, handwritten in a beautiful script.

Kate Tyler,

If you would like to learn more about
the legend of Arabella,
come to the Calloway House
at 8 p.m. this evening.
The guard will show you to my location.

Virginia Marguerite Calloway

Kate's first reaction was to wonder how the woman knew her name, and where to find her, and how much she knew about Kate's interest in the legend. But then she recalled introducing herself to the gardener and asking him if he knew anything about the legend of Arabella.

Kate was nothing if not flexible, as a journalist must be, and open for opportunities when they presented themselves. She put aside her thoughts of a quiet evening in her room, and asked Gilbert for assistance in renting a car. After reassuring him that she was familiar with driving in England, he arranged for a car to be brought to the inn at 7:15 p.m. He inquired about where she might be going, and if there was anything else that he could arrange for her. Reservations at a restaurant, perhaps? But she declined, saying that she just wanted to revisit a village she saw on the way to the Calloway House & Gardens the day before. And to herself, she hoped that it would still be a possibility after her meeting with Ms. Calloway.

When the car arrived, she found the address of her destination, entered it into the directional program on her phone, and started driving to East Stalton.

As she turned onto Blackbird Lane, leading to the Calloway House, Kate experienced a rising mixture of curiosity and apprehension. Both were reasonable, considering that she was naturally inquisitive and wanted to learn more about the legend. But she felt she had every reason to be nervous as well. The strange way that the book had come into her hands, and seeing the image of herself in it, was still unnerving to her. Still, this meeting with Virginia Calloway might reveal something of the mystery—and that revelation might be welcomed or unwelcomed.

No, her worry was unreasonable, she told herself, and tamped it down. It would be a privilege to meet the owner of the Calloway House, and a conversation with her might reveal a lot about what had been happening to Kate lately. She considered herself a good interviewer, and decided to treat this meeting as she would any other place or person of interest for her blog.

She pulled into the now-empty parking lot of the same medieval buildings she had visited the day before. A man in a guard's uniform stood by the front door. She parked the car, stepped out, and approached him.

"I'm Kate Tyler. Virginia Calloway is expecting me."

Without a word, he motioned her to follow him on a path that led around the old buildings, to the manor behind it.

They were soon walking down a long flagstone walkway toward the manor. There was still enough daylight to show the way, and Kate noted a well-manicured lawn on either side, with a scattering of trees and topiaries spaced throughout. A low hedge bordered the lawn on her left, and a grove of trees behind it blocked any further view.

Kate knew that the manor itself was mid-twentieth century, but it must have been built to appear much older—perhaps to blend in with the ancient buildings that it hid behind. The front was stone and extended up three stories. The lower half of the windows at ground level were hidden by large bushes, and one wall was partially covered with ivy growing up past the second floor. Several chimneys rose into the sky over the roof line. The entire building towered above Kate as they reached the front door.

The guard knocked three times, and soon the door opened. He stepped aside and motioned for Kate to enter.

A woman stood just a few steps into the foyer. She appeared to be in her seventies, and was tall and thin, with angular features. Her nose was long and jutted out over a receding chin. Her hair was thin and dyed brown. She wore a light-brown knobby tweed short-waisted jacket over a collared silk blouse. Her pleated, brown plaid skirt ended just below the knee.

She toyed with a pendant she wore around her neck, a look of wariness on her face.

"Kate Tyler?" the woman said, and Kate nodded.

After a span of eight chimes from a clock in the hallway, the woman spoke again.

Appearing to collect herself, she said, "I am Virginia Calloway. Welcome to my home. Please come with me."

From the outside, the manor house had appeared to be symmetrical, with a familiar, sensible logic to its structure. But as she followed Virginia Calloway deeper into the manor, Kate could see that it kept none of the proportion of the outside. She was intrigued by the warren of rooms and halls and stairways, turning right, then left, all equally narrow and cluttered with what she guessed were antiques, but she already felt uncomfortably lost in the maze that was this mysterious woman's home.

Ms. Calloway stopped in front of a set of intricately carved pocket doors and slid them open, revealing an enormous library. Bookshelves lined one of the walls from floor to ceiling. A massive fireplace filled the entirety of another wall, and an expanse of windows facing out over a garden covered another.

The woman waved a gnarled hand toward a sofa near the fireplace. Kate assumed she was being told to sit, which she did. She had been expecting something different in the room—a more refined space perhaps, again, a carryover from the imposing building itself. But the clutter in this room and the house that she had seen so far gave an entirely different impression.

The woman sat on the edge of a side chair across from Kate and folded her hands. When she didn't speak, Kate felt the silence and Virginia's piercing gaze weighing on her. She decided that she was expected to say something.

"Thank you for inviting me, Miss Calloway. I took a tour yesterday of the old Calloway House and the gardens, and as a travel blogger, I found it fascinating."

Ms. Calloway tipped her head quizzically. "A travel blogger? I am not certain what that might be, Miss Tyler." She removed a pair of wire-rimmed glasses and let them hang from a jeweled chain around her neck. "But it is no matter, is it? That is not why you have come, am I correct?"

"Well, I was hoping...I mean..." Kate suddenly felt tongue-tied, for reasons she could not explain, except that under the woman's intense scrutiny, she felt as if she were being scanned and measured, one feature at a time.

"Again, it is no matter what you were hoping. I asked you here for a reason. And that reason is to see you for myself. To take a good look at the woman who frightened my gardener."

"Mister McGregor?" Kate said. "I can assure you that I didn't frighten him at all."

"Well, of course you did. He came to me with such a tale, I could hardly believe him. But then, here we are—here you are—in the flesh."

Kate was surprised at this odd turn in the conversation. She hadn't been sure what to expect, but it certainly was not an accusation of frightening the gardener. And had there also been a fleeting look of recognition when they met? Yet another person that was startled when they met her? If so, she would be the fifth.

"Miss Calloway, your note—I assume it was written by you—said that if I wanted to learn more about the legend of Arabella itself, I should come here tonight. So I am here, and I would like it if our conversation could be about that. If not, I don't see any reason for me to stay, and I am happy to return to Rye right now."

"Very well," the woman responded coolly, after some hesitation. "My apologies for any embarrassment my comments may have caused you. I tend to speak plainly. I hope you will stay and have a cup of tea."

"Of course," Kate replied, pleased that Ms. Calloway had at least acknowledged her frankness.

Virginia picked up a small bell on the table next to her and rang it. Kate heard the sound of the doors sliding open behind her, and a man, whom Kate presumed to be the butler, appeared at Ms. Calloway's side.

"Samuel, please prepare a pot of tea. The special blend would be lovely."

He nodded and left the room.

Virginia turned back to Kate. "You said that you found the house and gardens interesting. What did you mean?"

The subject had been quickly changed, but Kate took the opening. Perhaps if she found common ground with Ms. Calloway on a subject they both were interested in, the evening might lead to learning more about the puzzling legend.

"I loved learning about the history of the house. You have preserved it so well. We don't have that type of architecture and history in the States. And from the minute I arrived, I knew the gardens were something special. The mix of colors, with the delphinium and hollyhocks in front of the house, was stunning. Everywhere I turned, there was more to see. And the scent of the lavender…I definitely want to bring that calming influence to my own gardens."

Ms. Calloway nodded. "Herbs are an excellent addition to any garden. I am an herbalist, as many of the women in my family were before me. Do you have an interest in herbalism, Kate? There is much more I could share with you that is not on the tour."

Kate brightened. "Yes, I would be very interested."

"Well, then, perhaps that can be arranged. How long will you be staying in Rye?"

"Until next Friday."

Ah," Virginia said, as the butler entered the room, "our tea is here. Thank you, Samuel."

He set the tray, holding a tall black teapot and two red teacups, on a low table in front of Ms. Calloway. She dismissed him and poured the tea, steam rising in wisps from the tawny liquid as it flowed into the teacups. She gave one of the cups to Kate, and as she did, Kate breathed in an herbal scent that she could not identify.

"This is an unusual aroma. May I ask what it is?"

"It is my own special blend of herbs," Ms. Calloway replied. "Please try the tea and tell me what you think."

Kate took a sip. "It has an earthy taste. And maybe a hint of mint?"

"You have an excellent palate, Miss Tyler." She also took several sips of the tea, before continuing. "You asked my gardener about the legend of Arabella." She set her teacup on the table. "Why? Where have you heard about the legend?"

Kate wasn't at all sure about how much to share with Miss Calloway. She was expecting a completely different conversation. One in which Ms. Calloway might begin by saying how much Kate resembled Arabella. Or maybe, wasn't it odd that there seemed to be such a resemblance. Something to reassure Kate of the coincidence of it all. Or that she might reveal some history of the legend. But this was not the exchange they were having, and without knowing Ms. Calloway at all yet, she decided to remain cautious.

"I read about it in a book that I found in a bookstore in Rye. *Ancient Tales of an Ancient Town* was the title, by Sir Archibald Mallard—"

"Well, that is simply impossible." Ms. Calloway dismissed Kate's claim with a wave of her hand. "I know of the book, of course, but it is certainly not something one just comes across randomly. In fact, its whereabouts are unknown, and have been for quite some time." She thought for a moment. "But perhaps you could describe the book to me?"

Kate gave as accurate a description as she could, noting in particular the embossed coat of arms on the cover, with its minor wear and tear, and then the way the book was arranged in tales.

"And where did you say you found this book?" Ms. Calloway said, now seeming a bit more intrigued.

"At a bookstore in Rye. A place called BOOKS. It's an out-of-the-way little shop, but—"

"I see. More tea, Miss Tyler?"

Kate nodded, and Ms. Calloway added to Kate's cup, the fragrant vapor once again rising around her. The fire warmed the room, and mesmerizing flames flickered in the fireplace. The logs crackled as they collapsed into the large grate. Kate sat back in her chair, trying to hear what Ms. Calloway was saying. She felt as if she was under a warm blanket as the woman began to ask her questions.

Suddenly, Kate felt a light breeze on her face. She opened her eyes and found that she was looking up at the sky. She sat up and realized that she was lying on a wooden bench in one of the public gardens of the Calloway House. She blinked a few times, trying to clear her head, wondering how she got there. She looked around but saw no one.

She was startled by a rustle on the ground in front of her. A large raven hopped closer, cocking his head as if she had invaded his territory. If she had, it was not anything she remembered doing.

Her tote bag was next to her on the bench, and she dug into it for her phone. She checked the time. It was eleven o'clock. The moon had risen high and full in the nighttime sky, lighting the looming form of the old Calloway House off to her right. The manor house was completely hidden from view from where she sat. She was alone and struggled to recall anything from the evening.

Kate knew she had been talking to Ms. Calloway and having tea with her. It had been an unusual herbal tea with a curious aroma. She realized that she couldn't recall anything after taking the first few sips. And she certainly did not remember how she came to be on a bench in the gardens.

She stood, a little shaky. Her head was cloudy, as if coming out of a deep sleep—not unlike the feeling she had when waking after her vivid dreams. But she could see enough by the moonlight to make her way from the garden to the front of the old Calloway House by following the path, and she quickly headed in that direction. The raven hopped along beside her as she walked.

"Shoo, bird," Kate whispered. "Go away."

But he would not leave her side.

She started to call out for help as she reached the parking lot but stopped herself. This might not be the place to draw attention to the fact that she was alone. She could see her car at the far end of the lot where she had left it and rummaged through her bag for the keys. She hurried to it, got in, and locked the doors behind her. The bird hopped onto the hood of the car, made a cawing sound, and then flew off.

She felt safer in the car and took a few deep breaths. Something had happened to her in Virginia Calloway's house. It seemed impossible that she could have been drugged. What possible reason could there have been?

She dismissed the thought. But she realized that she had not learned—or at least, could not remember learning—anything about the legend of Arabella, or what connection Ms. Calloway had with the strange tale. At this point, it was the least of her worries. She needed to return to Rye.

Kate punched the address for the Mermaid Inn into her phone and drove off into the night, eager to leave the mysterious Calloway House & Gardens, and the enigmatic Virginia Calloway, behind her.

Virginia's conversation with Kate had continued for several minutes after Kate received the full dose of the tea. But it was finally time for the questioning to end. After a few words of careful instructions, Virginia dismissed the butler and the guard to carry out her orders to take Kate to the garden.

Samuel slid the pocket doors closed as he left. Virginia crossed the room to a narrow bookshelf, pulled out a book, and pushed a button hidden behind it. The bookshelf opened inward, and Virginia entered her private study.

The room was small, and as chaotic as the library was, with its fill of books, papers, and journals. Virginia moved quickly to a particular box and sorted through it until a small notebook was uncovered. It was labeled 2000-2001, and had a cut-out picture of several different herbs taped on the cover. She leafed through the pages until she found the one she was looking for. The page had been folded down to mark it, and she scolded herself for not recalling it sooner.

She sat in a padded chair at a narrow writing desk set against one wall and flattened the notebook in front of her. The windowless room was dark except for the flickering glow from the fire in the library spilling in through the secret door, and she pulled the chain on a desk lamp, throwing off a wide swath of light.

This room and the workroom, where Virginia perfected her recipes for tonics and teas, were her sanctuaries. Decades of research and experimentation had been meticulously recorded, assembled, and catalogued. But the volumes of writings she had surrounded herself with were hers alone, and no longer for the world. Interest in Virginia's work had waned over the past three decades, and it had been a long time since she had published any of her research. But she had pushed on, as her grandmother, and indeed the generations of herbalists before her, had done, never satisfied with the latest trials and experiments, always seeking new knowledge.

It was shocking to see the young woman who called herself Kate Tyler. When Mr. McGregor had reported seeing her on the bench by Stalton Brook, Virginia had dismissed it at first. But more than once, he had seen the portrait of Arabella—a commissioned work that once hung in the hallway of the manor house, now relegated to this very room, where Virginia could see it as she worked. McGregor was a trusted employee, not prone to fanciful tales. If he thought he had seen someone who looked like Arabella, then she had to believe him.

When Kate arrived, she was exactly as Virginia had pictured her. She was more modern-looking than Arabella, of course. After all, there were two and a half centuries between the two women. But the likeness was undeniable, Virginia thought as she studied the small portrait of Arabella that stood on an easel nearby. There were questions she still needed to ask her, and would, but it was not yet the time to reveal to Kate her reasons behind them.

The special herbal tea had been prepared, and it had not been difficult to glean information from Kate—a gullible young woman, as it turned out. No self-control at all, like so many of the young people her age. Virginia drank the tea, and it never affected her that way. But her research over many years, built on the studies of herbalists before her, convinced her that there was a unique chemical reaction that took place in some people—especially women—that caused a somnolence after ingesting the *tonic*, as she thought of it. The person was conscious, but sleepy, and the effect of the drink was not only that the person's inhibitions about sharing information were relaxed, but there was often an immediate loss of memory of the previous conversation.

In Kate, the tea had the desired effect. But perhaps, due to her petite frame, she soon fell into a deep sleep.

Virginia ran her finger down the page of measurements and ingredients in the notebook in front of her and stopped when she found what she was looking for—a note to the side, in her own handwriting: "Adjustment needed for frame of subject."

She should have remembered. A misstep with Kate had amplified the effects of the tea. The ramifications were troubling. But there was nothing to be done about it now.

Virginia had instructed her security guard to carry Kate to a bench in the garden, where she was confident the young woman would soon awaken without any ill effects, and no memory of the evening. If questioned, the story would be that Kate must have wanted to take another walk through the gardens in the moonlight before she left for Rye. Of course, this must have happened without Virginia's permission or knowledge. She would say that Kate must have fallen asleep there, and then found her way home.

Virginia thought back to the information Kate had revealed to her before she'd fallen into a deep sleep. She learned that Kate had been adopted as an infant, with her twin sister, Becky, and that both of her adoptive parents were no longer living. And she disclosed that her biological grandmother's maiden name was Corbyn—a woman born in England, and who had died there after living in the United States for many years.

Corbyn. Was it possible then that there was a family connection? A connection between an English woman named Bessie Corbyn, and indeed, Kate Tyler, in the twenty-first century, and Arabella Courbain over two hundred years before? Virginia pondered the possibility. It was a common practice to modify surnames. Courbain could have been changed to Corbyn. Modern methods of genealogical research might be called for. But it was not something she had the time to do.

She flipped through an address book on her desk and found the name she was looking for. Rory Stimpith. She picked up the phone and made a call.

With no apologies for the lateness of the hour, and after firmly convincing Mr. Stimpith that the matter was of the utmost urgency to her, with reassurance of a very generous payment if the information was delivered to her promptly, Virginia sat back in her chair, satisfied that the man would use his extensive resources to quickly research the genealogy of Bessie Corbyn Howard.

What she had learned from Kate herself about her family history was important, no doubt. But perhaps the most stunning piece of information was what Kate shared while she was still awake—that she had seen the book of legends at Myrlie Shaw-Windham's bookstore in Rye. Virginia bristled at the thought. Myrlie must have known about the book. There would be no other way. She had sensed Myrlie was holding something back at the séance. Something that had interrupted the concentration of the circle. If Myrlie had voluntarily kept the book hidden from the Corvos Sisterhood, she would face the consequences of this betrayal. And it would be dealt with swiftly.

Virginia pulled open a drawer in the desk and retrieved a sheaf of rolled papers, loosely tied with a faded red ribbon. She laid them on top of the notebook, untied the ribbon, and smoothed out the yellowing diary pages written in her grandmother Mathilde's hand. These had been personally gifted to Virginia before Mathilde's death—the very documents that chronicled the origins of the legend of Arabella. Virginia ran her finger across the flourishes of Mathilde's penmanship on each of the pages and murmured the words of the story as it unfolded.

Mathilde had never known of the tale herself until after the death of her husband, Quentin Calloway. Soon after that, as Mathilde was going through his papers, she discovered a letter written by Arabella, and an etching of the young woman standing on a cliff in the midst of a terrible storm. She soon learned from family members that the letter and etching had been passed down through the generations of Calloways, since it was first found in Arabella's meager possessions by Devon Calloway, the younger brother of Arabella's lover, Ewen.

Mathilde had been captivated by the story of heartbreak and loss, and its heroine's desire to escape an unthinkable future. She became obsessed with the tale. And that it was part of her husband's family history made it even more thrilling.

A friend of the Calloways, Sir Archibald Mallard, had been a frequent guest at the Calloway House. During one of these visits, he had told them he was planning to write a book about the many legends of Rye and the surrounding area of Sussex. Later, after Quentin's death, and the discovery of the letter, Mathilde sought him out to tell him of Arabella's story.

She recounted a simple but tragic story of a young woman's hopes and dreams torn apart by fate, and her vow to return to live the life she was meant to live. A tale that reaches across the centuries, awaiting its fulfillment.

She showed him Arabella's handwritten letter and the original etching of her, both convincing provenance of the tale.

Sir Mallard then encouraged her to allow him to include it in his book. Mathilde wrote in her diary that while she knew that Quentin would never have approved of it, she was thrilled at the thought of a family story being included in a work by the esteemed Sir Archibald Mallard. The Calloway family learned of her plans, and they refused to allow the story to be included in his work. But after intense debate, they agreed that it could be published, stipulating that the Calloway name could not be included. And the story of Arabella became a legend.

Ancient Tales of an Ancient Town was published and over the ensuing years, Mathilde became even more obsessed with Arabella. Her writings revealed that she had attempted to contact Arabella through séances. This led to the creation of the Corvos Sisterhood, and it was Mathilde's wish that belief in the legend would carry on into future generations through the Sisterhood until Arabella returned.

Virginia drew her jacket close around her. The room had chilled, no doubt from the waning fire in the library. She had come to the end of the diary. She rolled the pages, tied the red ribbon around them, and slid them back into the desk drawer.

She never tired of reading her grandmother's words. They had been a comfort to her, even as her own hopes and dreams as a young woman had been dashed, when promises had been made and then destroyed. Virginia knew Arabella's pain and suffering because she herself had experienced her own. Arabella was closer to her than any living person since her grandmother had passed on. And if anyone tried to deny what Kate Tyler might represent to her and to the fulfillment of the legend...

It was simply unthinkable.

11

THE NEXT MORNING, AT SUNRISE, Virginia Calloway pulled on a pair of rubber boots and a slicker, and filled a small metal pan with bits of meat and dried bread. She exited the manor through the pantry door, onto a gravel path that led to her private gardens. The air held an undecided mix of mist and rain. The grassy leaves on a lemongrass plant drooped and bounced back to release an accumulation of water and the scent of lemon as she brushed past them.

When she reached the first gate, one of several in the gardens, she lifted a rusted latch and stepped in. She stopped briefly every few steps and called out softly, a short cry that caused small animals to scurry through the underbrush, and sparrows to break from the branches of the trees and soar away.

She reached the second gate. The garden on the other side was her own herb garden, secluded, away from the prying eyes of tourists. But she stopped and sat down on a stone bench, calling out again with a series of rattling noises and croaks and caws.

Virginia scattered the scraps of food at her feet as her brisk melody filled the air, bringing the whir of birds on the wing closer and closer. An unkindness of ravens set down and hopped about at her feet, feasting on what she had tossed there. She spoke softly to them all, encouraging them to eat. A large raven with glossy black feathers came, swooping down to sit regally behind Virginia's right shoulder. She greeted him and held out her hand. He pecked at the bits of food she offered him. Soon, the other ravens flew away, leaving the largest one to hop down from his perch on the bench and eat the remaining morsels.

In her childhood, Virginia had been taught the symbolism of the ravens by her grandmother Mathilde. She grew to admire their intelligence. She learned how to understand them, and she believed that they understood her. Some learned to mimic her voice, and she learned their sounds as well.

Her grandmother Mathilde claimed to have seen the very first swarm of ravens when she arrived at the Calloway House in 1895. As the bride of Quentin Calloway, she was the new mistress of the house. She told Virginia later that no one at the house had ever seen the birds in such numbers before. At first, they were frightening to everyone. They would soar over the roof of the house in powerful and menacing swarms, and swoop around the barns, creating a terrible racket, before finally settling in the trees. After a few minutes, they would, as if one bird, fly away. Mathilde learned that what she thought of as a swarm of ravens was correctly called an *unkindness*. But she, and eventually Virginia, never thought of them as unkind at all. They believed them to be clever and intelligent, and that their presence carried great meaning.

Mathilde was fascinated with the birds, although her husband and the workers on the farm thought they were a nuisance and did everything they could to drive them away. But they were unsuccessful. Mathilde began to wait for them by Stalton Brook, away from the farm. Sometimes the largest one would land on the bench where she sat, cock his head, then caw and fly away.

Mathilde had told Virginia that she and the ravens became friends, as she studied their ways. Soon, they came to Mathilde in her dreams. She began to believe that their constant presence in her subconscious and in her waking life were urging her to change course, to use her creative gifts—of which she believed she had many—in a different way. She believed that they were coming because she was the new mistress of the Calloway House, and that she was chosen to have a special bond with them.

Virginia pulled back the hood of her slicker to soak in the growing warmth of the morning sun, now shining low in the eastern sky. The mist was burning off, and she gathered up the few remaining crumbs on the walk and tossed them into the bushes.

Thoughts of her grandmother Mathilde were never far from Virginia's mind. Virginia herself was born in the closing years of World War II. As a teenager, when she was not at boarding school, and then as a young woman, she had spent time with her grandmother at the Calloway House. Her father's injuries from early in the war eventually became debilitating, both mentally and physically. Her mother, unable to cope, had turned to alcohol, and Virginia had found herself shuttled off to the Calloway House on many occasions. Mathilde took that time to pass on everything she knew about herbalism, and how plants in the wild could be used to heal all manner of illnesses. Virginia was eventually initiated into the Corvos Sisterhood. Finally, Virginia had found a place where she felt she belonged. Before her grandmother died, Virginia promised her that she would carry on the important work of the Sisterhood. It was now her own legacy, and Kate Tyler was the missing piece she had been waiting for.

12

MEMORIES OF THE PECULIAR EVENTS at the Calloway House shadowed Kate the next morning, and she began to look at Rye in a different light, wondering if the nods of passersby were a look of recognition, or if a stray raven landing on a street bench possessed a meaning that she had yet to decipher.

She scolded herself back to reality. Gilbert had arranged for the audio tour of Rye, which would take her to twenty-three of the most popular spots. She had already picked out the stops that seemed most likely to fit her needs and eliminated the places she had already visited. Rye was a compact town, and the entire tour would be an easy walk.

The tourists were already out and about, meandering along the sidewalks and appreciating the sunny morning. Kate walked down to the west end of Mermaid Street for the first stop on the tour—the Old Borough Arms, a three-hundred-year-old guest house. Underneath the Arms was the Mermaid Street Café, where she had eaten breakfast three days earlier, so she moved on to the next stop on the tour. The audio guide took her up The Mint to The Standard Inn, a popular pub and inn dating back to the fifteenth century, and then on to the Cobbles Tea Room, where she found herself practically at the back door of The Mermaid Inn. There was only a short distance between the two buildings, the tearoom being tucked away on Hylands Yard. The guide in her ear said that the tearoom had existed here since 1953, opened by two spinsters who began serving guests in the front room of their cottage, and had become a popular landmark in Rye since those early days.

Kate approached the host at the Cobbles, who, after a brief wait, took her to an outdoor patio. She was seated at a small white table surrounded by blossoms of every color. An assortment of flowerpots huddled together along the stone windowsill of the tearoom, overflowing with pansies in hues of plum and buttery yellows. Cherry-red Dianthus burst out of the hanging baskets anchored to the brick wall. The stark-white tables, each with its own unique filigree design, were decorated with a flowering plant in a simple clay pot. The patio was surrounded with a charming white picket fence, creating a relaxed ambience, perfect for breakfast in the sunshine.

"Good morning."

Kate turned at the greeting, expecting the server, but instead Miles Pixley was standing at the gate to the patio. She shaded her eyes against the morning sun and looked up at him. He was dressed differently than in their earlier encounter—no costume this time—but was still entirely in black—jeans, T-shirt and leather jacket.

"Well, good morning to you," she replied, wondering how he had found her.

"I wasn't expecting to see you again. Do you mind if I join you?"

She motioned to the seat across from her. "Please do."

And he sat down, stretching his long legs out next to the table.

" Is it just coincidence that you stopped at the Cobbles this morning?" she said.

"It's a regular stop for me. But finding you here was a coincidence. An added bonus, actually."

The server approached and took their orders.

"Are you sightseeing again today?" Miles said.

Kate nodded. "I'm planning to spend the day in Rye, and I've started the audio tour. This was one of the early stops, and I guess I got distracted by my stomach."

"Easy enough to do. Have you been to the Cobbles before?"

"I haven't. But I have been to the Mermaid Street Café. I enjoyed the rooftop view, of course, but the food was wonderful, too."

"Well, you have chosen two of the most popular tea rooms in Rye, so you clearly have good taste."

The server soon brought a pot of tea and two cups on a small tray. Miles had ordered an organic Assam tea, with small pitchers of milk and honey, and poured for them, his large hands managing the small teapot easily.

"Milk or honey?" he said.

"Both, please."

"Ah," he replied. "I see you know how to take you tea."

"I lived in London with my family as a young girl," Kate said. "My parents insisted on following the local customs when we could. I learned about teatime and other traditions. For example, I know that if I were to order a full English breakfast, I would probably not need lunch, or maybe even dinner, that day. It is pretty daunting to have all of that food in front of you."

"Yes, but on some mornings," Miles replied, "it is the only thing that will do to get you through the day."

The server approached with their simple breakfasts of toasted crumpets with a house jam, and a colorful dish of fresh strawberries, pineapple, and kiwi.

"How did you choose Rye to launch your blog, Kate? Of course, I love Rye, so I am biased. It is definitely worth writing about, but hasn't it been done already?"

"Yes, in some ways it has been covered in many of the travel blogs and magazines. But I'm hoping to find things to write about that are more off the beaten path, too. You know, get a real feel for the history of the town—what it was back when these buildings were built, and the streets were first paved with those cobblestones. I mean, just think about the centuries of people that have lived and worked here. The families that were raised here, and the stories those buildings could tell." She stirred the tea that Miles had set in front of her, and then pulled out her phone. "Could I ask a favor?"

"Certainly."

"Would you mind taking a picture of me for the blog? This is a great setting, and the lighting is perfect right now."

Miles took the phone from her as she situated herself with the bright flowers in the background. She turned on a huge smile, and he took several pictures.

"You are ridiculously photogenic, you know." As he gave the phone back to her, his hand lingered on hers for a moment. "The camera seems to love you."

Kate slid her hand away. Miles was still just as attractive as she had remembered him. She still saw a kind face, and felt he had an unassuming way about him—an unusual combination perhaps, but still just as risky. And the fact that he had a son, ex-wife or not, raised a red flag. The sensation she felt when he simply touched her hand was really the only warning she needed.

She decided forthrightness was the only option.

"Are you flirting with me, Miles Pixley? Because I have to tell you, I am in a serious relationship back in North Carolina." She kept her tone friendly, hoping that it would keep the conversation sociable.

He smiled and leaned back in his chair. "Thank you for telling me, Kate. Then, no, I am not flirting with you. I'm simply stating that the camera finds you extremely attractive, of course. And," he leaned forward, "I would suspect that anyone reading your blog would love to spend more time getting to know you, too—since you obviously love your work, and you are probably incredibly good at it." He took a sip of his tea. "It looked like you had a good time the other night. I hope the gang wasn't too wild for you."

"Not at all," Kate replied. "I really enjoyed myself. They seem like good friends."

"They are. But a little of them can sometimes go a long way. As you probably noticed."

"And how was your time with your son? I think Jeffrey mentioned it was his birthday?"

Miles set his cup down and sighed. "That didn't turn out quite as expected."

"I'm sorry."

He shook his head. "Thank you. I was hoping my ex would change her mind, but they decided to take Josh on his first visit to a zoo, not far from here. He's crazy about animals, so he'll love it. But enough about me. I didn't get a chance to ask you the other night, how long you've been doing the travel thing?"

"I've really just launched my website in the last few months. I did freelance before that. But *The Wayfarer* did take off with blogs about local places to visit in North Carolina. Hopefully, Rye will kick off more international locations." She spread a bit of jam on what was left of her scone and took a bite. "You haven't told me where you're from. Are you from Rye?"

"No, not originally. London, actually. But I've been here for about two years now."

"And what do you do for a living?"

When he hesitated, she quickly apologized.

"I'm sorry. Maybe that's none of my business. Or," she narrowed her eyes, "maybe you really are just a chivalrous but ne-er-do-well swashbuckler who frequents the pubs for...what is it called? The Rye Gang of Sussex Night?"

Miles laughed. "No, nothing like that. And the monthly event is called Rye Gang Night, by the way. For your blog, of course."

"I'll make a note of that. Let me guess, then. You are good at disguises. So you are either an actor, a pirate, or a spy?"

"Nice try! Actually, I'm a detective sergeant with the Rye Police." He pulled out his badge as if to show proof.

She looked him over. "Hmm. Not what I expected."

"It's my day off, as I mentioned."

"And what do you like to do on your days off, Miles?

"Well, I'm happiest somewhere on the river, or in the channel with my boat...and my son. Or tromping through the Rye Harbour Nature Reserve on a nice day."

He paused and refilled his cup with tea and offered Kate more. She held her cup for him to pour.

"Listen, the audio tour is great," he said, "but it won't take you outside of Rye. If you are up for it, I'd love to show you some spots that your readers might like. And with the news I had from my ex...I could use the company, to be honest."

Kate considered his offer for a moment. "Well, I really would love to go down to Rye Harbour and Camber Sands at some point. If there is ever a body of water nearby on my travels, I have to put my toes into it. And it looks like it might be a good day to do that. But I wouldn't want to impose."

"Not an imposition at all. Actually, I keep my boat at the marina. So if you would like to go down to the sea on the great River Rother, I would be happy to oblige, except that the tide is out which means no boating on the river—at least, not right now. But I do have a car to get us to Camber Sands."

His offer was enticing. She felt she had already set the boundaries with him, so she didn't see any harm in accepting his invitation.

"Then I think that sounds like a great idea," she replied. "I would appreciate it. As long as you don't mind helping me with more photos?"

"I'd be happy to," he said.

They finished their breakfast and walked a short distance to his vehicle—a Jeep Wrangler that looked out of place next to all of the compact cars lined up along The Mint. They climbed in, and he pulled out into traffic, driving along Mermaid Street to The Strand. A few minutes later, they arrived at Camber Car Park. After a short walk, they came to a wide path leading over a stretch of dunes, lined on either side with bushes and gnarled trees shaped by constant winds off the channel.

They followed the path over the dunes, and soon the shoreline itself was before them—seven miles of broad sandy beach, with the English Channel stretching out to the horizon. Beachgoers had already dotted the sand with their tents, chairs, and boogie boards, and Kate was quickly reminded of the famous Crystal Coast of North Carolina, one of her favorite beach spots in the world.

They reached the hard sand, and the sound of the ocean and gulls slowed them down to a calm pace, eyeing the thin line between water and sky in the distance. They selected broken shells beneath their feet and returned them to the channel with a hard throw. Kate slipped off her shoes at the water's edge and let the cold froth of the shallow waves lap over her feet, sinking slightly into the sand each time the waves retreated.

As they walked along, Kate turned her phone over to Miles.

"Here, I need some video content for *The Wayfarer*."

A gust of wind blew her auburn curls free, and she gathered them loosely, turned, and smiled back at him.

"Perfect." He hit the record button.

Kate began to walk backward along the beach, facing Miles, with the vast expanse of the water in view beside her.

"Here we are on Camber Sands in East Sussex, England," she narrated. "We're not far from Rye, so it's easy to visit both of these amazing places on a day trip. There are sand dunes here, and miles and miles of flat sandy beach. This is a favorite place to set up your tents and chairs, bring your boogie boards, and enjoy the surf. If you like to kitesurf, this is a great beach to come to. But just check in advance for designated areas where you can launch from."

Kate looked out over the water, and Miles followed her gaze with the video for a few moments, with just the sound of the waves and birds in the background. He turned back to her, and she began again.

"Camber Sands—a new favorite vacation spot for me. It's an easy trip from London. Lots of parking, miles of beach for an awesome family trip. I hope you can visit here soon."

Miles turned off the video and gave the phone back to Kate.

"You made that look very easy," he said.

"Really?"

"Sure. I don't think I could walk backwards and talk at the same time, and sound intelligent while I was doing it." He laughed.

"It took me a while to get the hang of it. I was used to expressing myself through my writing, and maybe a few still shots. But I love the way videos make the places I visit come alive to my viewers. And I'm still learning. I think of it as talking to my friends, and it makes it easier."

They soon came to a bench, set far enough back from the shoreline to avoid the high tides, and sat down.

"I confess, I've read some of your blog," Miles said, after a few quiet moments. "I can see you really love what you do."

"I do love it. It has its downside, of course. But I've always been a wanderer. They used to call me the 'Gypsy Journalist.'" She curved her fingers in air quotes. "It was my whole life. At least, until last year."

"And you are missing your home in North Carolina? And the people there? Or maybe something else?"

She glanced at him, her eyes questioning his curiosity.

"I am good at reading people, Kate. It comes with the job. You have been distracted ever since we got to the beach." When she didn't respond, he continued. "But you don't have to talk about it if you don't want to."

Kate shook her head. "No, it's okay, really. And you're right. There is something."

She debated how much to share with him, but decided it might be good to bounce what had been happening to her, off of someone else. And he would be in a unique position to give her a professional perspective.

"But it's a long story," she said.

"I've got time."

Kate took a deep breath. "It all started on Monday, the day after I arrived in Rye. I stopped at a little bookstore off of The Mint, and there was an elderly man working there. He made it sound like he was the owner. But I think he mistook me for someone else, and invited me in like he knew me and was waiting for me. We talked for a bit, and then he went behind the counter and picked out an old book."

"What was the name of the bookstore?"

"BOOKS was the only name on the storefront."

"And the book?"

"Ancient Tales of an Ancient Town." It's a collection of the tales or legends of Rye, published in 1904 by Sir Archibald Mallard. The man said it was just what I was looking for. I had only asked him for any books about Rye's history and folklore. I'll admit, I was curious about it. I asked him how much it was. He said it was twenty pounds, but then it looked like he wasn't feeling well, and he went behind the curtain, to the back of the store, and didn't come back."

"Then what happened?" Miles said.

"Later, after I looked at the book, it seemed to be much more valuable than twenty pounds—it was a signed first edition. So I took it back the next day. He wasn't in the shop, but there was a woman there. When I told her what happened, she acted very strangely and said my story was impossible. That I couldn't have talked to anyone else. Then she implied that I had stolen the book. I insisted that I hadn't, and told her I had left twenty pounds. Come to think of it, I don't know what happened to the money. I didn't think to ask her. But the look she gave me said that she was done talking and that I needed to leave. AndI did. Look." Kate took her phone back from Miles. "I took pictures of the book."

He scrolled through the photos and stopped at the one she had taken of the etching. He looked up at Kate and then back at the photo.

"Kate, this looks exactly like you."

"I know. How strange is that?"

"Can you text those pictures to me?"

Kate agreed and sent them to him.

"I've never heard of the legend of Arabella," he said, after scrolling back to the photo she had taken of Sir Mallard's writings. "What do you know about it?"

"Only what I've read. I certainly didn't learn anything from Miss Calloway."

"Miss Calloway?" he said. "The lady at the bookstore?"

Kate hesitated. She had not meant to mention Virginia Calloway's name.

"No." She shook her head. "But just as I was leaving the bookstore, the woman asked me if I had read the book, or if I had studied it at all—her words. I just told her I had not looked at it much."

"Was that true?" he said.

"Not really. I mean, the pictures I took prove it. I didn't want to lie about it, but I didn't really think it mattered much. And I probably wouldn't have, except..."

"Except what?"

"Except for the photo...and..."

Kate considered whether to tell Miles about the incident at the Calloway House. She had woken up that morning with a headache, which had dissipated after their walk on the beach. But she couldn't help but wonder if it was the result of what had happened the night before. And she had already slipped and mentioned Ms. Calloway's name.

She felt his gaze on her, waiting for her to say something, anything. She could almost see the wheels turning in his detective brain, listening carefully, making assessments about the truth or untruths of her story. But there was her likeness in the book, and she guessed that he couldn't ignore that.

Finally, she told him the rest of her story, briefly mentioning the incident at Opal's Tea Shop, then her meeting Mr. McGregor and receiving the invitation from Ms. Calloway and insisted that Miles should not make a fuss over it.

"And in the end, as I said, I never learned anything new about Arabella from Miss Calloway. It's all just a coincidence, I'm sure. Random events that are distracting me from why I am here in Rye. That's all it is."

"First of all," Miles replied, "I don't believe in coincidences, nor in random events. This doesn't sound right. I'm a bit concerned about what's been happening to you."

"Please don't be. Believe me, I've handled a lot in my travels. I know when something doesn't feel right, and if I have to remove myself from it, then I will. I was probably just overtired."

"But you don't remember how you got into the gardens, right?"

"Well, I woke up there—"

"And you don't remember how you got there."

Kate finally admitted that he was right. "No, I guess I don't remember. And I won't be going back there again. But it doesn't make sense that a woman like that would do anything to harm a person, right? I mean, she seemed a little eccentric, but the Calloway House and Gardens are famous, aren't they?"

"The Calloways have run the house and gardens as a tourist destination for years," Miles said, "and it's been in the family for centuries, if I remember the history right. You've seen how old some parts of the house are. I don't really know much about Virginia Calloway, though. Nothing that's come through our office, at any rate."

"All right, then, case closed," said Kate. "I am none the worse for wear, and I don't want to make a big deal about it. I'm just going to go about my business, which I am getting behind in, and I'll leave when the time comes."

"And when is that exactly?" he said.

"A week from tomorrow."

He reached in his pocket and pulled out a business card and his phone.

"Here's my number, Kate. Call me at any time, day or night, if you need to."

When she didn't reach for his card immediately, he held it out again.

"Kate, you are in my town now, and that means I will be keeping an eye on things. Please take my card. I insist. And if you would, please text me your contact information. This is strictly business, Kate."

She gave in again and texted her phone number to him after taking his business card.

"Enough about me," she said. 'You said you've lived here for several years?"

"Okay, I get the hint." He put his phone away. "Yes, about two years."

"Were you a detective in London, too?"

"For a bit."

"Do you have family there?"

Miles hesitated. "My mum and dad are there. My gran lives in Cornwall."

"No brothers or sisters, then?"

He turned and smiled at her. "Full of questions today, too, eh?"

"Well, I guess so. You don't have to answer if you don't want to. But you should know by now that I am naturally curious about people and places."

"I notice you didn't ask me more about the situation with Josh."

"I wouldn't want to pry about that."

"I appreciate it. It has been difficult."

He pulled up a photo on his phone and showed it to her—a beaming toddler with dark curls and bright-blue eyes, just like his father.

"He's adorable," Kate said.

"And he already knows it." Miles tucked the phone in his pocket.

After a few moments, he glanced over at her. Kate sensed he was deciding whether to trust her enough to open up to her about something that was on his mind, and that it probably wasn't what he was used to doing. Certainly not with someone he had just recently met. But somehow, she knew it would be okay with her if he did. Trust needed to go both ways. It was easy for her to feel comfortable with people quickly, but she guessed that it was not that way with him.

Something about the solitude of the beach had made it easier for her to share what had been happening to her over the last couple days. She hoped he would feel the same. Then she saw him take a deep breath.

"I was on the London Police Force when we met. My ex, I mean. She was a stunner, and so smart. I felt stupid around her. Not that she made me feel that way—I just could barely talk when she was around. Guess I was smitten from the day I met her."

He continued, gazing out at the horizon. "We were investigating an abduction—two kids went missing—and I was put on the case. Wasn't long before we realized that there was much more to it than we thought. It was a human trafficking ring. At least, that's what it looked like. They asked me to go undercover." He leaned forward, his arms resting on his knees. "I shouldn't have left her, but we thought it would be quick, a short-term operation. Phoebe was pregnant with Josh at the time. She didn't want me to go, but I thought I had to. Wrap it up quick, get the kids back to their parents, that's what I thought. But it got worse. I was in pretty deep, and they couldn't pull me out. We were so close. The ring stretched from the UK into Russia, so I was out of the country a lot. I guess the strain of me not being there was too much for her. She went into labor early. But I wasn't there." He swiped at his eyes and took a deep breath.

"I'm so sorry, Miles."

"When I did get out of it, I promised her I would be there for her. No matter what. But it was too late. She left, with Josh, and filed for divorce. We saved fifty-five kids, Kate! Fifty-five children went home to their parents. But I paid the price for it. In the end, it cost me my own son." He took a deep breath. "I will never forgive myself for that," he whispered.

Kate felt tears well up in her eyes—an understanding of what he was going through feeling very real to her.

"I know what a strain that can be on a relationship—not being there when they need you. I've had to deal with that myself. But you see Josh when you can, right?"

He shook his head. "I did for a while. But she hooked up with a guy with a lot of money and power. They got married, and she filed for full custody. Claimed it would be better for Josh. I've been fighting it. I'm sorry for unloading on you, Kate. You don't need to hear my problems."

"I can see it's been weighing on your mind, because of his birthday."

"I suppose. She called me today, too—of all days. Says her husband wants to adopt Josh, give him his name."

This landed on Kate hard. Her own history of not knowing about her biological family for so many years came flooding back to her.

"You can't let them do that, Miles! He's your son, no matter what." She shifted on the bench to face him. "Listen, my sister, Becky, and I were adopted by a wonderful family as babies. But I grew up knowing nothing about my biological family, except for my sister. Nothing. And just by chance, I found out last year that I have a brother. And now I know who my grandparents were, and my cousins. But to this day, I have no idea who my father was, and I don't know if my mother is even alive anymore. No one does. And it leaves a hole, Miles. It leaves a huge hole in my life, that I deal with every day. So don't let him go, whatever you have to do. He has a family. He has you, your parents, your grandma. They are still his family, too. You are his father. And if your ex and her new husband think he will be loved any more than he already is by changing his last name at this point, that's not true. And shame on them if they think that way."

Miles glanced at her. Tears were streaming down her face, and she wiped them away with her sleeve. He stood and walked away from her to the water's edge. He clasped his hands behind his head and stared out over the ocean as if looking for answers, for strength, for control of his emotions.

Kate could sense a battle taking place. She walked up to him.

"Listen, Miles, I'm sorry. I am in no position to give you advice."

"No need to apologize. Maybe that's what I needed to hear. And I'm sorry about your family situation, too. What you said came from a good place. I can see that."

She felt the urge to reach out to him, to comfort both of them, and for a deeper connection. But it would have been a mistake. She hitched her tote bag up onto her shoulder and slid her hand into her pocket.

"I'm glad I was here, then. And really, I know you'll do what is right for you and your son."

Miles nodded. He put his arm around her shoulder and gave a quick squeeze before letting go.

"Thank you for saying that," he replied. "Sometimes we just need to hear it from someone else, I guess."

The beachgoers were packing up and leaving as the tide was turning. The gulls hopped along the beach, ahead of the ripples from the channel.

"I think we should be getting back," Kate said, breaking the silence.

Miles nodded, and they made their way back over the dunes, to the car park.

13

MILES BEGAN TO RETRACE their drive back to Rye. Kate glanced over at him. He seemed to have put his own thoughts aside and was focusing on his driving. She had learned something about his character during the brief time they had spent together, and admired what she knew about him now. He was dedicated, principled, and her instincts were telling her that he was someone she could trust with even more of her story.

"I didn't really tell you everything about what has been happening to me, though," she said. "But if you don't want to talk about it now, I understand."

"There's more?" He glanced over at her. "I definitely want to know."

"Well, yes." Kate proceeded to tell him about her dreams and the similarities of the setting to the etching in Sir Mallard's book.

"And you said the scene was of high cliffs and boulders on the beach, with a lighthouse or fire of some sort?"

"Yes, that is what I keep seeing."

"Kate, do you have time for quick detour? There is a place I think you might want to see."

"Sure," she replied, and he changed lanes.

After about an hour, they pulled into a parking lot. A grassy field lay like a skirt in front of them, and beyond was the channel, blue and vast. Kate's pulse quickened.

"Where are we?" she said.

"This, Kate, is Beachy Head. I've been here before, and what you described in your dream reminded me of it. I thought maybe you would like to see it."

Kate slowly stepped out of the car. Something other than the channel loomed ahead of her, but she didn't yet know what it was. They followed a path toward the cliffs. The closer they got, the more anxious she felt.

"What is this place, Miles?" she whispered, when they stopped.

Miles had walked a few paces ahead, but then turned and looked back.

"Kate, are you all right? You're as pale as a ghost." He walked back to her and put his hands on her shoulders.

She looked up at him. "Just tell me what this place is."

"It's called Beachy Head. These are chalk cliffs, very similar to the White Cliffs of Dover. We're further down the coast, though. Kate, what's going on?"

She felt like she was rooted to the ground.

"Are you afraid of heights?"

Without answering, Kate moved away from him and finally took a few tentative steps forward. She was drawn and yet repelled by the approach to the edge of the cliffs. There was no fence, no barrier between the grass and the drop off to...she dared not look to see what was at the bottom of the cliffs.

"Do you want to leave?" Miles said.

Kate wanted to run. She wanted to get back in the car and go straight to the train, to the airport, and to home, as far away from there as she could get. There was a fear here, sinister and shadowy, even as the dazzling sun was reflected off the chalky white cliffs in the distance. It could have been night, though— such was the darkness she felt.

She was suddenly cold, and wrapped her arms around herself, clutching at her clothes. She wanted to flee, and yet she was drawn to the edge. She had to see what lay at the bottom of the towering cliffs.

Kate instinctively took Miles by the arm. "No. I need to see what...what is out there."

"Okay. We'll take it slow, then."

They inched toward the edge, not stopping again until they were mere feet away from the sheer drop-off. Kate felt Miles' tight grip on her arm and around her shoulders. She looked down. Jagged rocks stood like fallen sentinels on the beach. Off to the right of the rocks was a lighthouse. And to her left, more cliffs wound along the coast, edging the ocean like a bright-white ribbon.

She closed her eyes. A breeze blew her hair. Suddenly, in her mind, the sea became rough, the waves billowed, and there on the horizon was a ship, tossed in a storm. She was not in her own body then. She was Arabella, and there were voices—harsh, threatening voices—and laughter.

"Kate, Kate!" Miles's voice drew her back to reality. "What just happened?"

"She was here, Miles. This is where..."

"Where what?"

"Where Arabella met her fate."

Kate insisted that they leave then, and Miles guided her back to the car, supporting her as they walked. He drove for a few minutes and soon pulled into the parking lot of a pub. Kate said that she wanted to go back to Rye. That she wasn't hungry. The urge to flee was still pulling at her.

"Kate, I know you want to go, but we need to talk about this. Please, let's just stop here for a bit."

She finally agreed, and they walked to one of the tables in an outdoor seating area. Kate asked for a glass of white wine, and Miles ordered a beer. After a few sips of the wine, she felt calmer, and her hands stopped shaking.

"Do you want to talk about it now?" Miles said.

"I...I don't know." Her thoughts were swirling, darting around like fireflies in a jar.

"Kate, you told me that the legend was that Arabella would return to live the life she was meant to live, right?"

"Yes." She nodded.

"And we know that you favor the etching of Arabella."

"I look exactly like her."

"I agree. But we don't know where this actually happened. It's not in the legend, anyway, right? Did Miss Calloway say anything about it?"

"No. At least, nothing that I remember."

"Why do you think you had such a strong reaction at Beachy Head? Do you think it means something?"

She thought for a moment. There was no doubt in her mind that there was meaning to it. But it was hard to explain. She started slowly.

"Yes, I think it means something. This may be the place where Arabella...where she died. But Miles, it's more than that. I can't describe it, but I felt something very dark there. Something or someone..." She struggled to remember and explain it. "I'm not a psychic, Miles. I've never had *visions* or anything like that. But back there, I felt, for just a split second, that I wasn't me. It was like I was...her."

She emptied her glass, and Miles motioned to the server for another.

"You must think I'm crazy."

"No. I was there with you, and I could see that something was happening. Kate, you wouldn't know this, but as sad as it is, it's not uncommon for people to take their lives on the cliffs here. Maybe you were feeling something of that history, too?"

She agreed it was possible. "But this was more personal. I thought I heard voices there, too, and laughter."

She shivered, recalling the same laughter in the hallways at the Mermaid Inn, as she woke up from her dream the first night of her stay. But she kept this to herself.

"Is there anything I can do to help?" Miles said.

She shook her head. "I appreciate it, but this is mine to figure out. And I think that's what I need to do. There is a lot I don't know about that time in Rye—the smugglers' stories, what it was like for women back then. There must be places I can research it, right?"

"Sure," Miles said. "There's the library and the historical society in Rye. Great resources there, and online, too. It's pretty amazing the records that they've archived."

"Well, then, that's where I'll start."

14

KATE'S SLEEP THAT NIGHT was uneventful and dreamless, and for that, she was thankful. But the chilling memories from the day before lingered on into the morning—an uncomfortable reminder of their trip to Beachy Head. She was grateful to Miles for taking her there and supporting her as she relived Arabella's terror and realized that it was there, in that place, that she had decided her fate.

The days she was meant to spend in Rye were quickly slipping away. This was not turning out to be the trip she'd intended to have. For the day's itinerary, she had written in her journal, "Art Galleries, Antique Shops, Unique finds, discovering the art scene in Rye." But she was determined to set it all aside to focus on her research.

The Rye Library, her first stop, was just a short walk from the inn, and she turned right onto High Street. Like the thousands of Main Streets in the United States, High Streets in England were the backbone of the town, bustling with tourists and locals alike as they popped in and out of the shops crowded along either side, each one with its own personality and purpose. Some storefronts were brick. Some had wattle and daub exteriors, similar to the Mermaid Inn. But all retained the charm of the Old Rye.

Kate took her place in the stream of people. Just after she had turned the corner onto High Street, a small shop caught her eye. The sign over the door said, ESSENTIALS OF RYE. She stopped to look in the window and was drawn to a framed photograph of a nighttime sky with black birds skating across the moon, creating shadows on the landscape. As she gazed at it, the image triggered something in her mind, and after a few moments, she began to piece together connections she had not recognized before.

First, she remembered the brooch that Myrlie Shaw-Windham at the bookstore was wearing on her scarf. Kate sat down on a bench outside the store and pulled out her journal and a pencil and sketched the brooch as closely as she could remember it. It depicted two birds, similar to a crow or a raven, that appeared to be gripped in a battle. They formed the outside circular rim of the brooch. She drew them with their curved beaks open, and pressed the pencil down hard to blacken the center of their eyes. In its open talons, one bird clutched a small crescent-shaped moon. The other bird held three connected stars.

As the image formed on the paper, Kate realized she had seen the same image in other places. Ms. Calloway wore a pendant which was strikingly similar, if not identical, to the brooch she had seen on Ms. Shaw-Windham. And finally, over the entrance to the oldest part of the Calloway House, she remembered seeing two ravens carved into the wood. But there, they had been separated, with the moon and the stars sitting in between them. It hadn't meant anything to Kate at the time, but now she wondered if the pieces of jewelry had been based on the carvings in the ancient house. She wrote the word "origins" in the margin.

The images meant something. She wasn't sure exactly what yet, but she felt convinced that the woman in the bookstore, Ms. Calloway, and the Calloway House itself were connected, not only by the book and the legend of Arabella, but by this strange image of ravens in a battle with the moon and the stars.

Kate looked into the store window again and noticed even more images of ravens in other photographs, artists renderings, and jewelry.

A bell chimed as she opened the door and went in. The aroma of incense surrounded her as she made her way through the narrow aisles. Displays of teas and herbal remedies were scattered throughout the store. Along one wall were several shelves of books on meditation, yoga, veganism, and vegetarianism...and dreams. Kate's gaze landed on one entitled, *Dreams and You.* As she reached for it, a woman approached. A bright-blue scarf held back a mass of long white hair, and from head to toe, she wore the colors of a peacock woven into her shawl, blouse, and long skirt. Her face was lined with age, but kind and welcoming.

"May I help you?" the woman said.

Kate noticed a Russian accent in the woman's voice.

"I wonder if I could ask you a question," Kate said.

"Of course. I am Madame Zaytsev. What can I help you with?"

Kate opened her journal to the sketch she had just drawn.

"I have seen some images of this general design recently, and I wonder if you know whether it has any specific meaning?"

The woman adjusted her glasses and studied it for a bit.

"Well, of course, those look like ravens or crows. There have always been many meanings associated with the bird. And it looks like they are holding the moon and the stars in their talons?"

Kate confirmed that she had recalled it that way.

"Well," Madam Zaytsev said, "if I remember correctly, the birds together with the moon and the stars is a very old symbol. Centuries old, even. I haven't seen this exact design in anything I have sold here, though. I am curious, where did you see this?"

Kate hesitated, not wanting to involve anyone else in her recent experiences. Sharing them with Miles had been difficult enough.

"Oh, I think I saw it in an old book and in some jewelry, maybe. That's all. The photographs in your window of the black birds just reminded me of it."

"Did you sketch this? It is quite good."

"Thanks. I just like to sketch people I see, and places mostly, so I remember them," she said and then explained why she was visiting Rye—at least, the official version.

A smile spread across Madam Zaytsev's face. "Then please let me show you what I have here." She led Kate to several displays of artwork in the front window. "We have the works of several local artists and photographers. They often hold seminars here. And we have a wonderful yoga instructor who has classes upstairs."

They reached a display of essential oils and teas.

"I see you sell herbal teas here, too."

"Yes, yes, herbal teas." The woman nodded.

"Do you happen to have any that might make you very sleepy, so much so that you don't even remember things when you wake up?"

"Oh, well, of course chamomile is one of the more common herbal teas that have relaxing properties." She motioned for Kate to follow her to a display, and picked up an exquisitely decorated box. "This is a valerian tea. It is a natural sedative and mild tranquilizer. Also good for headaches and insomnia. But it sounds like you are talking about some of the more unusual and exotic herbals that might do that."

Madame Zaytsev thought a moment, before continuing.

"There are blends of herbals that have been studied over the years, that for some people are more like a drug. Perhaps valerian root combined with chamomile may create that type of effect—but very mild effect—of course. And some, in the hands of an expert herbalists, are medicinal. But," she laughed, "I don't have that knowledge. In fact, I am sure it's not legal to even prepare something like that—to drug you and make you forget! Oh no. That is for the *ancients* to keep that secret, I think!" She winked.

"The *ancients*," Kate repeated. "I'm not sure what it means."

"Well, England is a very ancient land, of course, just like my own country of Russia. I believe that the ancients are the generations that have gone on before us—before we were England, maybe even before the Romans or the Celts. Even in your own country, there were ancients that existed before you that are gone now, and their stories are gone with them."

She drew Kate by the arm to the front of the store.

"Look around you, my dear. In Rye, there is history that clings to the very stones. And those stories were handed down by oral tradition until they were written down much later. Personally, I like to think of the ancients as the women of the time—mysterious, knowledgeable in the healing arts, with herbs or with incantations, and interpretations of dreams. These are the women who gathered the wisdom into their hearts and handed it down from generation to generation."

"Do you think the ancients and their stories might be described in legends, then?" Kate said.

"Perhaps. But legends are not always true. People might believe them, and there might be a nugget of truth to them, but no one really knows if they are real or not."

"Have you ever heard of the legend of Arabella?" Kate said.

Madame Zaytsev thought for a moment. "No, I don't think that I have. What does this legend say?"

"Oh, nothing. Just something I heard."

Madam Zaytsev reached out and took Kate's hand. "May I ask you a question?"

The warmth from her hand seemed to spread up Kate's arm, comforting and calming.

Kate nodded.

"You asked about ravens. Often, ravens or crows appear in dreams, as a totem animal. This goes back to ancient times also. Have you been seeing ravens in your dreams, dear?" she whispered.

"Not ravens, no," Kate replied. "But..."

"But what?"

They were alone in the shop. A rhythmic and moody song played in the background—a flute and a harp joining in a soothing melody.

"I've seen myself in dreams. On a cliff overlooking the ocean. There is a ship—in a storm. I have this dream a lot."

"Ah, I see. This may mean difficult times ahead of you, dear. Perhaps even danger. But you have also seen images of the raven. Not in dreams, I understand. But all around you. This can be a symbol of a new phase in your life, a time to leave the past behind. There is magic and mystery all around us. Our dreams and the ravens are manifestations of so much that is hidden to mortals." Madam Zaytsev smiled and released Kate's hand after giving it a pat. "But it may mean nothing at all." She led Kate to a nearby display. "Now, I can recommend a tea that will maybe stop your racing thoughts at night. That might help you have a good sleep, right?" She picked up a small box. "Ah, here it is. Passionflower tea. Prepare one cup before bedtime. Just follow the instructions. It will quiet your thoughts, and you will sleep like a little babe."

"I think this is just what I need," Kate said. "You've been extremely helpful."

She paid for the tea, thanked Madam Zaytsev, and went out to the street.

Kate shaded her eyes from the bright sun as she stepped out into the busy sidewalk. Leaving the warm, calming surroundings of the shop jarred her back to reality. Perhaps the woman might have had some different advice if Kate had told her that it was not simply images of ravens she had been seeing, but physical ones at the Calloway House. But surely, those birds can be seen anywhere, she thought. If she looked hard enough right now, she would see them everywhere. She was sure of it.

15

AFTER FOLLOWING UP on two other investigations he had been assigned, Miles returned to the Rye Police station, made himself a cup of tea, and sat down at his desk. It was the morning after his outing with Kate, and he had been left stewing about the time he spent with her all evening and long into the night.

He had learned a lot about Kate Tyler in the brief time he knew her. She was genuine, caring and insightful. No one had ever talked to him about his personal situation like she had, and he had never opened up easily to anyone about it. She was very attractive, intelligent, creative, and adventurous.

He opened her website and looked at her profile picture. Yes, she was all of those things. Her deep emerald-green eyes had held his more than once, but there was a sadness there, too, and he sensed she had only exposed a small part of her past to him. The only flaw? She was apparently very loyal in her relationships, and to his disappointment, not easily swayed by his charms.

He shook his head and raised his cup to Kate's significant other in North Carolina.

"You're one lucky bloke, my friend," he murmured, and reluctantly exited *The Wayfarer* website.

He knew he needed to put aside his personal feelings, because he did have serious concerns about her situation. She didn't seem the type to make up stories to get attention, so he was inclined to believe what she had told him. But what was happening to her didn't make sense. She insisted that what had occurred at the Calloway House was a matter of simply falling asleep on a bench in the garden. Nothing to worry about. But it was highly unlikely that she would not be able to remember how she got there—unless there was some type of drug involved.

Her reactions at Beachy Head seemed genuine enough that he was concerned about how the incidents were affecting her physically and emotionally. And then there was the undeniable likeness between Kate and the etching in the book of legends.

If she were telling the truth, more investigation was needed. Rye was a safe town, even with hundreds of thousands of visitors every year, so the police department was always concerned when tourists were involved in any potentially dangerous situations. It wasn't clear that there was anything illegal going on, but there were enough unanswered questions for him to be suspicious, and he was determined to uncover the truth.

Kate said that she was planning to do her own research, but he would take a different approach using resources to which she did not have access. First, he needed to find out more about the bookstore and the book that Kate was given.

He started with a search of public records for details about the store. He found that it had been bought by Myrlie Shaw-Windham two years earlier, from the estate of Mr. and Mrs. Clive Beecham. They were an elderly couple who opened the store after World War II. The store was simply called BOOKS. Its social media presence was practically non-existent. The website was outdated. Not a recipe for success, he thought.

Next, he searched for information on the owner herself. Myrlie Shaw-Windham was fifty-five years old. She was not in a relationship, according to her social media profile. She had attended the University of Sussex, Brighton, and was retired from St. Peter's House Library at the University of Brighton. A lifelong interest in books, it would seem, since she parlayed her experience into opening a bookstore.

There were few photos available. But two interested him. One was of an elderly man and woman at a small pub in Rye Harbour. The names attached to it in the comments were Edward Bailey and Mildred Shaw-Bailey. Another one, dated later, was of just the man sitting in a chair next to a Christmas tree. He did appear to match the description that Kate gave, although the pictures were of someone a bit younger and perhaps healthier. A further search revealed that Edward Bailey and Mildred Shaw were married in 2010.

Myrlie Shaw-Windham's name search in public records revealed that she had been married at one point, and that she was divorced ten years prior. No children, as far as Miles could tell. There was nothing very helpful in his searches so far.

Next, he googled the name of the book *Ancient Tales of an Ancient Town,* and the author, Sir Archibald Mallard, and discovered that it was a rare book. Some of the attached links led to book reviews, all positive. He then accessed a stolen and missing book site. He scanned through the list of names for several pages, and then switched to a search for the title itself.

He wasn't surprised when he soon found that the book was listed as stolen. According to the website, it had been reported as such from the London home of Lord Arthur Cheswick in 1998, and had never been recovered. Lord Cheswick's library was extensive in its collection of rare books. Sir Mallard's book in particular was a signed copy from a small initial printing which was highly renowned for the etchings in it that had been created by the prestige engravers of the day—a coup for the author at the time. Miles compared the photos of the cover and the inside page that Kate texted him, and they matched the online images of the book. Kate must have had it in her hands at some point.

This gave the situation an entirely new significance. Miles wasn't sure how, or why, the old man would have sold the book—known to be stolen—out to a random customer in the bookstore. That didn't make any sense unless it was his plan to hand it off to someone like Kate, from another country, to take the risk away from him. Or maybe to protect his stepdaughter? But that didn't really fit with Kate's version of their interaction. So who exactly was the man?

If Miles believed Kate, which he really wanted to, then the man who sold her the book was Myrlie Shaw-Windham's stepfather, Edward Bailey. His residential address was the same as the bookstore. Miles knew that many of the businesses in that area of Rye had flats above them. It could have been possible then that the elderly man came downstairs when his stepdaughter wasn't there, met Kate, and sold her the book.

Miles was narrowing down the possibilities of the *how*, but the *why* was still a mystery.

Miles refreshed his tea and did an Internet search on the Calloway House & Gardens. The website itself was professionally done. Hubert Calloway was listed as chairman of the board for the public entity, with a small board of trustees also part of the management team. Notably missing, however, was the name of Virginia Calloway. And it wasn't clear what the exact relationship was between Hubert and Virginia, although they shared the Calloway name.

Miles tucked it away as an open question.

He skimmed through basic material on the website about their business hours and the history of the house and gardens. Compared to other public gardens in the area, the offerings seemed limited to tours of the medieval Calloway House, birdwatching and garden tours. But that in itself didn't raise any red flags.

A separate search of Virginia Calloway's name revealed bits of information on her connection to the Calloway House & Gardens, and then her work as an herbalist many years before, with a few published articles on the subject in professional journals. A studio photo dated 1985, matched up with the date of some of her published works. She herself had no social media presence.

Kate's retelling of her strange experience at Virginia Calloway's home was far more concerning than what had taken place at the bookstore, although Miles would need to check into both. He poured out the remains of his tea, left the police station, and drove first to the Calloway House & Gardens.

The public areas were not yet open when he arrived, but there was a guard near the entrance to the parking lot. After parking his car, Miles showed the guard his badge and asked to see Virginia Calloway.

The guard stepped away and made a brief phone call. When he ended the call, he told Miles to follow him, and they walked to the Calloway Manor. A butler greeted them and took Miles to the library, where he was announced to Virginia Calloway.

Miles quickly scanned the room and noted the clutter of papers, books and journals on every open space, and bookshelves stacked two-deep with more books. Dried herbs hung from nails in the walls and on the windowsills. The woman herself—who was seventy-five, according to his Internet search—was dressed in a long khaki skirt and a dark-green cardigan. His gaze was drawn to her hands—nails manicured with red polish, but knuckles scraped and dirty as if she had been working in the garden.

Ms. Calloway invited him to sit, which he did after finding a space on the edge of an upholstered side chair. She seated herself on a sofa near the fireplace and asked what his business might be with her.

"On Wednesday evening of this week, a young woman was invited here to speak with you." He took out a pen and a small pad of paper from his pocket. "Her name was Kate Tyler. Do you remember her?"

"Why, yes, of course, I remember the young woman. Charming. From America. We had a lovely chat."

"May I ask why she was invited here?"

"Certainly. My gardener, who had spoken to Miss Tyler on one of our tours earlier this week, happened to mention to me that she was extremely interested in the gardens. I invited her here to talk about it. I believe she said she was a 'travel blogger.' I wasn't sure what that was, but she explained it to me, and I was happy to share something about the Calloway House and Gardens."

Miles knew this was lie number one—at least, according to Kate's account. The gardens were not her reason for the invitation.

"How did you know her name?"

"My gardener knew her name, so I assume she introduced herself to him. He mentioned that particular tour often originates from guests staying at the Mermaid Inn, so I simply took a chance."

This was not the story that Kate had shared with him, but Miles took in what the woman told him and filed it away for future reference. Virginia Calloway was calm and collected, not revealing any concern about his questions up to this point. He began to study her body language more closely to see how she might reveal herself.

"Is that all, Detective?"

"Just a couple more questions."

Ms. Calloway nodded.

"Do you remember what time she left?"

"It was ten or ten-thirty. I don't recall the exact time."

"And how was she when she left?"

"Well, she was perfectly fine, of course. Now I must ask you a question, Detective Sergeant...Pixley, is it?"

He nodded.

"Is this young woman in some kind of difficulty? Is she all right? Was there some reason for her reporting this to the police?"

"Yes, she is fine. But apparently, she found herself on one of the benches in your gardens around eleven p.m., and she is not sure how she got there."

"Oh heavens, that is odd, then. She was escorted to her car by the guard, of course. You can ask him yourself if you would like." The question was answered smoothly and easily. "Should I ring for him?"

"No, ma'am, that won't be necessary. At least, not yet."

"Well..." Ms. Calloway rose and escorted Miles to the door of the library where the butler was waiting. "Perhaps she chose to go into the gardens after he left her? And fell asleep? As you can see, it is all quite open to the public, even at night. Perhaps that is something that needs to be remedied, I suppose. I will speak to my cousin Hubert about it immediately."

Ah, so Hubert Calloway was her cousin. Miles filed that piece of information away, too.

"One more question," he said. "Do you usually invite tourists to your private home to talk about the gardens?"

He finally noticed a flicker of surprise at the question, and a slight hesitation before she responded. She had probably rehearsed the other answers, but not that one.

"No. I don't suppose I do. Good day, sir."

Miles heard the door to the library slide shut behind him as he was escorted to the front of the house. He found his own back way to the parking lot, taking in his surroundings as he walked.

The old Calloway buildings loomed over him as he skirted them on the far end. He then walked to the entrance of the public gardens. Unless there was another way to walk from the manor to the interior of the gardens, Kate would have had to take the same route he just did. And he was told that the guard had escorted her to her car.

He quickly estimated how far Kate might have had to navigate between the manor and the public gardens, on her own or otherwise. It was a significant distance for someone who had no recollection of anything between having tea with Ms. Calloway and waking up on the bench.

He returned to his car. The guard was just stepping out of the guard shack as Miles drove by. He stopped and rolled down his window.

"Excuse me. Can I ask you a question?"

The guard nodded.

"There was a young woman visiting Miss Calloway Wednesday evening. Were you here at the time?"

"Yes, sir."

"What time did she leave?"

"I took her to her car around ten or ten-thirty. Then I got in my car and went home since I was done for the day."

"And did you see her leave?"

"No. But she should have been right behind me."

"Thank you."

The guard turned away, and Miles drove off. Again, he felt that the guard's answers were rehearsed, just as Virginia Calloway's were. Ten or ten-thirty seemed to be the prepared response. He was not yet convinced that what happened to Kate two nights before had not been a criminal act, being covered up by Ms. Calloway herself.

After returning to the station, Miles walked the four blocks down to BOOKS off of The Mint. He went in and perused the shelves of books marked as Mystery, and then others in the Crime section while waiting for a customer to leave. He soon returned a classic by Sir Arthur Conan Doyle to its place on the shelf and approached the woman behind the counter.

"Myrlie Shaw-Windham?"

"Yes, how can I help you?"

Miles showed her his badge. "Detective Sergeant Pixley. I'd like to ask you a few questions."

She stepped away to a nearby bookshelf. "What is this in regard to?"

Miles was not going to tip his hand yet about the status of the book, which he now knew had been stolen. Time enough for that later. He simply relayed the incident with Kate, and asked her if she recalled it.

"And she says she returned the book to you before she left your store."

"I am certain she did not," Myrlie replied, perhaps too quickly.

"She has photos of the book," Miles said. "She showed them to me."

"Well, if she has photos from the book, then she must have the book. She couldn't have gotten it from here. And you say she got it from an old man here?" Myrlie shook her head. "No, my stepfather lives here, but he hasn't spoken a coherent word in months. And he most definitely does not work here in the store. He isn't even able to leave the flat upstairs."

"May I speak to your stepfather?"

"Oh no, that would not be possible. You see, he is very frail, and as I said, he does not communicate. He suffers from dementia and sleeps most of the time. I don't think you would be able to learn anything from him, and it might be very upsetting to him to have a stranger in the flat."

"I would really like to try to talk to him, though, just to clear everything up. Perhaps I could come back tomorrow?"

"Well..." Myrlie hesitated. "I guess that would be acceptable. The afternoon would be the best time. But I must say, it sounds like this young woman is just trying to stir up some trouble. I can't imagine why, though."

Miles handed her his business card. "I will be back tomorrow afternoon, then."

"I doubt he will be able to help you, DS Pixley," Myrlie murmured to herself, as Miles left the shop.

When he saw her father, he would realize that he could not have been part of this incident. Even she could not see how he could have done it, but there didn't seem to be any other explanation. One thing was certain: Edward would not be alert when Pixley returned. Myrlie would see to it.

Opal Godwin came into the shop as Miles was leaving.

"Myrlie, please tell me who that gorgeous man was that just left here!"

"That, Opal, was Detective Sergeant Miles Pixley. He is no one we want to be involved with."

"Oh, well, that's too bad, I guess." Opal sashayed behind the counter, her round frame barely fitting through the narrow space.

"What are you doing here, Opal?"

"Is that any way to greet a friend, Myrlie? Really, you have been very touchy lately."

"I'm sorry, then. I hope you're feeling better after the other night at the séance."

"Yes, a bit, I guess. I don't mind telling you, I was scared to death. Nobody knew what was happening."

Myrlie thought back to Virginia's remarks after the others had left. The events during the séance were nothing compared to Virginia's threat that she would eventually find out what Myrlie was hiding.

"I've good reason to be touchy, Opal. And you should be, too. I don't like this. I don't like this at all."

"Well, I think it's exciting! I mean, I was shocked at first, seeing that woman come into my shop like that the other day who looked just like Arabella." Her eyes widened. "Myrlie, maybe Arabella was reaching out to me at the séance! I tell you, it was otherworldly, now that I think about it. The chills, the sounds...I swear I saw the candles lift up from the table. Just think—Opal Godwin chosen as the instrument of Arabella Courbain."

Myrlie rolled her eyes. Leave it to Opal to embellish the story.

"That's not what I am talking about, Opal. I mean, I don't need a detective snooping around here and asking questions." She motioned to Opal to follow her into the back room. "I need the name of the man we talked about. You know, the one that I might be able to sell some books to."

"Oh sure, no problem." Opal's eyes grew wide. "Is that why the detective sergeant was here? Does he suspect something?"

"Hush! I just need the man's name and number. And then you need to forget all about it, do you understand?"

Opal reached into her bag and pulled out her phone and searched for the name.

"Don't tell me you have the name in your mobile, Opal! What are you thinking?"

"I'm not stupid, Myrlie," she said, miffed by the implication. "I just put his initials in."

Myrlie sighed. "But you have his number in...oh, never mind. Just give it to me."

Opal gave her the number, and Myrlie wrote it down on the back of an envelope she had pulled out of the wastebasket. She had never wanted Opal to be involved with the books and her plan to deal with them. Opal was too flighty for her own good, and it was risky for her to know anything. But Myrlie had no choice. Opal had contacts through her brother, who had been released from prison the year before. Over several conversations, Myrlie had told Opal about the cache of stolen books. She hoped it wasn't the biggest mistake of her life. But she hadn't told Opal specifics. She still didn't know that Myrlie had Mallard's book of legends, a signed first edition—only that she had books that she wanted to move under the radar. And Myrlie wanted to keep it that way.

The bell on the door tinkled, and a group of tourists came in.

"Well, I've got to get back to the shop," Opal said. "I left Tonya in charge, so who knows what might happen." She tugged on Myrlie's arm, then with a wink, and in a loud whisper, "Good luck with the books."

Myrlie tucked the piece of paper with the phone number written on it, into her pocket and went to the front to greet her customers. When they didn't buy anything, she followed them to the door as they left and turned the Open sign around. She hurried upstairs to her flat, where she pulled the phone number out of her pocket, poured a Highland Queen whiskey, settled into a chair in the small kitchenette, and with a shaking hand, dialed the number.

"Yes?" a man's voice answered.

"This...this is Opal Godwin's friend. She gave me your number."

After a moment of hesitation, the man said, "What do you want?"

Myrlie knew to keep the discussion generic, in case anyone was listening. She took a deep breath and tried to sound confident, as if she did this all the time.

"That item that you wanted. I have it in stock now. Are you interested?"

"I'm not sure what you're talking about. But I'll be at the flea market in East Stalton on Sunday, Booth 25D. Just stop by there."

"Yes, of course. Thank you."

"And bring the item with you."

"Yes, I will." She ended the call.

16

AFTER HER ENCOUNTER with Madame Zaytsev, Kate located the Rye Library, a large brick building on a cobblestoned side street. She stepped inside and walked to an information desk near the entrance. After explaining what she was looking for, she was directed to the desk of Mr. Caleb Strawbridge, research associate. The desk was small but tidy, like Mr. Strawbridge, a short balding man wearing a sweater and bow tie. He looked up and adjusted his glasses as she approached.

Kate introduced herself and repeated her request.

"I am looking for any information on sea smugglers in the 1770s, especially in this area."

"I see. Well, we have many books on the subject of sea smuggling, so you are in the right place. It was at its peak in that century. Anyone in particular you are interested in? The Hawkhurst Gang? The Aldington Gang?"

"Well, I'm not sure. The name I have is William Courbain. I understand he was involved in smuggling in the 1770s. Maybe before and after, too."

"Courbain, Courbain." Mr. Strawbridge tapped a pencil on his desk and seemed lost in thought.

Suddenly, he swung around in his chair to a chest of card catalog drawers, and ran his finger across and down the front of it until he stopped and opened a small drawer. He flipped through the cards and pulled out one, then another, and then a third, and with those in hand, he began to walk toward a room at the back of the library. He turned, and when he saw Kate wasn't following, he waved for her to come along, which she did.

They approached a room with a sign above it that said, THE BANKS LIBRARY. At the door, he punched in a code on a keypad, and a set of glass doors swung open to a large room with built-in bookshelves along each wall, several desks down the center, and arrangements of comfortable leather couches.

"This is our main reference room. We should be able to find what you need here."

With the cards as his guide, he walked down a row of shelves, pulled the first two books out and handed them to her. The third book was located high above their heads, and he rolled a ladder to the spot and climbed up to the top shelf. He pulled a small book out of its place, descended the ladder, and led Kate to a nearby table.

"These are all research volumes and cannot be removed from this room, and they must be handled with care. These two," he pointed to the two books she had carried, "are recent, from the twenty-first century. But this little one here, this is much older." He opened the book. "Yes, 1938. No photos, please. And when you are done, please leave them here on the table and let me know when you are leaving so they may be replaced correctly on the shelves. Is there anything else?"

"Yes, one thing," Kate said. "Do you have a book called *Ancient Tales of an Ancient Town* by Sir Archibald Mallard?"

A look of surprise flitted across his face. "Oh, no, no. We have no copies of that book in this library. I would love to find one myself, but they are exceedingly rare. Well, if you need any help, I'll be at my desk."

Kate thanked him, sat down, and turned on a lamp in front of her. She carefully opened the first book, under the narrow swath of light from the lamp. She flipped through several chapters of the well-known reign of terror of the Hawkhurst Gang and others and read of their grisly ends. She scanned the pages for any reference to the name Courbain. The first book yielded nothing, and she moved on to the next.

The second book was a collection of lists: dates, ship names and types, the names of their captains, what they smuggled, and their fates. Each line had a reference to another page in the book where more detailed description was given. It appeared that anything that was known about that particular ship was in this book.

Again, Kate scanned the pages for the name Courbain, narrowing her search to the 1770s. The name did not appear, so she turned back a few pages and skimmed through the lists again.

Finally, she saw the name she was looking for.

William Courbain, Born: 1710, D: UNK
Captain of The Grand Lady
Carried tobacco, brandy, and other dutiable goods.

There was a reference to page 229. Kate took a small square of notepaper from a wire basket on the table, laid it on the page, then flipped to 229. A brief paragraph there, with additional information, was enough to let Kate know that Courbain was indeed a sea smuggler. He captained a ship called *The Grand Lady,* and it had been lost at sea in 1766.

Kate obeyed the rules and took no pictures, but she did make notes in her journal.

She finally set the book aside and opened the final one. It was smaller, less than a hundred pages, and had illustrations, along with brief notes about the customs officers in the 1700s. She did not find any references to Courbain or his cutter, *The Grand Lady*, but surprisingly she did find a reference to the name Calloway, and a simple statement.

Devon Calloway, Master of the revenue cutter The
Courageous
1764 to 1780
Armament 16 x 9-pounder guns
Nineteen cutters and brigs seized.

The dates triggered a thought. She checked her notes on William Courbain, and then went back to the reference of Devon Calloway. She tapped her pen on the page.

"They were both on the seas in 1766," she murmured to herself. "I wonder what the chances are that they crossed paths?"

After seeing these references, it struck her that the connection between the Courbains and the Calloways might have gone back centuries, too, and that Virginia Calloway's knowledge of the legend might go beyond a simple interest in the subject, as Kate had first thought. She had also seen the symbol of the ravens in three places: at the architecture of the Calloway House itself, in the brooch worn by Ms. Shaw-Windham, and in the pendant that Ms. Calloway wore around her neck. It was critical now for her to find out the connection between these two families.

After recording this final piece of information in her journal, Kate let Mr. Strawbridge know that she was done with the books and left the library. She walked along the Strand Quay for a few minutes, until she came to the Rye Heritage Centre. At the information desk, Kate asked whether there were archives she could research to find something about a particular sea smuggler in the 1700s. She was told no, but they referred her to the Rye Historical Society, located on the second floor of an art gallery on Cinque Ports Street.

Kate pulled out her map, oriented herself once again, and set off for the Cinque Ports Street. The door to the Rye Historical Society was at ground level, adjacent to the art gallery entrance. Once inside, she took a steep, narrow stairway to the second floor. A sign on the door at the top of the stairs gave the hours of the business and said, PLEASE COME IN. Kate turned the door handle and entered.

The worn wooden floors creaked as she walked toward a desk near the entrance. An elderly woman sat at the desk. Her hair was full and white, and she wore it swept into a classic chignon. She was dressed in a tailored light-green suit, with a strand of pearls and drop-pearl earrings as her only jewelry.

She smiled as Kate approached. "May I help you?"

Kate introduced herself and explained her reason for being there. The woman motioned for her to sit in a chair in front of the desk.

"How fascinating!" she said, as if no one had ever asked for such a thing before. "Well, you must meet my husband, Guilford, then. He is the expert of that era." She pushed a button on an intercom. "Guilford, dear, can you come to the front? We have a guest."

Soon, Guilford appeared. He was tall, at least six feet, and his salt and pepper hair brushed the top of the doorway as he stepped through it. He was as formally dressed as his wife, in a gray suit, vest, and tie. The pair seemed to be a perfect match, and not what Kate expected to find in this room over an art gallery.

Guilford introduced himself and his wife, Winnie, and asked again how they could help. Kate gave as thorough a response as she could.

"Specifically, I am interested in a sea smuggler known as William Courbain, and his daughter, Arabella Courbain. Oh, and if possible, any link they might have to a Devon Calloway back in the 1700s."

"I see," Guilford said. "Winnie, dear, I believe there are several references in the 1700s Room that might be helpful. Let's start with those and see where they take us. Follow me, Miss Tyler."

"How long have you been here?" Kate said, as they walked.

"June first, 2001, we set up shop. Winnie and I are retired teachers, and were concerned about certain items of historical value that were not being made available in one place for the public. There is so much history here in Rye and in East Sussex, as you can imagine, going back centuries. The historical sites here are doing a bang-up job curating the history with their own displays and presentations, but there was not one place for all the rest of it—the pieces that didn't fit in anywhere else. Mostly, things that people got tired of hanging on to. Eventually, we started the Rye Historical Society, and became a repository for just those types of things. No matter how small or seemingly unimportant it is, we want it. We catalog it, preserve it, and make the connections to other documents that perhaps no one has thought of. It has been very fulfilling work."

They had walked down a hall to what Kate assumed to be the back of the building, and entered a room on their right. On the door, a sign said 1700-1799. The space he called the 1700s Room was surprisingly expansive. Kate would not have guessed the square footage of the historical society from looking at the outside of the building.

The room was immaculate, although its age was showing. Bookshelves and file cabinets were lined up along the walls, all neatly marked. Winnie had walked on ahead of them and stopped at a filing cabinet at the far end of the room. She pulled open a drawer and selected a file folder, then carried it to a table in the center of the room and leafed through it. Kate noticed that Winnie had never searched a card catalog, or a computer list of any kind. She had simply walked directly to the right room, to the right cabinet, and pulled out the right folder.

"This might be a start for you, dear," Winnie said.

A pad of paper and a pen appeared next to her, again courtesy of Winnie. Kate thanked her and sat down.

"This is a list of smugglers and their ships in the 1700s," Winnie said. "There are some that are very well-known, but we pride ourselves on having collected documents and information on some of the lesser known as well. If you find anything of interest, please let us know. And if they are available, we can find other cross-references for you."

"If you have any information on the Calloway family," Kate said, "or a link to William Courbain, I would love to see that, too."

"I'm sure that if we have it, I will be able to find it. I'll be back in a moment." Winnie scurried off.

Guilford lingered behind. "The name Calloway is quite prominent in East Sussex. Are you looking for information on the Calloways of the Calloway House and Gardens?"

"Yes. I visited the house and gardens the other day."

"I see. And you are looking for a link to the Courbains? I don't think we have ever had that particular request before. Intriguing." He lingered for a moment, before announcing, "I'll leave you to your research, then."

Left alone in the room, Kate ran her finger down the columns, searching for any mention of the name Courbain. The materials Winnie had provided Kate were, in some respects, duplications of the information she'd found in the books at the library—lists of ships, their captains and dates, but without any indication of what the dates meant. She would have to ask Winnie or Guilford.

Finally, she found what she was looking for.

William Courbain, Born: 1710, Died: UNK.
Captain of The Sally, cutter, 1752 to 1759
Captain of The Grand Lady, cutter, 1760 to 1766.

There was no mention of ships after *The Grand Lady,* and Kate wondered if this was the last ship that he captained.

She found Guilford and asked him about the single dates that were listed in one of the columns. He told her that those were most likely the dates that the smuggling ships interacted with authorities, usually the customs officers.

Kate returned to the 1700s Room and went back to the line where Courbain was mentioned, and wrote down the dates with a note, "Customs involved?"

The Grand Lady seemed to be the last mention of Courbain's ship.

Kate's next search was specific to the customs officers in the same era as Arabella and her father. Again, Winnie was a whiz at finding exactly what Kate needed. These records were much more detailed since they were official government records, and they confirmed what Kate had uncovered at the library: Devon Calloway was a customs officer in Romney Marsh from 1760 to 1785. This fit in with the dates of his time as master of the revenue cutter, *The Courageous,* from 1764 to 1780. After that, he was involved in local government, and for a brief time was a member of parliament.

"Thank you, Winnie," Kate whispered to herself, as she added to the notes already in her journal.

A few minutes later, Guilford returned and laid a large book on a table adjacent to where Kate was working, and she wheeled over to it in her chair. He opened to a page that had been marked with a piece of paper.

"I think you will find this very interesting. This is a report from the revenue officers themselves, not just a historian's reference. It would be the official notice of what happened."

Kate read the article that he pointed to.

On Thursday morning, 17 November 1766, the smuggling cutter, The Grand Lady, was seen 4 leagues WSW off Romney Marsh, armed with swivel guns and small arms, and had a crew of 20 men. HM Revenue Cutter, The Courageous, armed with 16 x 9-pounder guns and a crew of 30 men, Devon Calloway, Master, set out in pursuit. After a running battle, The Grand Lady was sunk. Many of the crew were killed and several wounded. Several escaped, including the master. Estimated 20 bags of tobacco, 300 casks of spirits, 200 gallons of brandy, silk cloths, and tea were lost when the smuggling cutter sank. A reward of 300 pounds was offered for information and capture of the master of the smuggling cutter, William Courbain.

The information was stunning in its detail, and exactly what Kate had been hoping to find.

"But there is no record of whether Courbain was ever captured?" Kate asked Guilford.

"Winnie is still researching it, but often, a sea smuggler's fate is unknown unless they were taken to trial and convicted of their crimes. If captured, and if the smuggler was not released because of the bribery of some official before his trial, the punishment was often death. And in that case, there would be a record of it. But nothing so far—at least for Mister Courbain."

Kate spent the afternoon delving into the archives and chatting with both Winnie and Guilford. She learned more about the smuggling trade in a couple hours from Guilford than she might have learned in days of searching the Internet.

"You must remember that in those days," he said, "it was common for the locals to side with the smugglers. After all, the smuggling or 'free-trade,' as it was known, gave people jobs—getting goods off the ships, packing them on horses and in wagons to take them inland, where they could be sold duty free. People looked the other way in many instances. The smugglers were ruthless, with no respect for the law during that time. A revenue officer's job put him at major risk on the seas, and on shore from the smugglers. According to this account, Mister Calloway put his own life at risk by chasing down *The Grand Lady,* since it is reported to have been heavily armed."

Suddenly, the stories that Kate had been researching and finding in the dusty archives were becoming more real to her. Like her dreams, they reflected the lives of real people, real tragedies, and real struggles. Life was not easy, especially for a young woman in those days. Promised to a man she did not love, giving up her son for his own safety, Arabella had borne the weight of the world on her shoulders.

"How would the revenue officers find the ships?" Kate said. "Did they just patrol the coastlines?"

"They might have," Guilford said. "There were several places—Hastings, Pevensey, Bexhill, and of course, Rye—that were known to be easier for the cutters to unload their merchandise, and easy for men known as 'luggers' to get it inland. But sometimes there would be tips. A rumor here and there about when a ship might be coming in, to the right ears, and the officials would try to intercept."

"But you said that people didn't really want the smugglers to get caught," Kate said. "Why would they tip off the officials?"

Guilford sat on the edge of the table and began to weave a story.

"Imagine this, if you will. A man and his wife make their living by fishing. Barely enough to put food on the table, but this is the life they have been given. Their young son, their only child, is desperate to help his family. He hears of a way to make some money, and even though he is a good boy, he begins to work as a lugger. But the sea smugglers are evil men, and the young man is killed during a fight between the smugglers and the men on land helping them. Over money, or stealing from the smugglers, whatever it may be. His parents have now lost their only son. Their retaliation? Perhaps the only thing they can do is to give information to the revenue officers about this ship—when and where it lands, what they carry, how many men are on board, and so forth. In the end, it may seal their own fates since the smugglers had their own way of doling out justice. But it is their only way to avenge the loss of their son."

Kate was drawn in by Guilford's skillful storytelling.

"That is so tragic," she said.

"Yes. Eventually, the smugglers became so violent and so indifferent to the law during that era that the sentiments of the citizenry turned against them. They were finally rooted out and killed or arrested and imprisoned."

Kate looked back at the official report of the battle between *The Grand Lady* and *The Courageous*. The armament on *The Courageous* was meant to inflict heavy damage on the ships they pursued. And the smugglers no doubt were as heavily armed. There would have been fierce fighting between the ships. It would have been remembered as a battle between the customs officers and the smugglers, between the crown and those who dared disobey. In reality, though, it was a battle between two captains, Devon Calloway and William Courbain—between right and wrong.

November 17, 1766—a date that Kate would not be able to forget.

Winnie soon rejoined them, carrying a tray of a teapot and cups. Kate set aside her notes on smuggling.

"Winnie, do you also keep genealogy records here?" Kate added milk and honey to her tea.

"Yes, we have access to some. Is there another search you would like to do?"

"I'd like to do a search for the names Courbain and Calloway, if I could."

"Of course," Winnie replied. "It might take days to do a thorough search for either of those names. But the Calloway name is so prominent in the area, perhaps the family themselves could shed some light on their ancestry?"

Kate expected that she was correct, but Kate wasn't sure if it would be a good idea to approach Virginia with that question.

"You may be right, Winnie. Maybe I'll check into that."

Guilford had joined them, and Kate asked him about the book *Ancient Tales of an Ancient Town*.

"By Sir Archibald Mallard, if I remember correctly?" he said.

"Yes, that's the one."

"Well, we have no copy of the book here. It is very rare, I think. We would love to have one of them ourselves, of course, but haven't had the opportunity."

"Do you know anything about Sir Mallard?" Kate said.

"As I recall, he was a well-known historian. But his book of legends put him on the map, so to speak. It was very well-received. After that, he became rather eccentric in his thinking, wanting to see truth in all of the legends, whether they had any veracity or not. He became a recluse in his later years."

And Kate had held the book in her hands, casually carried it around in her tote bag, perused it on the rooftop of the Mermaid Street Café and in the Mrs. Betts room at the Mermaid Inn. This was not some random book that a man had pulled out of a box. It carried a mysterious aura with it, no doubt from its strange history.

Winnie then brought Kate several books on The Calloway House, as it was known in the 1700s, before the gardens were added, including a history of the house, back to its beginnings in the fifteenth century. Some of the information was familiar to Kate, as she had heard the guide give the background during the tour. But some was new to her, and she made notes in her journal.

Kate eventually gathered her things and asked one last question.

"How recent are your records here, say from the 1940s to the present?"

"We have records from that time, up until the year 2000 only," Winnie replied. "The most thorough records are the newspapers we have digitized."

Kate was surprised, since she couldn't remember seeing a computer anywhere in sight.

"Can they be searched by a name, then?" she said.

They both nodded, and she followed them to a smaller room with a computer in the corner. Winnie left to attend to other tasks, and Kate ran a search for Virginia Calloway, focusing on the years 1940–1980.

Kate almost missed it, but finally, she found an article of interest.

On February 14, 1971, *The London Times* society section announced that VIRGINIA MARGUERITE CALLOWAY, OF LONDON, IS ENGAGED TO TERRANCE HELMSFORD BILLINGS, ALSO OF LONDON. The announcement went on to list Mr. Billings's education, recent accomplishments, and plans for a career in law. No mention was made of Virginia's accomplishments. The wedding date was set for January 1, 1972.

Kate made notes about the engagement announcement, and then searched further for the wedding announcement, although it occurred to her that Virginia Calloway was still using her maiden name. But she knew that there could be many reasons for that.

Her search revealed no wedding announcement. Sadly, she soon discovered an obituary stating that Terrance Billings died in London on December 25, 1971, after a brief illness.

Kate wrote down the details, recognizing now that a tragedy in Ms. Calloway's past such as this could have had a lasting effect on her entire life. This revelation, along with a string of other seemingly unrelated information, had drawn Kate further into the mystery.

She looked up as Winnie approached her.

"Is there anything else we can help you with, Kate?"

She closed her journal and put it back into her tote bag.

"I don't think so. I can't thank you enough for all of your help. I couldn't have managed this without you and Guilford."

"Of course. It was our pleasure! We don't get many visitors here, so it was delightful to have you stop by today. You have given us some interesting questions to pursue as well."

She pulled up a chair and sat down next to Kate. "I did want to share with you some personal knowledge that might be helpful, though. Virginia Calloway, the current resident of the Calloway House, and I...well, we attended the Stonewell School for Young Women together, in our teen years. I recall that she had quite a bit on her shoulders at the time. What with the Calloway name and legacy."

"Can you tell me about her during that time?" Kate said.

"She was a shy girl. I seem to remember that she had a challenging time with her family then, and lived with her grandmother at the Calloway House quite a bit—on holidays and that sort of thing."

"Have you stayed in touch?"

Winnie shook her head. "Oh no. We went our separate ways after graduation. We led completely different lives, you see. I went into teaching, met Guilford, and we married and started our family. And this historical society has been our passion for many years now."

Kate shared with Winnie what she had found in the newspaper articles about the engagement and death notice.

"I had forgotten about that incident," Winnie said. "It was many years ago, of course. That would explain her keeping her maiden name, then, wouldn't it?"

Kate agreed.

"I'm afraid I don't know what her life has been like since then. Perhaps the house and gardens take up much of her time." Winnie continued. "One piece of advice, if I may. Sometimes there are pieces of history that we don't ever see here in the historical societies or in the libraries. They are secreted away in personal collections, tucked away in boxes in attics or in dusty basements, often because they are the parts of people's lives that perhaps should never see the light of day. Now, I'm not suggesting you knock on Virginia Calloway's door and ask if she has any secrets she wants to share." She smiled. "But I sense this may be something personal with you?"

"In a way, yes," Kate replied.

"In any event, it may be the only place you will find your answers."

Kate gave in to an impulse and hugged Winnie as Guilford smiled on from the doorway.

"Thank you both so much. You have been very generous with your time, and I really appreciate it." She handed them her business card. "If you find anything else that might be relevant, would you let me know?"

"Of course, Kate," Guilford said. "Please stop by and see us again."

He walked her back to the door at the top of the stairs. Kate said goodbye and walked down to the street. She found an outdoor table at a nearby café on Cinque Ports Street and ordered a light supper. As she looked back over her notes, she was amazed at how much she had learned in just a few hours of research.

Over two centuries ago, the Courbains and the Calloways had been connected. Perhaps they had continued to weave in and out of each other's lives over the next two hundred years. Perhaps not. But now, they had converged again, bringing Kate from her home four thousand miles away, for some new purpose, one she had yet to discover. One thing was clear: the year 1766 was pivotal in the lives of Arabella Courbain, William Courbain, and Devon Calloway.

That evening, the lights in the library at the Calloway Manor flickered off and on. Exasperated at the inconsistency of the electricity lately, Virginia Calloway lit a small taper, switched off the lights, and placed several tall candles around the room. She often preferred candlelight to the brashness of the electric lamps, especially on solitary nights like this. The candlelight would not be enough to study her latest journal entries or write notes about her discovery of a new herbal blend that could be a remedy for arthritis, but she was tiring anyway, and she sat down in her chair in front of the fire and closed her eyes.

Outside, the wind began to swirl through the gardens of the manor, whipping leaves from the trees and snapping branches against the tall windows. Gray clouds scuttled across the sky, black birds slashed through the air, their faint cries disappearing into the night.

Suddenly, all was silent for Virginia Calloway. She no longer heard the wind or the crackling of logs collapsing into the fire. Her mind was filled with a vision of a young woman on a cliff overlooking the ocean. It was Arabella, and she held out her hand to a figure coming toward her.

"You have finally come," Arabella said. "I have been waiting a very long time."

Arabella then turned, as if looking directly at Virginia.

"Time is short. A new course has been set. Kate is ready. The ravens have foretold my wishes, and you must carry them out. But Kate must be here, with you, in order for the legend to be fulfilled."

Virginia was startled by the sonorous gong of the grandfather clock in the hall. The vision vanished. But it had been as clear to her as if the two women had been standing in front of her.

Arabella had spoken and made her wishes known.

Of course, Virginia thought. *She was waiting until I was alone and prepared to hear her voice. Now I understand.*

Police investigation be damned. Virginia was no longer concerned with the mundane consequences of the law, now that Arabella had spoken. She would invite Kate to the Calloway Manor once more.

17

MILES, WEARING THE APPROPRIATE WORK ATTIRE of a gray suit and tie this time, returned to the bookstore for his meeting with Ms. Shaw-Windham and Mr. Bailey. It was early Saturday afternoon, and he stepped into the cheerless atmosphere of the shop, thinking that Myrlie Shaw-Windham was not doing herself, or her stepfather, a service by presenting her business in such a light. To draw people in—and there were plenty of tourists to draw from in Rye— he thought there should be a warm, welcoming environment, with colorful displays and inviting chairs and couches to counteract the unrelenting gloom from the alleyway. Books, she had. Ambiance, she did not. As often as he himself had walked around Rye in his role as a police officer, this particular alleyway had eluded him, and for good reason, he thought.

And Myrlie herself—as he noted the stern look he was getting from her when he entered the store—was too much of an austere librarian caricature. A stark contrast to the warm and friendly shopkeepers he knew in other stores along The Mint. Customers were a business owner's livelihood, and the good shopkeepers would do whatever it took to make their visitors comfortable and satisfied.

But not Myrlie Shaw-Windham. There was no greeting from her when she recognized him.

"I still don't know why you need to see him," she said, before he could even say a word. "He is not able to communicate, as I told you yesterday."

"Perhaps. But I would still like to meet him, if you don't mind."

She flipped the sign on the door to Closed and taped a note on it: BACK AT 2:00 P.M.

"Come with me, then." It was a command.

Miles followed her to the back of the store and through the curtained doorway.

"This can't take long," she said. "I need to open back up as quickly as possible. Saturday is my busiest day."

Miles doubted that it was, but he kept his thoughts to himself, knowing that he would spend as much time there as he needed to, regardless of her claims.

Myrlie reached the top of the stairs and opened the door. Miles noted that a deadbolt on their side of the door was not locked. He theorized that Myrlie may have made sure it was unlocked for his visit. At the very least, it was a hazard for anyone such as Edward living there with no exit. At least, none that Miles could see.

He followed Myrlie through the small, cramped living room to a bedroom door which was partially open. She pushed it open a bit further. Miles looked in and saw a thin, elderly man lying on a bed. He appeared to be dressed in pajamas and was covered with a light blanket. The room was sparsely furnished with bed, dresser, and bedside table. A pair of wirerimmed glasses lay open on the table within his reach.

"May I go in?"

Myrlie didn't respond but motioned him into the room with a wave of her hand.

"Mister Bailey?" He approached the elderly man.

When there was no response, he tried again.

"Mister Bailey?"

"He won't answer you. I already told you that."

Just then, Mr. Bailey's eyes fluttered open. He coughed lightly and appeared to be trying to focus his eyes on the man standing over him.

Miles leaned down slightly. "Mister Bailey, I'm sorry to bother you. I'm Detective Sergeant Miles Pixley, Rye Police. Could I ask you a few questions, sir?"

The old man blinked a few times, and Miles recognized the emptiness in his eyes—the vacancy of a man living in a world devoid of understanding, emotion, and communication.

"You see?" Myrlie announced from the doorway. "He can't communicate with you. I told you. But he's well-taken-care-of if that's what you are wondering. I do everything for him, and I'm happy to do it. I won't put him in a home. That's not what Mother wanted, so I will keep him here as long as I can."

Miles straightened up. In spite of Ms. Shaw-Windham's declaration that she was happy to do whatever was needed for her stepfather, Miles doubted that she was ever happy to do anything in her life.

He glanced around the room for any signs of obvious maltreatment but saw nothing. There were no pill bottles in plain sight, but neither was there water available if Mr. Bailey needed it. He had seen enough.

"Thank you, ma'am. We can go now."

Myrlie led him back through the flat and motioned for him to go down the stairs first. Behind him, he heard the turn of the key in the lock and knew that she had just locked her stepfather in the flat.

Miles looked back at her as he heard the click of the lock.

"It's for his own safety." Myrlie sniffed and motioned him to move along.

She escorted Miles to the door of the bookstore, flipped the Open sign, and ripped the "Back at 2:00 p.m." note off the window with one quick tug.

"Seems to me like this young woman is just wanting to cause trouble," she said. "Got a lot of nerve, if you ask me, with her wild tales of talking to my stepfather. You can see he could never have done what she says he did."

"Yes, ma'am, it would seem that way. Thank you for your time."

Miles heard the shop door slam behind him, it's bell protesting with a dull clang, as he headed down the alleyway to The Mint. The sunshine on the main street was welcoming after the dreary environment of BOOKS and the flat above it.

As he walked back to the police station, he turned over in his mind the facts he knew. The description Kate had given him of the man in BOOKS who supposedly sold her the book of legends matched the man he had just left. It would have been very unlikely that she could have met him anywhere other than in the shop, as she claimed.

Kate had visited with Ms. Calloway at her home. Neither one denied that. But the reasons each gave for the visit were not the same. Someone was lying, and he thought it was probably Ms. Calloway. Her written invitation to Kate could prove that.

No one had actually seen Kate drive away after her visit with Ms. Calloway. Or at least, no one was owning up to it. She could have been placed in the garden after being drugged with something in her tea. But there was no real proof. And by her own admission, Ms. Calloway was not in the habit of inviting people to her house, and yet she did.

The book in question, *Ancient Tales of an Ancient Town*, was in fact a rare book that had been stolen years before, but its whereabouts were unknown. Except, Kate had photos of it, so she must have had it in her hands at some point. The date stamp on the photos he saw indicated that they were taken just four days earlier, proving that she did have possession of it at that time.

Myrlie Shaw-Windham claimed that Kate did not return the book. Kate claimed that she did. Again, someone was lying, and it was probably Ms. Shaw-Windham, who of course would do anything to avoid being caught with a stolen book. Kate would have no reason to lie about having it, and she had volunteered that information willingly. And Ms. Shaw-Windham was most likely willing to let Miles see her stepfather so that she could prove her claim that he could not have spoken to Kate, knowing that most of the time, he was as uncommunicative as she had asserted.

Final fact: Edward Bailey was not being cared for in the manner that he deserved. Of that, Miles was sure. And that situation needed to be remedied as soon as possible.

18

KATE STARTED OUT EARLY the next morning, taking a bus to Rye Harbour Village, about nine minutes from Rye. A two-mile walk along the paths of the Rye Harbour Nature Reserve would do much to clear her head and give her back a semblance of normalcy. Too much had happened to her in the last few days, and she needed to get back on track—again.

A walk through the Discovery Centre at the beginning of her hike opened Kate's eyes to the important efforts to preserve the diverse wildlife and habitats found there. She was given a map of the nature reserve trails to follow, and she started out at a fast pace.

The route she chose was an easy walk along the River Rother. She soon passed the iconic Red Roofed Hut which sat between her path and the river. It was a simple black hut capped with a startling-red tin roof and contrasting white door and shutters, sitting small and alone against the backdrop of the river and the gray morning sky.

Kate walked on, soon reaching the path's closest point to the English Channel. Feeling the sting of the wind-whipped water, she pulled her hood closer around her face. She continued on the section that turned away from the mouth of the river, followed along the shoreline, southwest, until turning across the shingle and grassland, back to her starting point. Among the wealth of plant and bird life on the reserve, she recognized sea kale and yellow horned poppy that seemed to thrive in the harsh pebbled ground. Terns and gulls screeched and wheeled overhead. The birds had been her only company on her walk, with no other hikers on the trails that she had noticed. It was refreshing to be away from the crowds in Rye, and she realized she had not thought about Arabella since stepping foot on the nature reserve.

Kate knew that the reserve was a treasure, only made possible by the hard work of the staff and volunteers, and she wanted to do it justice in her blog. She flipped back through the photos she had taken along the hike, and made a few voice memos on her phone, describing this unique treasure. The hike had given her a better appreciation of this section of the English coast, and further deepened her love of East Sussex.

Kate reached the entrance of the reserve, and after speaking to the volunteers there, walked to Rye Harbour, another picturesque village between the mouth of the River Rother and Rye, which deserved a few days of exploring all by itself. The river was busy with all manner of crafts, from small motorboats and commercial fishing boats, to large commercial tankers moving along the waterway.

She chose an outdoor table at a small pub for an early lunch, and as she was finishing, she heard a familiar voice calling her name from somewhere out on the river.

"Yoo-hoo! Kate! Over here."

She turned and saw Lillian from the Mermaid Inn, balancing her stocky form in a rocking motorboat, waving her hat in the air. She said something to the driver of the boat, and he pulled up to the dock leading to the café where Kate sat. He secured the boat and helped Lillian as she hauled herself up the short ladder to the deck.

"Fancy meeting you here, Kate."

Lillian huffed from the effort of her ladder climb and pulled up a chair from the next table. She grabbed a few napkins and wiped water off her face, still catching her breath.

"I've only just been on the water a minute, and already I've been *baptized!*" She laughed.

A server approached, but Lillian waved him away.

"No time to eat, I'm afraid. I've booked Clive and his boat for the afternoon, Kate. I couldn't convince the Crossthwaites to come. It would have been good for them to try something different. But no matter. That's their choice, their loss. There's plenty of room on the boat. Why don't you come with me down to the channel?"

Kate didn't hesitate. Being in a boat on the river would give her an entirely different viewpoint from what she had experienced on her walk that morning.

"I would love to, Lillian. Thank you."

Kate paid for her lunch and then followed Lillian down the ladder to the waiting boat, *The Channel Chaser,* still rocking from the swells of the passing watercrafts. Certain that she could not let Lillian best her, Kate managed to seat herself and don a life preserver safely.

"This is what it's all about, Kate!" Lillian settled herself on the cushioned seat. "Taking advantage of everything you can. But I don't need to tell you that. This will be great for your blog. Let's go, Clive!" She pointed to the east, where the channel awaited them.

Lillian was in her element, shouting "Ahoy!" to boats passing by, waving her hat with abandon, her gray braid flying in the breeze. The greeting was enthusiastically returned, and Kate found herself forgetting her job, neglecting thoughts about how she would write about this in her blog, and just enjoying the moment.

She reached her hand out into the spray from the river and wondered what effect ripples made by her hand here in the Rother might have on the English Channel that would soon be in front of them. Would the small movement vanish in the length of the river? Or would it gather in strength and size and become a wave that shivered ships in the sea?

"Believe it or not, this is my first time on the River Rother!" Lillian shouted over the sound of the boat's motor, bringing Kate out of her thoughts. "Don't know why I haven't done this before, but here we are now, and glad for it." She was smiling from ear to ear. "Clive has been here all his life. Got this boat when he was twenty-one, been taking people up and down the river for a long time. Right, Clive?"

Clive smiled and nodded. "It's a fisherman's life here on the river, though, still today."

They passed sailboats, catamarans, and motorboats of all types and sizes on the river. People waved to them from the banks and the breakwater as they motored by. A misty spray from the low waves spit at them, but Clive kept up his pace as they bounced along. Soon, the choppy water graduated from a green to dirty brown, signaling the open channel ahead, and Clive finally slowed the boat.

"Over there on your right, that's the Red Roofed Hut," he said.

They idled for a moment, just at the mouth of the river, and Kate took photos of the hut from a new perspective.

"I wanted us to make it all the way out here so we could see the English Channel!" Lillian shouted, her voice competing with the wind and waves. "Never seen it from here in all my travels. Marvelous. Just marvelous," she murmured.

Kate silently agreed.

Soon, Clive turned the boat around and headed back up the river. He expertly pulled into a slip, tied the boat up, and helped the two women climb up a short ladder to the dock. The quaint village of Rye Harbour offered a variety of places to eat, shop, and stay, and she and Lillian soon found a table at a small restaurant after bidding farewell to Captain Clive and *The*

Channel Chaser. While Lillian ordered her lunch, Kate pulled out her journal and began to sketch.

She sketched Clive and his boat, the docks and quaint shops across the river, and her recollection of the breakwater as it reached the channel. A slight breeze ruffled the pages of her journal and rippled the water of the river, now sparkling in the afternoon sun. The thrum of passing boats and the happy voices of tourists blended in a soothing melody.

Lillian's enthusiasm was contagious, and Kate realized it was the most peaceful she had felt since her arrival in Rye. She had almost forgotten about her dreams, the book and the etching of Arabella, and her experience at the Calloway House. But Lillian soon brought her out of her reverie.

"Well, what do you think, Kate? Worth the trip, right?"

"Absolutely, Lillian. Thank you for inviting me along. I could get lost in the simple beauty and peace of this place. What an uncomplicated life it must be here."

"Oh no, Kate. Any life that depends upon the water and the weather is not uncomplicated. These fishermen struggle like everyone else. They have good days and bad days. Good years and bad ones. But it's a life they love, and they wouldn't trade it for anything. Same with the shops along here, I'm sure. Most of them depend on the tourist trade, and that can be somewhat unreliable and seasonal."

"Of course," Kate replied. "I didn't mean to minimize their livelihoods. I guess it's simply good to be able to do what you love."

"Yes, that is the most important thing in life, isn't it? Let's have a pint, then, Kate, to cap off our afternoon."

As they enjoyed their ale, Lillian began to pull brochures out of her ever-present tote bag.

"Aha! Here it is." She had landed on one in particular. "What say we go to Camber Castle, Kate? Have you been yet?"

She shook her head.

"Just think," Lillian continued as she perused the pamphlet, "a sixteenth century castle built right on the Sussex coast of England, near Rye and Winchelsea, by good old King Henry the Eighth to protect against French invaders. And what happens? The harbor silts up over the years, and the castle is rendered completely useless, and ends up at one and a half kilometers from the sea. But there it still stands, almost five hundred years later."

Kate agreed to the side trip, and they returned by bus to the starting point near Rye to begin their hike.

They walked for about a mile on a trail across the flat fields that surrounded the castle. Kate sensed the desolation of the spot as they approached, the ancient bastion having crumbled bit by bit over the centuries, worn away by time and weather.

"What do humans do with ruins? Why do we keep them?" Kate said to Lillian, as they stood looking up at the great stone walls that towered above them, grass growing there like tufts of an old man's beard.

This was not a castle built for a king's dwelling, as the name might imply, so it was not the stuff of fairy tales. It was meant to be a fort to protect England throughout centuries of wars and battles and invasions. Even though its usefulness was never fully realized, the reason for its existence, however fruitless, and the feat of its construction, still mattered. And so it remained, beaten down by the elements, eroded and deteriorating. The enemies of the past had retreated with the sea when violent storms cut off direct access to the channel, leaving Camber Castle stranded in the middle of a field, abandoned like the artillery of a fleeing army.

Still, it remained, in ruins—its bulk, its towers, its walls and gates, the very soul of it, now fused with the flat fields surrounding it. Flocks of sheep grazed nearby, the castle merely rocks in their way.

Kate closed her eyes and imagined the centuries of memories here, now ancient and quiet, silent like the ground. There were no enemies here except for the deliberate advance of time.

In the hazy distance, far across the pastures, modern wind turbines turned, moved by air sliding across their monstrous wings. New and old coexisted here, as with the rest of Rye. Kate wondered if Camber Castle would outlive the wind turbines.

"Well," Lillian said, subdued now after her earlier excitement. "We sure do build things to last, don't you agree, Kate?" she asked, but it was more of a statement of fact, to which Kate could wholeheartedly agree.

They turned their backs to Camber Castle and began the journey back to the present, back to Rye.

"I have to thank you, Lillian. You have helped me clear my head today," Kate said, before parting from her friend in the lobby of the Mermaid Inn, now far away from her dreams, questions, doubts, and fears.

"It was my pleasure to have you along, Kate. Well, my joints are aching from that hike, so I'll say goodbye, dear. You'll have a good rest tonight." She patted Kate's arm before heading off to her room.

19

THAT EVENING, KATE DECIDED to stay close to home and capture the feel of Rye at night. The day, as physically demanding as it had turned out to be, had refreshed her. But the research from the day before soon started creeping back into her brain. The time she had spent at the library and with Winnie and Guilford had given her some answers but had also raised more questions.

She stepped out of the inn, onto Mermaid Street and into a fairy-tale scene. The cobblestones had turned golden in the light of the streetlamps. Muted lights from homes along the ancient pathway illuminated their stoops and created a delicate patchwork of brightness and darkness far down the street. The distant view of the fields of Rye, over the descending rooftops, was bathed in a bluish haze as the sun lowered into the horizon.

Kate took a few pictures, then turned onto West Street, to Market Road, a familiar route by now. She soon came to an alley which she quickly realized was behind Opal's Tea Shop. The shop would have been closed at this hour, but a light came through an open door. She guessed it led into the kitchen.

She heard arguing and thought she recognized the voices. One sounded like Ms. Shaw-Windham from the bookstore, and the other was similar to the high-pitched voice of the older woman from Opal's Tea Shop. And since they were two of the people who thought they had recognized Kate in Rye, she wanted to hear more. Over the clatter of pots and pans, their conversation was not clear, and Kate tiptoed forward.

Suddenly, there was a commotion around the trash cans in the alley. Two cats raced off into the street, howling and spitting, and the noises brought the tea shop owner to the door. Kate quickly stepped back into the shadows and squeezed herself back against a fence.

"What is it, Opal?" Myrlie said, from inside.

"Nothing, Myrlie. Just some cats." She set the trash can lids back in place, looked around again, and went back inside, closing the kitchen door behind her.

Kate breathed a sigh of relief, stepped out of the shadows, and came face to face with Miles.

"Miles!" she cried out in surprise, then lowered her voice to a whisper. "What are you doing here?"

He put his finger to his lips, and they hurried out to the street.

"I'll tell you why, but not here. My car is just over here."

"How did you find me?" Kate said, trying to calm the pounding in her heart.

"Coincidence." He noted the doubtful look on her face. "Yes, coincidence again. I'll explain soon. I promise."

They got into his Jeep.

"Well?" Kate said.

"I didn't mean to frighten you, really. I apologize for that." He pulled out onto Market Road.

"And how did you find me?"

"Pure chance, honestly. I saw you taking pictures along Market Road, but then you walked into the alleyway behind the tea shop. I started walking over to see if you needed help with your pictures, and then the cats started brawling in the trash cans."

"Scared me half to death," Kate said.

"I didn't want you to be seen, either," Miles replied.

"Well, neither did I."

"So why were you there?"

She hesitated briefly. "I was just walking around town to get some night photos for my blog, as you know. I was near the tea shop, and I heard loud voices. I realized it was the two women from the bookstore and the tea shop. And I guess I thought it was strange that they knew each other."

"And?" Miles said.

"And what? I was trying to hear what they were arguing about. Maybe it wasn't a coincidence that they were the two people in Rye who thought they knew me, and they were together, and I wanted to know more. Now it's your turn."

Miles pulled into an empty parking lot by the harbor.

"I need to know if I can trust you," he said.

Kate got out of the car, and Miles joined her.

"Me? Really, Miles? After all we've been through in the very short time we've known each other? Listen, I've had a long day, and I'm tired, so can you take me back to the inn? This is ridiculous. I feel like I'm being interrogated. Or is that it? Is this a police interrogation? Answer me, or I will start walking back on my own."

He raised his hands in surrender. "Fair enough, Kate. But listen, I did some digging into that book you told me about. And it appears that it is on a list of stolen books."

"Oh," she breathed, the news taking her by surprise.

She took a step toward him and lowered her voice.

"Do you think Miss Shaw-Windham knows about that? That it's stolen?"

"I have my suspicions. And there's one other thing. She lives and cares for her stepfather, Edward Bailey, in the upstairs flat. I checked some sources in social services, and apparently, he is in the early stages of...well, I can't divulge that. Let's just say, they confirmed that he probably could not have talked to you."

"But he did talk to me, Miles! He was very coherent. Maybe a little confused since he thought he knew me—just like the others who seemed to recognize me. But very friendly and...I am telling you the truth. All of it."

"I know. And I believe you. But there is something going on there. I talked to her—"

"You what?"

"I did my duty as an officer and went to follow-up on information I had about a stolen book."

"You shouldn't have done that."

"I am doing my job, Kate. And I thought you'd appreciate it."

She thought for a moment. "Well, I guess..."

"You might as well know the rest, then. I saw Mister Bailey myself today, and he is as she described. He could not communicate with me."

"And you are sure it was him?"

"From the description you gave, yes, I am quite sure. And there's more. I also went to the Calloway House yesterday and talked to Miss Calloway—"

"Oh, great. Miles, I told you that I didn't need you to make a fuss about that."

"It's too late now, Kate. There is something strange going on here, and I am trying to make the connections."

"What did Miss Calloway tell you?"

"She said that you had tea, you left, escorted by her guard, and as far as she knew, you went home. The guard confirmed her story, and there were no cameras that I saw to challenge their claims. But she lied, Kate. She said she invited you there to talk about the gardens. That can be disproved by the invitation you received, right?"

"Yes, of course. It's in my room."

"Good. Can you tell me anything else about what's happened since you got here?"

"Nothing more than what I have already told you. I promise. So have you talked to the tea shop lady yet? Just for good measure?"

"Her name is Opal Godwin. And no, I haven't talked to her yet. But I will if I have to."

Kate sighed. She studied his face, and in the dim glow of the harbor lights, she could tell he was genuinely concerned about her, and she began to relax.

"I do appreciate you looking into this," she said, "but I am beginning to regret ever coming to Rye. This is all too strange. And honestly, I'm not sure what to do at this point."

"You don't need to do anything," he said.

"But Miles, now I know you are interested in the stolen book and what happened to me at the Calloway House, but there is something more personal going on here. Who was this woman Arabella? I am beginning to wonder if I am actually related to her. I've been thinking about the name Courbain and my grandmother's maiden name, Corbyn. Could there be a link there? I definitely look like Arabella."

Kate leaned against the car and looked out over the harbor as it settled for the night. The day had been one of highs and lows, of revelation and more unanswered questions. And now, with Miles's professional involvement, she felt she was losing what little control she had over the situation.

"I didn't expect any of this, Miles, and I am torn between chalking it up to mere coincidence, and wondering if there is really something to it all. What if I am related to Arabella? And are these women connected to her and the legend, somehow? And where does this stolen book fit in?"

"My main concern is your safety and the whereabouts of the stolen book," Miles said. "I can't tell you whether to pursue any ancestral connection to Arabella. But if you want my advice, for your own safety, I would stay away from those three women and their businesses. And as far as the book goes, I'll open a criminal investigation, which you won't need to be involved in."

"But I have pictures of it on my phone, Miles. And I supposedly got it from a man who doesn't even communicate. That's not going to look good for me, is it? And don't forget, I have to leave in five days, too."

"Just let me worry about that for now," he said, "and you won't have to miss your flight. I'll follow where the evidence leads, but honestly, I'd take your word for what happened over Miss Shaw-Windham's account of it any day. We'll work that out. I'm not sure she's taking care of her stepfather in the best way, either."

"Well, as much as that does concern me—I mean, he seemed like a very nice man—I just can't get involved with that right now," she said.

"Of course not. I wouldn't expect you to." He pulled his keys out of his jacket pocket. "I can take you back to the inn now, if you like."

"Thanks. I would appreciate that," she said. "I am tired. And if you heard about my day, you would understand."

"Would a drink at The Tudor Bar at the inn be out of line? You can tell me all about your day?"

"Well, it all started at the nature reserve."

"You mean, you went there without me?" He feigned insult, smiling, and they drove back to the inn.

20

AFTER CLOSING HER BOOKSTORE late on Sunday afternoon, Myrlie backed her Fiat out of a small garage in the alley behind BOOKS, and turned onto The Mint. The East Stalton Flea Market was well-known in the area, and she had frequented it many times, looking for old books for herself. An hour later, she found a parking spot near the market, got out, and locked the car.

The flea market was housed in an old school building that had been unused since the 1950s, when a new school was built. Local antiquers soon discovered that it would be a great spot for a flea market, so the building was leased and then rented out to a variety of vendors. Over the years, it had become famous for its huge collection of antiques, collectibles, and unique handcrafted items.

Myrlie bought a ticket at the entrance, received a map of the building, noting the location of each vendor, and searched for 25D. The booth she was looking for was on the second floor, and she took the narrow stairs at the front of the building.

Booth 25D appeared to be at the far end of the second floor, and she made her way toward it, apprehensive about how the meeting would go. A few people were perusing the items at the entrance to the booth. Myrlie approached slowly, looking for the man she was to meet. She didn't know what he looked like, but she would know his voice—deep and gravelly, with a smoker's cough.

When the people left, she straightened her jacket, smoothed down her hair, and took a closer look into the booth. The air reeked of cigarette smoke, which settled into the close space like an early morning haze. Myrlie coughed lightly and stepped in, looking for the proprietor.

A man sat in an armchair at the back of the booth, a knife cradled in his large fingers. He swiftly turned and twisted the knife into a block of wood, the shavings falling in a heap on the floor at his feet. He was bald. His large head settled neckless on broad shoulders.

"Excuse me," Myrlie said. "Sir?"

He looked up, his jowls unfolding onto his chest.

"What do you want?" he said in a voice familiar to Myrlie from their brief phone conversation.

She stepped closer. "We spoke. Yesterday. About an item I have for you."

He slowly set down the block of wood and his carving knife.

"Come here, then," he replied.

Myrlie stepped around displays of records, magazines, and books, and as she reached him, he stood with difficulty and motioned for her to follow him. They went into a small room behind the booth.

"Do you have it?" he said.

"Yes, of course." Myrlie pulled the book, in its protective cover, out of a large tote she carried, and held it out to him. "It's *Ancient Tales*—"

"Quiet!" He grabbed it from her. "I'll do the talking here."

Myrlie nodded.

He studied the book, using a magnifying glass to examine the details of the etchings, the author's signature, and some worn spots on the spine.

"I'll give you three thousand pounds. Not a penny more."

Myrlie was stunned. "But it's worth so much more than that," she whispered. "No, no, I won't take anything less than five thousand."

The man handed it back to her. "Sorry. I can't help you, then."

Myrlie stood there, not sure what to do next. The man squinted at her.

"Maybe you don't know how this works," he growled. "You have something you want to unload. I pay you what I think it's worth to me, then I have to do the work to find a buyer. Easier for you than it is for me. I don't care where you got it from, I'm not asking any questions."

"How do I know I can trust you?" she said.

"Ha! Lady, you are in the wrong business, then. I think we're done here." He stepped back out into his booth.

Myrlie followed him. He went back to his carving, and she left the booth and walked a few feet down the row of merchants, maneuvering through the throng of buyers hurrying to make last-minute deals.

She slowed at the booth of an antique clock dealer. Wall clocks, mantel clocks, grandfather and grandmother clocks were packed together in the small space, with only the *tick-tock* of the hands sounding out the seconds. Suddenly, from somewhere buried in the horde of timepieces, she was startled by the sound of a cuckoo clock. It was off by seven minutes—itself an irritating state of affairs to Myrlie. But it was also an infuriating reminder that time was running out. Ever since the last séance, she felt the pressure mounting. There had been a change in Virginia—a desperation to see the legend fulfilled, that had not been as evident as it now was.

Virginia had treated her badly then and was clearly suspicious of something. Myrlie hoped that she was not sensing anything about the book of legends, but Virginia's intuition had often surprised her.

That woman, Kate Tyler, who had shown up at the bookstore, looking as she did, had been a shock. But even worse, she was a threat to the plans Myrlie had so carefully been crafting to make her escape—to leave the struggling bookstore and her ailing stepfather, and start over somewhere new and exciting. The police were suspicious, and she could not afford to have any of the stolen books found in her possession. This book and the others were her ticket out. The value of Sir Mallard's book no longer had anything to do with the legend of Arabella, although it was a well-written translation of oral legend. It had, at one time, been a legend that she herself had embraced. Now its value was reduced to simply how much money it could bring her.

The dealer's offer was nowhere near the price she wanted, but she knew she had to get rid of the book, somehow and soon. And the amount that he quoted would at least be a start.

She returned to his booth and approached the man again.

"I accept your terms. When and where do we—"

"Tuesday. Come back just before closing, when it's not busy. Bring it in a box with other books—ones that don't need *special handling*." He used his fat fingers for air quotes. "If I still like what I see, I'll pick it out with two or three others."

"And the money?" she said. "Cash?"

He shook his head at her naivete and went back to his carving.

"I have others," she said. "Other books."

Once again, he hefted himself off of the chair again and impatiently motioned her to the room behind the booth.

"Are they of similar value?" he replied.

"I don't know. I could do some research, I guess."

"Listen, I don't know where you got these books, and I really don't care. But you might not want to have a search history on your computer for this type of merchandise, if you know what I mean."

She huffed. "Sir, I am not ignorant in the use of a computer. How do you think I found out about this one?"

"Well, let's see how it goes first," he said. "Put a list of the others inside the book, and I'll take a look at it."

"That is acceptable. Thank you very much." She left, pushing her way through the crowds, back to her car.

She slumped into it and tossed her tote on the seat next to her, breathing her panic away. Once her heart had stopped racing, she closed her eyes and retreated into a vision of a cozy apartment on a quiet street near the beach in Spain, with window boxes that she would fill with red and yellow flowers, and sand that she would sweep from the front walk, and a sunrise that would gently awaken her through her bedroom window. An open book or two would be waiting for her in a hammock on the patio, and she would spend her day steeped in a world of adventure and romance.

She would be there soon.

21

THE EARLY DINNER CROWD was gathering in the Dr. Syn dining room at the Mermaid Inn as Kate was leaving it. Just before the Sunday dinner hour, she had secured a meeting there with the manager of the Inn, who had graciously shared the history of the inn, its secret rooms, its connections to pirates and smugglers, and its famous ghost stories. He was very interested in her blog and told her that he himself had been a travel journalist at one season in his life.

"But now that I'm settled here in Rye, I never want to leave!"

Kate could tell that he loved his job, and that the Inn was a very special place to him and everyone who worked there. She made a note to comment in her blog about the wonderful staff at the Mermaid Inn.

She had indulged in the Sunday roast for her noon meal at the Inn—a British tradition consisting of roast beef, Yorkshire pudding, gravy, vegetables, and a sweet dessert—and for Kate, enough food to last the entire day and evening, through to the following morning. But it was an experience that she had missed since leaving England as a young girl, and she was not going to pass up the opportunity to treat herself to the meal. So her late-afternoon meeting with the manager simply consisted of a glass of local wine and an appetizer provided by the inn.

As she reached the front entrance, she heard Mrs. Crossthwaite calling her.

"Kate! Over here." The woman scurried toward her, leaving her husband behind. "Kate, I'm so glad we caught you. We're about to leave for the Ghost Tour. You are going, aren't you? Lillian is on her way just now. Isn't it thrilling!" She turned and waved at Leonard. "Dear, come, come! We are meeting here in the lobby, not down by the kitchen, for heaven's sake."

Leonard began to trudge toward them.

Kate had decided earlier that she would go on the tour. She already had a ticket, and the information she had just gathered from the manager had piqued her interest even more.

"Yes, I'm going, of course," she replied. "Wouldn't miss it."

Isabelle clapped. "Wonderful, then. It's a bit gloomy out, but all the more to add to the ghostly atmosphere, right?" She shivered. "Oh, there's Lillian now."

Lillian approached them, looking at her watch. "Everyone's running a bit late, I see. Maybe the ghosts aren't cooperating tonight?"

Other guests were slowly gathering at the front door of the Mermaid Inn, and soon a young man in formal but dated attire of tails and a top hat began to round them up.

"Are we all here for the Ghost Tour, then?" he said. "Everyone have their tickets handy? Does anyone need a brolly?"

A few raised their hands, and the tour guide handed out umbrellas to those that needed them.

"Wonderful. Well, just file past me here. I'll take your ticket, and then we'll all meet on the sidewalk out front."

The group did as instructed and went outside. It was not dusk yet, but the air was misty, and the sky alternated between dark and light as the clouds raced across the sky in front of a full moon, creating the illusion of nightfall. Everyone had been instructed to dress warmly, and Kate had brought a hooded jacket in case of rain.

The young man stepped to the front of the group.

"Welcome, everyone. My name is William, and I will be your guide this evening. Or should I say, your conductor of this symphony of spirits. This aria of apparitions, perhaps?"

He got a twitter of laughter from the group. Kate had expected him to fall into a well-rehearsed patter, and she was not disappointed.

William continued. "Rye is known as the most haunted town in England, and for good reason. Why, you are staying at one of the most famous of all of the haunted spots in Rye—the Mermaid Inn. Now, is anyone in Room five, The Nutcracker Suite? Or perhaps Room seventeen, Kingsmill?"

There were a few nods.

"Well, in the Nutcracker Suite, you might have seen a lady in white. She has been known to walk through the room, stop at the foot of the bed, and then move on. Now, the Kingsmill Room was named after Thomas Kingsmill, second-in-command of a smuggling gang. The wife of George Gray, the founder of the Hawkhurst Gang, has been seen in the rocking chair in that room, and those who have seen her report an icy chill surrounding them."

"What about Room sixteen?" Lillian said. "I've heard some tales about hauntings in that room."

"Ah, that would be the Elizabethan Chamber. One of our guests claims they saw ghostly duelers fighting with swords, right in that room! Then they claim to have seen the winning dueler drag the other's ghostly body right through the inn and drop it through a trap door."

Isabelle let out a sharp gasp and clenched her husband's arm.

"Leonard, we are right next door to Room sixteen! I might not sleep a wink tonight." She turned to Kate. "But isn't it fun?" She giggled.

Leonard simply rolled his eyes.

"Stay sharp as we walk the streets of Rye," William continued. "You never know what you might experience. Come along, then. We've got lots of ground to cover. Let's see what other haunted places we can find."

The group was mesmerized at the tales of the supernatural told by William as they turned from Mermaid Street, onto the narrow cobblestoned alley known as Trader's Passage, and then onto Watchbell Lane. Further on, as they reached Watchbell Street, William drew them all close.

"Be vigilant now," he whispered. "If the light is just right, you might just spot a small boy wrapped in a white sheet."

Suddenly, a low cry and a flurry of leaves swirling in front of the group held them back. Each person tried to identify the source of the sound, but no one was there.

"Let's move on," William whispered, "and leave this apparition behind us."

A dog howled in the distance. Thunder rolled over the fields in a long, sonorous grumble. Birds scattered up into the darkening sky off roofs and power lines. Now, every noise drew a gasp. Every movement created nervous chatter among the group. But they walked on.

The intrepid but subdued band of ghost hunters finally arrived at Church Square. St. Mary's Parish Church rose up in front of them, a massive stone edifice surrounded by an ancient stone wall. William motioned them to gather round, and spoke softly.

"This beautiful church dates back to early in the twelfth century, and is the oldest building still here in Rye. Some of the headstones you see here date back centuries as well. This will be just a walk-through folks, so please keep to the path and stay together. We don't want to *disturb* anyone. Follow me."

The wind had picked up a bit, and the rumble of thunder came closer, bringing with it a heavier rain. Some of the group had dropped out, but Kate knew they were nearing Mermaid

Street, and she decided to finish the tour with Lillian, the Crossthwaites, and some others.

Suddenly, Isabelle grabbed Leonard's elbow. "Dear, that stone there—it looks absolutely ancient. Look how it's almost tipped right over! I'm going to take a closer look."

"Isabelle, he said to stay on the walk. It's wet back there. Isabelle," Leonard whispered loudly, but his wife was determined.

She crept closer to the headstone.

"Leonard, there's something..." She let out an ear-splitting scream. "Leonard, there's a man here. Come quick!"

Her cry brought everyone running to where she stood. Just as William was about to ask her what was going on, a body—one that had apparently been leaning against the headstone—tipped over onto the ground. Kate pushed to the front of the group.

"Oh no!" She stifled a cry as she knelt beside the still form. "It's Edward Bailey!" She shook him, and he began to rouse a bit. "Quick! Someone call an ambulance."

William joined Kate, next to Edward, and others held their umbrellas over them. Lillian joined them, expertly checking his pulse, then covering him with her own coat. Edward wasn't dressed for being outside, and his shoes—the same tattered slippers he wore the day Kate had met him—were soaked through.

"Do you know him?" William asked Kate.

"I met him at a bookstore. How could he have gotten here, though? He must be drenched to the bone."

As Lillian and the others gathered to make Edward comfortable, Kate stepped away and dialed Miles's number. He answered on the first ring.

"Kate?"

"Yes, Miles, it's me. You need to come to Saint Mary's Cemetery right away. We found Edward Bailey out here by himself, and he is not in very good shape. We've called an ambulance, but can you please come?"

"I'll be right there," Miles said.

The pulsing wail of the ambulance grew louder as it approached the cemetery. The emergency crew was soon hurrying to where Edward lay, and they began their examination.

"Isabelle, Leonard, let's go back to the inn." Lillian pulled the Crossthwaites aside. "There's nothing we can do here, and we could all use a stiff drink." She looked at Kate. "Are you coming?"

"Not yet. I want to make sure Edward is okay. I'll be along later. And thank you for helping, Lillian."

Lillian nodded and hurried off with the Crossthwaites, the three huddled close under one large umbrella.

Miles soon arrived and approached the ambulance team. Then he went over to Kate, who was standing not far from where they had found Edward.

"What happened, Kate? How did you happen to be out here?"

"A ghost tour that turned scary for everyone. Missus Crossthwaite found him by accident. I don't know how long he's been here, but he was just sitting against the headstone, and fell over."

"Well, there is no way he should be out at night," Miles said. "And his stepdaughter keeps him...well, she knows he shouldn't be out. I'll send an officer over to the store and see if they can find her."

Paramedics put Edward onto a stretcher and into the ambulance. One of the team came over to speak to Miles.

"We'll take him to hospital, but there's no identification. You said that you knew him?"

"Yes, his name is Edward Bailey," Miles replied, "and he lives with his stepdaughter, in a flat over a bookstore off of The Mint. We'll try to contact her and let her know where he is."

The man nodded and joined the others in the ambulance, and they drove off, the sound of the sirens quickly fading into the distance.

Miles turned back to Kate. "You're drenched. Let me take you back to the inn."

Kate thanked him, and they hurried to his car. As they pulled onto Church Square, Miles called the police station and gave details about what had happened.

"They'll send officers to find Miss Shaw-Windham," he told Kate. "She'll have some explaining to do this time."

Myrlie parked her car across the street from the bookstore, and as she stepped out, noticed a police car parked on the other side, almost blocking the alley. Two officers got out as she started across the street. She froze as they approached, gripping the tote containing the stolen book tight to her side.

"Myrlie Shaw-Windham?"

"Yes, that's me. Is there a problem?" She walked past them, into the alley.

"Does your stepfather, Edward Bailey, live here with you?"

"Yes." She then realized the door to the store was ajar, and pushed it open easily.

"The door was that way when we approached, ma'am. We did enter the store to make sure there were no problems. We're here to tell you that Mister Bailey was found in the Saint Mary's Cemetery this evening. A group of people found him and called an ambulance and the police. He's been taken to hospital."

Myrlie dropped her tote onto the wet cobblestone as her hand flew to her mouth in shock.

"But that's impossible! Is he okay? Is he..."

"He was alive when they found him, ma'am, but that's all we know. You'd better go to hospital and see for yourself."

"Thank you. Of course."

The police officers left, and Myrlie picked up her tote, stepped into the shop, and pulled the door shut. She ran to the cellar and hid the book, checking the lock twice as she closed the storage room door behind her.

She hurried back to her car. This was not good at all. How did he do it? How could he possibly have wandered off... again?

The police were involved for a second time now, and it wouldn't look good for her, to be so neglectful of her stepfather. And where would she tell them she had been?

She had to think fast, since she was sure that questions would be coming from social services, at the least. But at the very worst, from the police.

22

AFTER DROPPING KATE OFF AT THE INN, Miles went back to the police station to make his report. His instincts had been telling him there was more to the story of the mysterious book. He did a further search on the Internet to see if there were other books reported as stolen or missing around the same time as the *Ancient Tales of an Ancient Town*. He got a few hits, but then made a call to a contact in London who specialized in stolen books and art.

His London contact was surprised that the book in question had surfaced, since it was known to have been stolen in 1998. Miles asked him about other books missing around that same time, and his contact confirmed that there were several— the thefts thought to be perpetrated by the same person or people—and he said that he could send Miles a list.

An hour later, Miles compared the list his contact had sent him, to his own Internet search, and was growing more confident that some, or all, of the books could be in the possession of Myrlie Shaw-Windham. Although, how she might have come to have them was still a question in his mind.

As he was driving home, his phone rang and he answered it.

"Hey, Pixley," said a voice on the other end.

"Garth. I haven't heard from you in a while."

Garth was a paid informant that Miles had known for several years. He had an eye and ear for the trafficking of stolen articles, and after he was released from prison—five years for fencing jewels—Miles had found him especially useful, and surprisingly honest and trustworthy, in some of his cases. A number of tips from him had led to the recovery of stolen goods.

"Actually, I was thinking of calling you," Miles said.

"You don't say?" Garth replied. "That is a coincidence, then, because I might have a bit of information for you."

"Oh, and what's that?"

"I may have discovered a bit of mischief going on, Pixley. I mean, it might be some high-dollar goods in play this time. You're not on speaker are you? I mean, this is confidential, right?"

Miles assured him that he was alone.

"What have you got, Garth?"

"Are you familiar with the East Stalton Flea Market?"

"Yes, very. What about it?"

"Well, there might be some mischief going on there, as I said. There's at least one item, and maybe more, that might be 'changing hands,' so to speak."

"I see. And what booth might this mischief be happening in?"

"Ah, ah, ah, Pixley! Aren't you forgetting something?"

"You get the usual. Same as always. You know you can trust me on that."

"Well, I'm not too much on trust, right, Pixley? After that little incident—"

"Let it go, Garth. That's in the past. Are you going to give me the information or not?"

After a moment, Garth replied, "I guess the arrangement is acceptable to me, then. When can we meet?"

"Right now."

"Now? Why the rush?"

"I have my reasons, and they don't involve you. Same place. Say, in twenty minutes?"

"Same place, then. Twenty minutes."

Miles took the next left and headed out into the countryside, away from Rye. He soon pulled into the parking lot of a small pub. It was dark inside the bar area, and Miles was careful to avoid grazing his head on the low beams as he made his way to a booth in the back. Garth was already there, drinking a pint. Miles slid into the booth across from him.

"What's with the sunglasses, Garth? You know that doesn't work for me. And you don't need them in here."

Garth touched the rim of his glasses but didn't take them off.

"I was hoping you wouldn't mind."

"Off with them, Garth."

He slowly pulled the glasses off, revealing a swollen blue and yellow bruise, and a small, stitched cut below his right eyebrow.

"There's a story here, of course, Pixley. You might even find it amusing." He laughed nervously and took a swig of beer.

"Does it have anything to do with what you need to tell me?" Miles said.

"No."

"Then we'll leave it for another time. What have you got for me?"

"So no friendly greeting? No, 'How are you doing, Garth?' Right to business, then?"

A server approached, but Miles waved him away.

"I think we're past that," he said. "Now, what have you got for me?"

"Okay, okay. Here's the thing. I'm spending my usual Sunday afternoon, browsing the flea market. I love collectibles, you know. Especially angels...or dogs...or angels with dogs..."

"And?"

"And so I'm standing at booth twenty-five-C, and the owner, a good friend of mine, Errol, says 'Hey, Garth, come in the back with me. I have something you might be interested in.

It just came in. I haven't even unpacked it yet.' So I go with him to the back of his booth, and while I'm waiting for him to find it...oh, Pixley it was perfect—beautiful angel wings—"

"Just get on with it, Garth."

"Oh, sorry, I got distracted. So I'm standing there waiting for Errol to find it, and I hear, from the next booth, a man and a woman talking. They were talking low, but you know I've got acute powers of hearing. I wouldn't be in this business if I didn't."

"And what booth would that be?"

"Uh, well, probably twenty-five-D, I would say. It's at the end of the row, next to Errol's place."

"How could you hear them?"

"Well, there's storage rooms behind the booths, and it sounds like the two people moved back there, so I step back there just for a minute on Errol's side while he goes back out front for a customer. The door in the storage rooms between the booths was jammed open a wee bit at the bottom for some reason. Must be, the guy next door hadn't noticed. Very careless of him, I'd say. Anybody could be listening, right?"

"And could he hear you?" Miles said.

Garth took a swig of his beer. "I wasn't saying anything."

"And what did you hear?"

"Well, the man asks the woman if she 'had the item.' She says she did, and she must have showed it to him then. I didn't think much about it, but then she starts to say something else, and he shuts her up real quick-like."

"What did she start to say?"

"Not sure. Sounded like ancient tales of something or other."

Miles leaned back in the booth. "Go on."

"Then he tells her what he'll pay, but she wants to argue with him about it."

"How much did he offer?"

"Three thousand pounds, I think. Well, then, like I said, she wants to argue about it, and he says, 'Well, he can't help her.' Then—and this is the good part—he starts to tell her how the whole thing works!" Garth clapped his hand down on the table. "He says if she wants to unload something, he pays her, then he finds the buyer, and how it's his risk, not hers, and how he didn't care where it came from, and he wasn't asking any questions. You know the drill."

"And?" Miles said.

"Just then, Errol comes back, so I step back inside, he finds the angel, and, oh Pixley, I couldn't take my eyes off it, you know—"

"But what else did you hear, Garth? Anything? Did you see anything?"

"All in good time, my friend. All in good time. You know I like to spin a story just so."

"Yes, I know that," Miles said, trying to keep his impatience in check.

"So we go back out to the front of Errol's booth so I could pay him—because I really wanted that angel—and I see a woman leave twenty-five-D."

"Can you describe her?"

"Well, severe. Kind of witch-like, actually. That's the best word to describe her. Black hair, pale face, all dressed in black, red lipstick. But then, not a minute later, she comes back to the booth, and my antennae are up again."

"Okay, then what happened when she came back?"

"I think they must have come to some agreement. I couldn't hear much then, because Errol was going on and on. I really tried to listen, though, because I thought it might be a bit of valuable information that I could pass along, you know? I think the woman said she had some others, too."

"Other items?"

Garth nodded.

"Okay, that's good Garth. Anything else?"

"Nope. That's about it. But that's worth a little something, right?" He rubbed his fingers together.

Miles pulled some cash out of his pocket and slid it across the table.

"Our usual."

Garth smiled and grabbed up the money.

"Are you sure there's nothing else?" Miles said.

"Well, there might just be. And I'm using my keen powers of deduction here, but I think it's a book, and here's why. For one thing, the guy carries that type of merchandise. So," Garth tapped his forehead, "I checked it out on a hunch. Because I want to make it worth your while, my friend. When I get home, I do a look-see on the computer for 'ancient tales,' because it reminded me of something. Well, a certain rare book called *Ancient Tales of an Ancient Town* happened to show up on a stolen book website. And I'm thinking this is what they were talking about. Oh, this could be the big one, Pixley. A feather in your cap if you solve this one. So don't forget it was ol' Garth that helped you out, eh?"

Miles sighed in exasperation. But it all made sense. The woman Garth saw must have been Myrlie Shaw-Windham, and that was probably where she was when Edward sneaked out of the flat and ended up in the cemetery, cold and wet. He had already heard from one of the officers that she had returned to her flat and was going to the hospital to see Edward.

The information was worth more than Garth could ever know. Miles thanked his informant, threw some money on the table to pay for Garth's beer, and then some extra, and left the pub. Once in the car, he dialed Kate's number, but there was no answer. He left a voicemail.

"Kate, it's Miles. I think I have this figured out, and you need to stay away from Myrlie, Opal, and Virginia Calloway. I know I already told you this, but it's really important. Myrlie Shaw-Windham's involvement with the book is a police matter now. I'm going to check on Edward, then head home. Call me if you need anything."

Miles called the hospital and was told that Edward was stable, but that they were keeping him at least overnight for observation. Social services would be checking into his living arrangements, but as of now, the nurse felt it was clear that he would not be returning to live with his stepdaughter.

Satisfied that Edward was being well-taken-care of, Miles went home.

23

KATE RETURNED HER UMBRELLA TO THE STAND inside the door of the Mermaid Inn. After the chill of the rain, and finding Edward as they did, she was exhausted. But as she walked past the Giants Fireplace Bar, she saw Lillian there near the fire, with a drink in her hand.

Lillian looked up when Kate entered the room. She nodded and waved her over. Kate took off her wet jacket and laid it over the back of the chair.

"Well, you're a mess, Kate, and I don't mind telling you. Looks like you could use a hot toddy."

Kate agreed, and Lillian motioned to a server, who took her order.

"Isabelle and Leonard went right upstairs," Lillian said. "Not sure if they'll sleep a wink tonight after that scare. How is that man?"

Kate twisted her damp hair back into a loose bun and sat down.

"They took him to the hospital," she replied. "He was in pretty bad shape."

"You knew his name. Did you know him?"

Kate didn't want to go into too much detail, but Lillian seemed genuinely concerned.

"I met him at a bookstore off of The Mint. I don't really know him, but he seemed like a very nice man. I can't imagine why he would have been out on a night like this, and he certainly wasn't dressed for it."

"Such a shame," Lillian said. "Well, let's talk about something else, then. How is your blog coming? I took a peek at it. It's very good, but I haven't seen any postings for the last couple days."

The server brought Kate's drink, and she took a sip, relishing the warmth spreading through her body.

"You're right," she replied. "I guess I've been neglecting it. I've gotten...well, distracted."

"That can easily happen when you travel. I got so distracted on a safari in Kenya by some tragic conditions with the locals that I didn't leave for three months. Worked in a clinic there. I was trained as a nurse at one time in my younger years, and they welcomed my help." Lillian looked distant for a moment. "Yes, lots can distract you when you travel."

Kate knew exactly what Lillian was talking about. But she honestly could not remember a trip where she had gotten so far off track as this one. Except maybe for her disastrous trip to Rome the year before. She had gotten the flu, and had had to come home early, losing out on her assignment and any future ones for the magazine she was writing for at the time.

"You've led an interesting life, Lillian. What else have you done?"

"Well, I worked as a nurse in London, right out of college. But I found out pretty quick, I didn't care for the bureaucracy. Just make people better the best you can is what I thought. Eventually, I quit nursing. Then I worked for a newspaper for a while after that. That's when I learned to love traveling. I did the newspaper thing for a while, then worked as a nanny—anything I could to help support my new travel addiction. Now I just live off an inheritance that should feed my wanderlust for the rest of my life." She chuckled at that.

"Do you mind if I ask you a personal question?" Kate said.

"Shoot."

"Were you ever married? Or find that a relationship got in the way of what you loved to do?"

"Well, my traveling got in the way of any relationships I might have had. And I say, *might have,* because none ever got very far. I sacrificed a lot in my life to do what I loved. There was always another place to go, another adventure to be on. I don't regret it, mostly, but it was always a choice. How about you?"

Kate thought about it for a moment and then shared with Lillian about her life back at Howard's Walk.

"I have to be honest with you. I think I was running away a little when I came here—back to a life I thought I missed and needed. Travel has always been in my blood."

"I'm not the one you have to be honest with, Kate. You have to be honest with yourself. You and I, we aren't the same. Yes, we both love to see the world, visit new places. But the life you just described back at Howard's Walk is everything I don't have, never had, and never will have. And I guess I couldn't miss what I never had. But you...you've already got it, and by God, if I were you, I would never let that go. Not for anything." Lillian swallowed the rest of her drink. "Time for me to head up to my room. Will you be okay?"

Kate smiled. "Yes, Lillian. And thank you for the talk. I guess I have a lot to think about."

"You'll figure it out, dear." Lillian gathered her things. "Just find what you were meant to do, and do it the best you can. That's my motto."

Kate sat for a while, nursing her drink by the warmth of the fire. It occurred to her that nothing really changes over the centuries. People are all meant to do something with their lives, and they really only have one chance to do it—one life in which to live it. Arabella may have thought that she could come back one day and live the life she was meant to live, but that really was the heart of a legend or folklore—a desperate dream of a young woman who had lost all hope.

Slowly, Kate was beginning to be more comfortable with having Arabella in her thoughts and dreams. Maybe the two of them weren't so different. The more research she did on Arabella, and the more she learned about her, the more real she became. Maybe it wasn't the legend, the hyped-up story that resided in a book of ancient tales, that Kate needed to be concerned about. Maybe it was the truth about Arabella that needed to be found. Maybe by finding the truth, Arabella could live out her eternity in peace. And there was more truth to be uncovered. Kate was sure of it.

She finished her drink and started to walk back to her room. Gilbert waved her down as she passed the front desk.

"Miss Tyler, glad I caught you. I have another message for you."

Kate took an envelope from his hand. It was the same monogrammed stationery and handwriting as the last time— from Virginia Calloway. It read:

Dear Ms. Tyler,

I recall that you mentioned an interest in herbalism during your visit here. I am happy to say that I have arranged for you to be my guest at the Calloway Manor, if you are still interested in that area of study. It will be a wonderful opportunity for you to take back what you have learned to your own gardens in the States. I will personally ensure your comfort here, and every need will be met. If convenient, a car will pick you up at noon tomorrow.

Sincerely,

Virginia Marguerite Calloway

24

ARABELLA DID NOT VISIT KATE in her dreams that night. But her sleep was, nonetheless, sporadic and invaded by other visitors. Worry about Edward Bailey and what part she might have played in him being out on such a rainy night. An unease about her conversation with Lillian that revealed some truths about Kate's reasons for being in Rye. But mostly, if she did accept the invitation to the Calloway House, would she be successful in finding out the truth about Arabella, and how she herself was connected to this legend?

Kate could decide not to accept the invitation. She could find other places to visit during the rest of her stay in Rye. She had pages of notes in her journal that needed to be transcribed into the blog, and she was missing photos to go with some of her writing. But her plans for the entire trip had already been disrupted, and it was more than just adjusting her itinerary on the fly as opportunities came along. It was so much more than that. Regardless of Ms. Calloway's reasons for the invitation, and as appealing as that might be, Kate's reasons for accepting would be something much more than her interest in herbalism.

Kate sat up on the edge of her bed, sunlight sifting in through the window. At that moment, she felt lost—a feeling that she thought would never surface again. When she had finally come to terms with creating a home at Howard's Walk with Ben and her friends—a challenge that she embraced wholeheartedly—she thought that the feeling of being adrift and alone had passed. The fears that she was without family and without a place to call home, she thought they had been buried, along with the pain of losing her twin sister, Rebecca. She thought she had moved on. But now, something was pulling at her in a way she had never expected.

Something had brought Arabella to her in her dreams. Something had brought her here to Rye. Something had been triggered in her at Beachy Head, starting a chain reaction of events that had led her to this point. There were too many unanswered questions for her to simply ignore them and walk away.

Miles had advised her not to have anything to do with Opal and Myrlie, and especially Virginia Calloway. And for good reason. But if she accepted Virginia's invitation to Calloway Manor, she would go with her eyes wide open this time. After her last experience there, she did not trust Virginia Calloway. But her instincts told her that the answers to her questions about what really happened to Arabella Courbain were in that house, and she intended to find them.

The invitation had been made. She would accept it, knowing the risks, and pursue the truth.

After calling the number on Virginia's invitation to accept, she called Ben.

"Kate, is everything all right? It's really early here. "

She hadn't even thought of the time difference. She apologized and assured him she was fine.

"I haven't heard from you in a while," he said.

Kate suddenly realized, with a sinking feeling, that he was right.

"I thought you might call me, too," she said weakly, knowing that it was no excuse for her not to call him.

"I know you've been busy there. So what's up?"

She brushed aside what seemed to be indifference in his voice.

"I just wanted to let you know I had a change of plans here. It's really a once-in-a-lifetime opportunity to spend a few days at a place called the Calloway House and Gardens near here.

"That's great, but I thought you wanted to spend your time in Rye."

She sighed. He was right, but she wasn't ready to go into details. Not yet.

"I did," she replied. "But plans can change quickly on these trips."

"Well, don't worry about things here. Everything's fine. Billy's doing great. The gardens are moving along now that the rain has stopped. Listen, if they know anything about roses at those gardens, I guess you could see what we might be missing so we can fill in any gaps here."

Kate promised she would. Leave it to Ben to think about what was good for the gardens, she thought. She knew that it should also be her focus, but explaining otherwise would not be easy.

Kate missed Ben terribly at that moment, and told him so. But what she didn't admit to him was that she knew she should have asked him to come with her. She knew that, but it was too late to change it now. That had also been on her mind, and she realized that it might have been her biggest worry. Did she detect a hint of regret in his voice, too? Or resentment, perhaps? She knew Ben wasn't that type of person, and that's why she loved him. But hearing his voice now, she felt too far distant from him to even begin to tell him everything that she was feeling. He was an ocean away, and when she admitted it to herself, she knew she had run away from those feelings, even in Rye, and she was still running. She had let this unexpected turn of events with the legend of Arabella get in the way. She vowed to herself to make it right when she returned to Eden Springs.

She could hear him yawning over the phone.

"Sorry, I forgot about the time difference," she said again. "I'll call you soon, I promise. And Ben, you can call me at any time."

"Okay. I'm going back to bed. We'll talk soon." He ended the call.

Kate set her phone aside and rubbed her temples. Time difference or not, he was abrupt with her, and that wasn't like him.

Put it aside, Kate.

She picked up her phone again. Her next call was to Miles. She left a brief voicemail to let him know that she had gotten his message about avoiding Myrlie, Opal, and Virginia Calloway, and that she had no intention of going anywhere near the bookstore or the tea shop. But she told him that Ms. Calloway was another matter. She had to find out more about the missing pieces of Arabella's legend and told him about her invitation to the manor.

When he returned her call—and she knew he would—Kate would just have to convince him that she would be safe.

Just before noon, she checked out of the Mermaid Inn and left messages for Lillian and the Crossthwaites. They had her contact information, and she let them know that she truly hoped that they would keep in touch.

Right at noon, the car from the Calloway House & Gardens arrived, as promised, and the porter helped Kate with her bags. She realized she was moving even further away from her original plans for the trip. But it was something she had to do.

25

KATE WAS QUICKLY ON HER WAY to the Calloway House & Gardens after checking out of the Mermaid Inn. When they arrived, the driver skirted the public parking area in front of the Calloway House and stopped instead at the end of the long flagstone walkway in front of Ms. Calloway's manor. He pulled Kate's bag out of the trunk and walked on ahead, the rolling bag thumping along the uneven stones.

The noon sun gave a brighter look to the house—unlike the dismal nighttime view of her first visit. The surroundings were still intimidating as she thought back to the last time she had visited Ms. Calloway. But the bench where she had awoken that night was out of sight. There weren't any ravens lighting near her that she could see. She took a deep breath and braced herself for whatever might be ahead.

Samuel, the butler, greeted them at the door.

"Good afternoon, Miss Tyler. I will take you to your room to freshen up, and then you will meet Miss Calloway for lunch in the dining room there." He pointed to his left.

Kate followed Samuel as he took her further into the house than she had been on her previous visit, navigating the maze of hallways and stairs that seemed created to confuse anyone who did not live there. Kate doubted she would be able to find her way back to the dining room without a map.

They took a stairway to the second floor, and Samuel opened the door to a bedroom that was spacious and filled with light. The furnishings were antique, but not as well-preserved as at the inn. Several faded oriental rugs partially covered the dull hardwood floor. A large four-poster bed, in need of a dusting, sat against one wall.

Kate unpacked a few things into a small closet and dresser, then freshened up in an en suite bathroom with fixtures that looked original to the house. She went to the windows to see if they could be opened to help freshen the air in the room. She turned the handle on one of the multi-paned windows and swiveled it outward, letting in a fragrant breeze from the gardens. Just as she was ready to leave to find her way back to the dining room to meet Ms. Calloway, her cell phone rang. It was Miles.

"Kate, I got your message. What are you doing at the Calloway House?"

"Well, hello to you, too, Miles. And I told you, I was invited to come and stay for as long as I wanted to. But I still need to leave here on Thursday and get back to Rye. I really think it's fine, though. You don't need to worry. It'll just be for a couple days so I can find out more about Arabella."

She heard a sigh on the other end.

"Yes, and I also said to stay away from those three women and their businesses. And yet you decided not only to visit the lion's den, but move in? Nothing has changed since we talked the other night. If anything, it's worse. I'm still worried about you."

"And I appreciate your concern," she said in a firm voice. "But what I haven't told you about was what I found doing research last Friday."

"And what was that?" Miles said.

"Well, back in 1766, Arabella's father, William Courbain, captained a ship called *The Grand Lady*. He was a sea smuggler, and on November seventeenth of that year, it was attacked by a revenue cutter called *The Courageous*. And guess who captained that ship?"

"I have no idea," Miles said.

"Devon Calloway," Kate replied. "That can't just be a coincidence."

"No, probably not. He could be related to Miss Calloway. So what happened to the ship?"

"Which one?" Kate said.

"Well, both, I guess."

"*The Grand Lady* was sunk, but a few men escaped, including William Courbain. There wasn't any record of him being captured that I—that we—could find. *The Courageous* survived. And get this. Winnie, the lady I met at the historical society, said that she knew Virginia Calloway back when they were students together at a boarding school."

"And how is that relevant?" Miles said.

"I don't know, but she said Virginia really kept to herself, and maybe had a hard time with her family growing up."

"Well, this is all this very interesting, and I am not sure how you dug it all up, so kudos to you for getting this far. But my feeling is still the same, Kate. Be careful. She may not like it if you start asking personal questions."

"I'll be fine," Kate said. "There is nothing to worry about."

"If there is nothing to worry about, why are you whispering? And where are you right now?"

Kate sat down on the bed. "I'm in a bedroom on the second floor of the house. Okay, so I get your point. This is all a little bit cloak and dagger. But I'm really just here to see what I can find out from Miss Calloway about Arabella. And the gardens, Miles, they are incredible. I know I can learn a lot from their gardener. I do have that much in common with her. And she asked me here to teach me more about herbs, which I really am interested in. Listen, if I sense anything is wrong, I'll call for an Uber and go back to Rye. It'll only be for a couple days, anyway."

"I don't like it, Kate. If I can't get in touch with you, I'm sending in the troops, understand? Keep your mobile nearby, and promise me you'll call me first before you call for a car. Do I have your word on that?"

Kate relented. "Yes, you will be the first person I call."

"And Kate?"

"Yes?"

"I want to see you before you go home. Please let me take you to the train station."

"I promise I will do that. And thanks. Listen, I've got to go. Having lunch with Miss Calloway. I'll talk to you soon."

She ended the call and checked herself in the mirror. Satisfied, she took the steps at the end of the hallway to the first floor, and after a few wrong turns, found her way back to the dining room.

Ms. Calloway was already seated at the head of a long table. She smiled and welcomed Kate, pointing to a seat near her. Kate thanked her for the invitation to lunch and sat down.

"You are quite welcome, Kate. And please call me Virginia."

"Thank you, Virginia."

Kate laid a monogrammed napkin on her lap and studied the room. Dappled rays of sun stole through the trees, through a wall of tall windows behind her, glinting off a crystal chandelier over their heads, and laying shadows across a stunning table setting. Stark-white peonies and blushing-pink roses burst out of a crystal vase in the center of the table. The design on the china place settings imitated the botanical gardens Kate had seen on the estate, with colorful florals and butterflies. The water goblets were crystal—probably Waterford—and the silver was monogrammed with an elaborate "C."

"What a lovely table, Virginia," Kate said, receiving a slight nod from her host.

The butler brought their lunch of grilled fish and salad, and for a few moments, the two women ate in silence. The room reminded Kate of the television shows she had seen located at large English estates. Howard's Walk was not nearly as grand as the Calloway Manor, and Kate felt out of place at her seat in the large room. But on closer scrutiny, the room was not all that the exquisite table might have hinted at.

Signs of aging appeared not only in the cloth covering on the table, but in the rugs and curtains, just as they did in her own bedroom. The wallpaper showed slight wear at the ceiling, and the parquet flooring was dull. Kate realized that, other than the staff working in the public areas, she had only seen the butler, the guard, and Mr. McGregor, and a few gardeners. She wondered if the small house staff was just a preference, or if finances had dictated it.

Virginia appeared to be focused on her meal, but Kate felt a sense of urgency to get to know her host as quickly as possible because of her limited time there. She silently scolded herself for judging the appearance of the room, and decided that perhaps another compliment would start them off in the right direction.

"This fish is delicious." Kate smiled. "Is it trout?"

"You are too kind," Virginia replied. "And yes. It was caught this morning. We stock our own pond and have trout quite often here at the house. And the salad greens are from our gardens."

"That is wonderful that you grow and harvest your own food right here on the property, then. We've done that at Howard's Walk, but only on a small scale. I do hope to grow that part of the business. We have a lot of farming in our area of North Carolina. All types. And wineries and breweries now, too. Do you supply local restaurants or farmers markets, too?"

Virginia responded with a puzzled look, and a simple, "No."

Kate knew her nerves were showing. She was here to learn, and so far, she had mostly rambled on about herself. She drizzled a light vinaigrette on her salad to slow herself down, and after a bite, continued.

"I'm curious, though. I learned quite a bit about the house during the tour last Tuesday. I wonder if there is anything else you can tell me that wouldn't be on the tour?"

Virginia laid her fork aside and dabbed her napkin to her lips.

"As you can imagine," she replied, "I have never taken the tour myself. No need at all. I know every corner of the old house and the gardens. My cousin Hubert arranges the tours and all of that. But although you might know this already, the house has been in the Calloway family since Jarod Calloway built the oldest part in 1472. The other additions were done later. The buildings were found to be unlivable for all practical purposes, in 1955, and so the manor house, this house, was built, and it has been occupied since that time."

"Then you have lived here since 1955?" Kate said, pleased that Virginia was finally opening up.

"Not exactly. You see, the latest generation was not allowed to live here until the previous generation had passed. My grandparents, Quentin and Mathilde Calloway, lived here, and my parents lived in London. Unfortunately, both of my parents, and Grandfather Quentin, died before Grandmother Mathilde. She lived to be one hundred years old. I came to live with her in 1975, since I was the next generation that could take residency here. It was her wishes that I do so, and as it turned out, it was just prior to her death that same year. But I spent a fair amount of time here before that as well, in my younger years."

Kate recalled this same detail from her talk with Winnie.

"And the Calloway House and Gardens?" she said. "They opened in 1985 to the public, if I remember correctly."

"Yes," Virginia replied. "Although, that was never my idea—to have people tromping through the place where we lived and worked, the house and the gardens. They like to say they are birdwatching, but I think they are a bunch of busybodies that don't know a sparrow from a barn swallow, and just want to get on the property." She picked up her fork and stabbed at a piece of fish. "But it was decided, against my better judgement, that the house and at least part of the gardens should be open to the public. Upkeep, you know. It can be rather costly. And I didn't want to see it all go to ruin. So it is now The Calloway House and Gardens, and I simply live here."

"I see," Kate said. "But surely you have your privacy from the public? With this house and your private gardens?"

"I suppose I do. But it is not as it once was—a real working farm where we grew most our own food, raised our own meat, lived the way we wanted. Other than the vegetables and fish, and some laying hens, we do very little of that now."

She looked pensive and distant, and Kate waited for her to continue.

"Yes, that is all gone." Virginia finally looked at her guest. "But someone like you comes along, and it brings back memories." Her eyes were piercing, and her gaze suddenly made Kate uncomfortable. "It brings back...so many memories."

"Memories of what?" Kate said. "If you don't mind my asking?"

After a slight hesitation, Virginia replied, "Memories of younger days here at the Calloway House and this manor. Simpler days." She looked out the window, as if to some invisible place from the past. "Springtime, when everything was fresh and new. When plans for the gardens made in the winter were put into place. Long summer days spent lying in a boat on the Stalton Brook, and floating wherever the ripples cared to take you." She turned back to Kate, her wistful demeanor gone. "Then in the fall, it was back to school, and the Calloway House was left behind until the next visit."

"It sounds wonderful," Kate said.

Virginia's dark eyes flashed. "It was. For a time. But that is all gone now." She rang for the butler and pushed her chair back. "I expect you are anxious to see the manor gardens, am I right?" She stood and began to walk to the door.

It seemed that the time for polite lunch conversation and a brief glimpse into Virginia's past was over, and Kate quickly followed her host. She reminded herself that she was a guest in the house, and there were other things that she hoped to accomplish there. But she and Virginia seemed to be in a dance, one with secret moves and unfamiliar music, and Virginia was leading.

Kate walked with Virginia down a long hallway that soon opened up into a large foyer that, at first glance, Kate thought would have been better suited at the front of the house rather than the back. But when she saw the view from it, and its stunning design, she understood.

The foyer was circular, and in front of her, Kate looked up at a massive wall of windows, two stories high. The early afternoon sun beaming through a generous scattering of stained-glass panes threw tinted rays onto the tile floor. Rich shades of emerald and crimson, plum and golden yellow seemed to flow around Kate's feet. The remaining glass panes were covered with delicate etchings of flowers, herbs, fruits, and vegetables. Kate was mesmerized as she took in the exquisite artistry.

"Virginia, this is amazing!" Kate stepped closer to the windows, reaching out to trace the etched flowers.

The details of the etching were so real, she felt she could pluck them from the glass, into her hand.

Out of the corner of her eye, she caught Virginia smiling, seemingly pleased with her guest's reaction. But her smile disappeared as quickly as it had shown itself.

"The Calloway family has a long history of engravers and artisans," Virginia said. "These windows were made by others, of course, when the manor was built. But many of the designs, especially the florals and fruits, were first drawn by a Calloway centuries ago."

"It is simply breathtaking," Kate said.

She was so entranced that she didn't notice what was beyond the windows until Virginia opened a glass door to the outside. The door fit so perfectly into the design of the windows that it was almost invisible. Kate was reluctant to leave the beauty of the space, until she stepped out onto a wide stone patio and looked out over gardens that were beyond anything that the public was afforded on their tours of the Calloway House & Gardens.

It seemed that everything in the garden was in bloom at that moment. The scene was lush and bright. The emerald-green grass lay like a carpet in front of them. Groves of trees dripped with tender new blossoms, their fallen petals creating a mosaic on the grass. Further along the grassy path, banks of flowering shrubs rose up on either side. A pebbled walk led to a stone archway covered with climbing roses of every hue. The archway reminded Kate of the gates at Howard's Walk. Both were inviting. But here, with the permanence of stone rather than a simple latched gate, there was an air of mystery about what was on the other side.

"Virginia, you have created something wonderful here. I had no idea. I mean, the public gardens are beautiful, but this... this is simply amazing."

"Yes, well, it is a legacy of the Calloways, I suppose."

"That's what I would like Howard's Walk to be. My legacy. A place of tranquility and learning, where families can gather. A place of healing. Something that people will continue to admire, long after I'm gone."

Virginia leaned down and plucked a leaf from the carpet of grass and tossed it into the bushes.

"Cousin Hubert has it in his head to open all of this to the public, too, but I have steadfastly refused. I told him it would be over my dead body. But I suppose that someday it will happen, since I have no descendants." She hesitated and turned to look at

Kate. "Is that of concern to you, Kate? Are you concerned about what might happen to the Calloway House and Gardens when I pass on?"

Kate thought it an odd question, and chose her words carefully.

"I don't have a personal interest, of course. But as someone who has received a similar inheritance, yes, I understand the concern you must have. Heirlooms are important ways to pass down a family's legacy. I know that it is something I also will have to decide—someday."

Virginia waved a dismissive hand. "Of course, I was referring to your own home at Howard's Walk."

Kate was doubtful that Virginia had simply misspoken, but she let it pass without comment.

"But surely, for everything you have here," Kate said, "you must have other relatives?"

"Yes, of course. Only cousins and their children, though. And none of them have ever lived here, so their understanding of what this place truly means is dubious, and their motives for wanting it could be questionable. But another, more direct descendant of another Calloway—" Virginia cut herself off and was silent.

"If there were another direct descendant," Kate said, trying to fill in the blanks without crossing a line with her host, "the idea that they might have an interest in the estate after all this time is quite far-fetched, don't you think? How could they possibly feel entitled to anything?"

"Well, I suppose anything is possible." Virginia sighed. "Shall we return to the house now? We have a busy afternoon ahead of us."

"Of course," Kate said, as they turned back.

Kate had to hold her impatience in check. Perhaps she was hoping for too much too quickly. She had decided to accept Virginia's invitation, and now she was here. And thinking back on the conversation so far, she had learned important pieces of Virginia and her life. The thoughts she had shared about her past at the Calloway Manor as a young woman reinforced what Kate had learned from Winnie at the Rye Historical Society. Virginia lived simply and was not a big fan of the tourist activity caused by the public part of the Calloway House & Gardens. She was proud of her own personal gardens, and was concerned about what would happen to them after she was gone. And she worried about her cousin Hubert pushing her to open the entire property to the public.

It was understandable that Virginia felt she was the protector of all that was here. And as personally revealing as her conversations with Virginia were so far, Kate was left with more questions than when she'd started. She was peeling the layers away, but had many more to go. And the mystery of Arabella still hung suspended between them.

As they walked, Kate said, "Virginia, I appreciate that you said this was an open-ended invitation, but I'll need to return to Rye on Thursday. I'll stay overnight there, then take the early train to London on Friday to catch my plane."

"Very well," Virginia replied, as they neared the house.

She stopped and inclined her head toward Kate.

"But then, wouldn't it be lovely if you decided to stay?"

26

JUST AS KATE WAS ABOUT TO RESPOND to Virginia's cryptic comment, they came to a small shed attached to the house, tucked away in a courtyard which was well-hidden from the sight of visitors, and even workers in the gardens. Virginia unlocked the door and went into the shed. She pulled a chain above her head, and a single bare bulb lit the area.

Kate stepped in behind her and scanned the room. Two of the walls were lined with work benches that held various sized bottles, boxes, and books. Above the workbenches were tiers of small drawers, each labeled in a neat script. A large stainless-steel table stood in the center of the room, completely empty, the surface polished to a high shine. The wall to Kate's right held a large, deep sink, a refrigerator, and open shelves stacked with various sized bowls. A variety of utensils hung from a hook over the sink. Kate realized that what had appeared to be a nondescript shed from the outside, was instead a well-designed, temperature-controlled workroom.

Virginia moved around the area methodically, wiping the top of the stainless-steel table with a cloth, then brushing bits of debris from the workbenches into her hand and tossing them into a wastebasket by the door. Kate sensed a clear difference in how this room was cared for, compared to the general upkeep of the manor.

Virginia folded the cloth, set in in a basket by the sink, and took a seat on one of two stools at the table.

"This is where I do my work, Kate. It's changed from where I started out, of course. I created what you see now. But the traditions which I was taught as a young girl and a young woman, from my grandmother and other herbalists of that era, I brought it all here with me. And there are new methods now, better ones, that I have developed myself, and that I have learned from others."

Finally, the woman was opening up about something. It was clear that she must love her work with herbs, so it was easy for her to talk about it. And Kate understood. She had learned from her own grandmother's writings in market bulletins and journals about gardening, plant propagation, and so much more. But then she had also learned new methods from Ben and her friends, who were trained in more modern techniques. Kate had integrated both the old and the new into how she worked in her own gardens now. A look of understanding went between the elder Virginia and young Kate.

"What you brought with you, though," Kate said, "the soul of the thing. Some things never change, am I right?"

It was only the second time that Kate had seen even the slightest hint of a smile on Virginia's face.

"Yes, indeed," she replied. "Perhaps you and I are beginning to understand each other."

"Perhaps we are," Kate said. "I will admit, though, that all I know about herbalism, I could fit into a teabag."

"I see. Then let your education begin."

Virginia took two plain white aprons from a hook on the wall, gave one to Kate, and put the other on herself. She stepped to the sink and turned on the water.

"First, when working with herbs, your hands must be clean and dry." She washed and dried her own hands, then stepped aside for Kate to do the same. "Keep drying," she admonished, when Kate set down her towel. "Moisture, light, heat: it all causes oxidation in the herbs, and must be avoided."

Virginia opened one of the small drawers above the workbench and retrieved a small opaque bag.

"A beginner must be trained in the basics first. It took many, many years for my grandmother to teach me the mystery of herbs—how they can sustain and heal the body." She opened the bag, breathed in the aroma, then handed it to Kate. "What do you smell?"

Kate put her nose to the opening in the bag and thought for a moment.

"I honestly can't place it." She looked at the label on the bag. "Betony: Stachys officinalis." She stumbled over the Latin pronunciation. "You grow this here, right? I think I saw this in the garden earlier."

"Yes," Virginia replied. "Betony's reputation for healing goes back centuries. In the Middle Ages, it was grown in the monastery infirmary gardens. Its popularity has waxed and waned over the years, but I still keep it in the garden and use it in herbal tea and as a gargle."

She retrieved another bag labeled "Skullcap," and shook a few dried bits of the herb out into Kate's hand.

"I use this in combination with other herbs as a restorative. And in tea, it has a calming effect at bedtime. You see, to truly understand herbs, you must learn how and where they grow, the soil they thrive in, and when they are best harvested. You must learn the taste of the herbs, the feel of them, and in turn, how they make you feel. As you put it, there is more to herbal understanding than what you will find in a commercial teabag, or what passes for tea these days. No, to understand the potential and power of herbs, you must never stop questioning, searching, and learning."

Virginia closed the bags of herbs and returned them to their designated drawers.

Kate glanced up to the shelf lined with thick books with titles like *The Art of Herbal Medicine*, and *Ancient Use of Herbs in Medicine*, feeling both impressed and overwhelmed.

"Virginia, I really appreciate you taking the time to show me your workroom and some of the basics, but I think that with my time here being so limited, it would be nice to learn a simple herbal tea recipe maybe. I know that it has taken you a lifetime to accomplish all of this. I only have a couple days here."

"I see," Virginia replied, after a moment. "Well, perhaps we could manage that, then." She reached for a large bowl and brought it to the table, and then again gathered bags of various herbs from the drawers. "We'll make something to energize us this afternoon."

Virginia took a digital scale from a cupboard, set it on the bench, and placed a small, thin-sided bowl on it. She pushed a couple buttons on the scale, then she showed Kate how to measure the herbs—gunpowder green tea, lemongrass, and pennywort—by weight into the small bowl, one at a time, and then after each measurement, pour them into the larger bowl.

"Now we slowly mix the herbs together with our hands, like this." Virginia slowly lifted, then sifted the ingredients in the large bowl, through her long, thin fingers. "Now you try."

Kate copied her movements while Virginia filled an electric kettle with water and set the temperature to seventy-nine degrees Celsius. When it reached the right temperature, she poured a bit into a teapot—white and hand-painted with botanicals and butterflies—to warm it. She showed Kate how to swirl the water around to warm the teapot, and then instructed her to pour the water into the sink.

Virginia handed Kate a measuring spoon and asked her to measure out thirty milliliters of the combined tea ingredients into the bowl on the scale, and from there, into the teapot. The water in the kettle had maintained its exact temperature, and Virginia then poured it over the tea.

"We'll leave this for about ten minutes." She put the lid on the teapot.

Virginia rummaged around in a cupboard under the worktable and pulled out two teacups that matched the teapot. As she was doing that, Kate walked around the room, looking more closely at what appeared to be journals on the shelves, with dates going back decades. One journal was labeled *Valerian 2000–2015*. Kate suddenly recalled what she had learned at the Essentials of Rye, about valerian. Madame Zaytsev had said it was a natural sedative and mild tranquilizer, and in the hands of the right herbalist, would be medicinal, but that it would not be legal to prepare anything that might act like a drug.

Kate recalled her words: *That is for the ancients to keep that secret, I think.*

Virginia had been taught the traditions of herbalism from her grandmother, who had most likely had that same experience from her mother, and on it went for generations before that. From the *ancients*. This knowledge was as ingrained in Virginia as her DNA. It was part of her psyche. It was her soul and her companion. And she believed that she had no one to whom she could pass on the legacy. Not just the material things—those did not seem as important to her. Or even her house and land and her precious gardens. They would be taken over by someone, in the future. But her knowledge, her skill, her wisdom—her belief in the power of plants, which kept her curious, searching, and learning. It seemed that there was no one who cared to learn all that Virginia could teach.

There were other books on the shelves. *Holistic Health and Tonics, A History of Chai Tea in India,* and an entire row of books dedicated to various herbs that Kate had never heard of. At the end of the row were several more journals on mugwort, lavender, and catnip. And finally, one simply labeled *Dreams*.

These collections must have been the entirety of Virginia's existence—the sum of what she dedicated her entire life to. A life that, perhaps, she saw slipping away too quickly now. For all the mystery and improbability that Kate felt about the legend of Arabella, and what Virginia might see as her connection to it, Kate suddenly felt a clearer understanding of the woman and the desperation she might be feeling.

Kate had been so immersed in Virginia's teaching for the past hour that she had almost forgotten about Arabella. But Mr. McGregor had said that Virginia would be a source of information about her. And on Kate's first visit, Virginia had invited her to the manor to talk about Arabella. And Kate knew now that there was a definite link between at least the Calloway name and Arabella Courbain. At some point in history, their lives had intersected.

Kate had not planned on bringing up what happened that first evening, with Virginia. She was a guest in one of the most famous homes in East Sussex, and to directly accuse Virginia of drugging her and leaving her on a bench in the garden—it would be the height of impoliteness. But Virginia clearly had knowledge to concoct any sort of herbal drink that might have put Kate in a deep sleep. She had to wonder that if there were a connection to Arabella's story, what would happen if she simply asked Virginia about the incident?

When the ten minutes were up, Virginia poured the tea into the cups and handed one to Kate, rousing her out of her thoughts.

Kate tested the temperature of the tea before tasting it, and in a few moments, it was perfect for drinking. She recognized the component of green tea, and the aroma of the lemongrass as she sipped.

"How do you like the tea, Kate?"

"It smells lemony. It's very nice."

Virginia merely nodded and picked up her own cup.

Kate pointed at the journals. "I see you have a journal here on Valerian, from 2000 to 2015. Were you studying it for all that time?"

"Yes, those are my notes from a fifteen-year exploration of the herb. I still investigate it occasionally, as a new idea might come to me."

"What is the herb used for?"

After the briefest of hesitations, Virginia replied, "I combine it with other herbs for a tea that helps alleviate insomnia."

Kate turned to face her. "Can it make you forgetful... about something that might have happened, after you drink it?"

Virginia stiffened. "No, of course not. Valerian does not do that."

"But combined with something else, maybe?" Kate said. "Other herbs? Or drugs?"

Virginia shook her head. "No, no, never drugs. Perhaps it could cause a different reaction in the hands of an expert in that particular herb—combined with something else, of course."

An expert who has been studying it for fifteen years.

"But why do you ask?" Virginia said.

Kate set her cup down on the table. "I had the strangest thing happen to me on my first visit here. The night when we first met. I know that we had tea together. It had a strange aroma, and I remember getting very sleepy. We had been talking about Arabella, but then the next thing I knew, I found myself on a bench in one of your public gardens. It was eleven o'clock. There was no one around, so I drove back to Rye. I just can't imagine what happened." She nerved herself to ask, "Do you know?"

The question bounced against the silence that was suddenly between the two women.

Kate knew that her direct question held consequences. Virginia Calloway might be insulted, and with good reason. She might ask Kate to leave. And if that happened, Kate would never learn what she needed to about Arabella. But at the moment, it seemed to be the most important thing for her to know. The question had to be asked. And she needed to begin there. Virginia's answer would be very revealing now that Kate knew what she had told Miles.

Virginia seemed to collect herself. "Well, I'm sure I don't know. We were having a lovely conversation with our tea, and after a bit, you decided to leave. The guard would have escorted you to the front of the old buildings. I assume, to the parking lot. The gardens are accessible at that hour. Perhaps you went for another walk through them?"

There was a knock on the door.

"Well," Virginia appeared relieved by the interruption, "I think we've had enough education for today, hm?" She opened the door to Mr. McGregor.

"Pardon me, Miss Calloway. You wanted me to show Kate the gardens this afternoon? I can take her now, if you like."

"Yes, Mister McGregor, I think that would be very good. We seem to be done here. Kate, you may go with Mister McGregor now. I will see you in the morning at eight, for breakfast. Supper will be brought to your room this evening, at seven."

She nodded at Mr. McGregor and quickly left the workroom.

27

KATE REMOVED HER APRON and put it back on its hook, then walked with Mr. McGregor to the gardens.

"What would you like to know, Kate? I think I can share a bit of knowledge with you."

Her brain was whirling from the disrupted conversation she just had with Virginia. What she would like to know was more than Mr. McGregor could tell her. But she refocused her attention on what he was saying, and hoped for another chance to speak frankly with Virginia.

They had reached the same gravel path she recalled from her first visit through the Lavender Garden. These were the gardens that the public was allowed in. But Kate knew now that the real gem was hidden from their view.

"If I remember correctly, these gardens have been here from the eighteenth century." Kate pulled a folded brochure out of her back pocket and opened it up. "It says here that Edith Calloway was an avid botanist and created the gardens in the late 1700s. And that some of the plants came from all over the world."

"Yes, that's true, miss. She and many other women of the period were devoted to the study of botany, although not accepted in a field that was dominated by men at the time. There was a definite divide between what was suitable for women in botany, versus men. Men were considered the scientists. Women were more apt to be the artists, and fine ones they were. And they used their knowledge of the herbs, in the healing arts. Still do today. Their contributions were very impressive."

He stopped in front of a border planting. "Edith Calloway did encourage importing plants from all over the world. It was a popular thing to do back then. For example, this is a globe amaranth, native to Asia."

The magenta flowers mimicked its name—globe-like flowers swaying atop leggy stems.

"And this one." He lifted the fern-like leaves of a low shrub. "This is sweet bush, or Comptonia peregrina. Comes from your part of the world." He pointed to an expanse of trees in the distance. "Further out in the woods over there, we have a kraal honey thorn. Not something we want near the public because of its thorns, but it's a plant that originated in South Africa. And the birds like the berries. So we let them deal with the pointy parts." He winked.

"Virginia is really the keeper of all of this, isn't she?" Kate said. "This must be a massive amount of work."

"We do what we can on the day-to-day work. But yes, Miss Calloway takes all of this very seriously. It's in her blood, I guess you could say. If you have the opportunity, ask her about the medicinal properties of these plants."

They walked a bit further.

Then Kate turned to him. "Mister McGregor, how long do you think it would take to learn all of this?"

"All of this?" He spread his arms out. "A lifetime, miss. Maybe many lifetimes."

He stepped away onto an adjacent path to say a few words to a man navigating a wheelbarrow along the garden's edge, then walked back to Kate.

"Did you see the rose garden, miss?"

"I'm afraid not," Kate replied, and he motioned her to follow him.

They soon walked down a slight incline, and the rose garden appeared before them. Kate pulled out her phone and showed Mr. McGregor pictures of Rebecca's rose garden at Howard's Walk, dedicated to her late sister.

"But mine are nothing like you have here. I do recognize some of the varieties—the rugosa rose and the Felicia shrub roses."

"Aye, that's right," Mr. McGregor said. "Yes, this is one of my favorite places on the estate."

After a few moments, he said, "I'm a straight-speaking man, Miss Tyler. And I have a question for you, if you don't mind."

"No, not at all."

"Why are you here?"

His forthrightness took Kate by surprise.

"Well, I was invited by Virginia—"

"Miss Calloway rarely invites people to the manor. And never overnight guests."

"Perhaps," Kate said. "But it's true. I know we share an interest in gardening, and she invited me here."

"I see. And the legend of Arabella? I recall you asked me about that the last time we met."

Mr. McGregor was indeed straight-speaking, but his tone was gentle, and the question kindly worded.

"Yes, sir. And I am assuming you are the one who spoke to her about my interest in Arabella? Are you not?"

He nodded. "Fair enough. Yes, it was I."

"To answer your question, then, I have not been able to talk to her."

Alfie had run off, and Mr. McGregor called him back. The dog leapt and jumped his way back to his master's side. The old gardener leaned down and rubbed the dog's head.

"What do you know about the legend of Arabella, Mister McGregor?"

He hesitated. "I know that in Virginia Calloway's mind, the legend is alive and well."

"What do you mean?"

He motioned to a gate up ahead. "Through that gate is one of the herb gardens."

He had walked on ahead of her, but Kate stopped.

"Mister McGregor, what did you mean?"

He turned back. "Miss Calloway will be the one to ask about Arabella. Just keep trying."

Kate shook her head, frustrated with the vague answers she was getting from Virginia, and now Mr. McGregor. She would simply have to do what he suggested, because she was not going to let it go.

"Mister McGregor, I do appreciate the tour, but would it be all right if I did some weeding? That bed of betony looks like it could use some tending to. And the sage, too. I think I'd like to get my hands in the soil."

Mr. McGregor looked skeptical, but pulled a pair of gardening gloves from his coat pocket.

"Certainly. If you like, miss. You might need these."

"No, thank you. I'll be fine without them."

"Suit yourself. I'll be right over here if you need anything."

Kate knelt at the edge of the plantings and began to work. She hadn't gotten a complete explanation from Virginia on what happened at her last visit, but from the change in Virginia's demeanor, Kate knew she had struck a chord. It would be naïve to think that Virginia did not have the ability to concoct a drug, or mixture of herbs to act like a drug.

Kate would have loved to read the journals in her workroom, but the door had been locked, and was probably kept that way. She had noticed even more journals and books in the library, which had been open the couple times she had passed it. Kate would have to think of a way to get a closer look.

Then a thought occurred to her. If Virginia had been so careful about journaling her work on herbs, would she have been as careful about other things pertaining to Arabella?

The puzzle would be solved here, at the Calloway Manor. Kate was sure of it.

Dinner was brought to her room, precisely at 7:00 p.m., as promised. Fish was on the menu again, with grilled vegetables this time, and a bottle of sparkling water, and lemon and blueberry parfait for dessert. She savored the meal, which she admitted to herself was expertly prepared, but soon realized that she didn't know the protocol for her tray of dirty dishes. She started to leave them outside her door, but decided that was probably not the polite thing to do. She wasn't in a hotel.

Another thought came to her, and she put on a light jacket, grabbed her journal and pen and the dinner tray, and found her way down to the first floor. After a few wrong turns, she located the kitchen and left the tray on a counter.

The house seemed empty. The distant gong of a clock counted out the eight o'clock hour.

Kate unlocked the kitchen door that led to the outside, and tested it before she closed it. She did not want to find herself locked out of the house.

She got her bearings and headed in what she hoped was the direction of the bench where she had found herself on her first visit to the manor. After gingerly crossing through several vegetable beds when there wasn't a clear path, she reached the same wooden bench and sat down.

She drew her jacket closer around her. The warmth of the day had dissipated as dusk settled over the landscape. Kate thought back to the night when she had found herself there alone in the garden. So much had happened since then. Bits and pieces of the puzzle had been found—or had found her. She wondered if it had been a wise decision to come to the Calloway Manor at Virginia's invitation, but here she was.

She was also not sure whether Virginia really grasped that Kate was leaving in three days. It seemed she was simply pacifying Kate when she acknowledged it.

Virginia's words came back to her: *Wouldn't it be lovely if you decided to stay?*

It was really too farfetched for Kate to believe that Virginia would actually want or expect her to stay. No, Kate had already made it very clear. And she realized that she needed to confront Virginia about it, once and for all.

The view from the bench to the public gardens was a different perspective for her, and she sketched for a while until the darkness overtook her. She closed her journal and activated the light on her phone to find her way back to the kitchen, through the vegetable gardens. As she was walking, she noticed movement off to her left. Tall bushes mostly hid her view, but she could see that someone was walking on the other side of them. It looked like Virginia, but Kate could not be sure. The person appeared to be wearing a cloak of some kind, but that wasn't surprising, considering the lowering temperatures.

She dismissed it and continued back to the house and up to her room.

28

THAT EVENING, as the sun dipped into the western horizon, Virginia Calloway left the manor and walked to a winding dirt path that led to the ancient Calloway buildings. The path took her down a slight hill, to a plain wooden door tucked underneath the oldest section of the building. She pushed aside the ivy that had grown over it, completely camouflaging the entrance, and inserted a large brass key into the lock before turning it twice. The door creaked on its hinges as she pulled it open.

Immediately inside the entrance, a pull chain hung down from the ceiling. Virginia reached up with her fingertips, pulled the crystal bead at the end of it, and a series of bare lightbulbs flickered overhead, lighting her way down a long tunnel. The floor of the tunnel was stone, laid out in symmetrical blocks, each cut to fit perfectly with the next. The ceiling and walls were whitewashed, and occasional rivulets of water skimmed down the surface, from the arched ceiling to the gray stone below.

Virginia locked the door behind her. Only one other woman had the key. She would allow access to the others, and then it would be locked behind them.

No one except Virginia's Calloway's security guard, her trusted butler, and the Sisterhood knew what this entrance led to. Cousin Hubert knew of the door, but Virginia had assured him that the area behind it was completely unusable, and he had never questioned it.

The tunnel she was now standing in was underneath the section of the old Calloway home that was over five hundred years old. At some point, this area, and the rooms off to the sides of it, were used for storage. But now it was essentially empty. Or at least, that's what Virginia wanted everyone to think.

At the end of the tunnel, she opened a door into a cavernous room. She lit a taper candle that she had carried with her, and stepped in. There was a fireplace at the far end of the room, but there would be no fire tonight. It hadn't been used in over a century, and she never wanted smoke to be coming through the chimney to alert anyone to a presence in this space. The women she had invited were familiar with the conditions there, and would be dressed appropriately for the damp chill that pervaded the room.

Virginia walked to the front of the room slowly, reverently. At times, this was her place of solitude and contemplation. But often, it was the room where she held the secret meetings and seances of the Corvos Sisterhood.

Virginia set the thin taper into a candlestick on the fireplace mantle. A half-circle of chairs had already been placed in front of the cold stone hearth. She began to prepare the room.

In the center of the half-circle, Virginia placed an ornate pedestal. It was made from solid mahogany, almost supernaturally giving off its own light. The filigree carvings along the legs of the stand were sculpted into the slender pieces of wood like delicate knots. She unwrapped a marble candlestick from a velvet cloth and set it on top of the stand. Lastly, a white pillar candle was placed on it to be lit later as part of the ceremony.

From a wooden chest that sat against the wall on one side of the room, Virginia pulled a wide banner. She unfurled it and hung it on a gilded stand. The banner was black, with silver embroidery depicting two ravens gripped in a battle. The ravens formed the outside border of the image, their curved beaks open. One bird clutched a small crescent-shaped moon in its talons. The other held three connected stars. The banner had been the defining symbol of the Sisterhood in this room for over one hundred years. Her grandmother Mathilde had designed and sewn it herself. It was one of Virginia's most cherished possessions.

With this last piece in place, the room was ready. Virginia had called an urgent meeting of the Corvos Sisterhood. There were pressing matters to be discussed.

She thought back to her conversation with Kate. Virginia had not expected Kate to ask her about her first visit there. She had been surprised by Kate's boldness, and it was unfortunate that her ruse had brought doubts to Kate's mind. It had been a risk to use the tea to obtain the information from her, but a necessary one. In the end, Kate would need that kind of fortitude when she finally accepted her role at Calloway House. And it had to happen soon. The vision of Arabella, and her direct words to Virginia only three days earlier, had contained an urgency she had never realized before. And Virginia would not let Arabella down.

There was another reason for urgency. Only the week before, Virginia's cousin Hubert had approached her with a dire story—and she knew it was only a story—about the financial circumstances of the estate. He was trying to force her hand, telling her she could move to a much more manageable situation. Then they could open up more of the estate, draw more people, create a much more lucrative operation. Either that, he said, or she would have to release her own funds to staunch the flow of losses that he was seeing. He claimed that keeping the old Calloway House & Gardens as they were right now, for occasional tours, was simply not a profitable enterprise.

It was all about the money to Hubert. Virginia regretted ever putting him in charge of the business part of the operation— no, truthfully, she regretted ever agreeing to make the Calloway House & Gardens a business entity in the first place. But she couldn't worry about that now. Fate had revealed another plan. Kate—Arabella—had returned to take her rightful place at the Calloway House.

But first, there were other urgent matters. The Corvos Sisterhood, the one other constant in Virginia's life that gave her purpose—her legacy from her grandmother Mathilde—was at risk. The Sisterhood had been betrayed by one of its own, and that had to be dealt with.

Soon, she heard the sounds of footsteps in the hallway. The door opened, and three women entered, single file, and they silently took their seats. A few minutes later, Myrlie, Opal, and Tonya were admitted, followed by a woman who locked the door behind them, and they sat down. The women all wore identical long, hooded red cloaks and red leather gloves. Their eyes were on Virginia, who now stood at the front of the room.

She stepped to the pedestal, nodded to each of the women, and lit the candle. The flickering light cast an eerie glow and highlighted Virginia's angular features. After a few moments, she spoke.

"Sisters, you have been summoned here for some very grave news. Nothing has ever shaken the Sisterhood as this information has. Some of you are aware of it already."

She looked at Myrlie, then and walked up to her.

"Sister Myrlie, you have betrayed the Corvos Sisterhood."

A gasp went up. Myrlie pressed herself back into her chair as Virginia laid out the claims against her.

"You have, in your possession, a book. A book that belongs to us, to the Sisterhood. More than that, it belongs to the ages. In keeping the *Ancient Tales of an Ancient Town* to yourself, you have betrayed us, the memory of Arabella Courbain, and the very legend itself."

The women looked at each other questioningly.

"I don't know what you are talking about," Myrlie whispered.

"Oh, but I know that you do," Virginia said. "To add to your betrayal, you have witnessed, with your own eyes, the one we believe to be the return of Arabella. And you made the grave mistake of keeping this to yourself. What do you have to say about this unfaithful act?"

Myrlie said, "I-I don't know about any b-book. But yes, I have seen the woman who looks like Arabella. Perhaps it is just a coincidence, Sister Virginia. Perhaps she is not Arabella. She is from America. Shouldn't we consider the possibility that she is an imposter? I would hate to think that you could be taken in by someone like that."

"You are missing an important clue, Sister Myrlie," said Virginia. "I have learned that Kate Tyler's grandmother was an English-born Corbyn. Did you know that?"

Myrlie shook her head.

"No, I don't suppose you did," Virginia said. "The name 'Courbain' could have been changed, generations back, to 'Corbyn.' Now, do you still mean to argue with me about the reality of what is right in front of you?"

"N-no, of course not, b-but did we ever really think this day would come?"

Virginia's featured hardened. The betrayal and distrust went much further than she even thought. For one of the Sisterhood to even imply that the legend might not ever be fulfilled was unthinkable.

"Your doubts are very revealing," she said. "You have been playing me for a fool all these years?"

"No, of course not!" Myrlie said. "I guess I just never thought—not in our lifetime—that it would really happen. What are the chances, after all? The legend doesn't say when she will return. Really, what are the chances, after two hundred fifty years?"

Virginia watched her warily as Myrlie fought to make her case.

"Sister Virginia, have you also seen her?" Myrlie said.

Virginia turned and walked to the front of the group.

"Yes, I have met her. I have talked to Kate Tyler. She is the image of our Arabella. And she will begin to live the life that Arabella was meant to live—just as the legend requires. Arabella's son, Richard Courbain, whose father was Ewen Calloway, should have taken his rightful place here, as Ewen was the elder Calloway son. Fate chose another path for Richard—one unknown to us. But the legend still remained. And it remained and was treasured for a reason. And because of that legend, his true descendent, Kate Tyler, will take his place here.

"Grandmother Mathilde told me very clearly: 'My ancestors have chosen this time for the legend to be fulfilled. They will not allow their dynasty to slip away, scattered into the future, any longer.' And I have been chosen as the one Calloway to see it fulfilled—to receive Kate here as Arabella."

The woman who'd carried the key to the room said, "Has she agreed, Sister Virginia? Has Kate acknowledged that this will happen?"

"No, not yet. But she will. She is here, now, at the manor. Soon, she will realize that her life here will be a life of learning the ancient ways, of the art of herbal healing, of reclaiming her inheritance, and living the life that Arabella was meant to live. It will happen. The line will end without her. I have been chosen as the Calloway who will see it all happen. I have received foreknowledge of this in seances and dreams. You have all believed this with me for many years, steadfast and loyal." Virginia turned her piercing gaze to Myrlie. "Except for one of you. Sister Myrlie, you will bring the book to me—directly to me—tomorrow, without any further delay. You have shown your disloyalty to me and to the Sisterhood. You are no longer worthy to be part of us."

Virginia turned and walked out of the room. The Corvos Sisterhood stood, as one, and faced Myrlie, who sat pale and trembling in her chair.

"Opal? Tonya?" Myrlie whispered, hoping for a sign from her friends that she was not being completely rejected.

After all, they had seen Kate Tyler, too. But they turned away and followed Virginia. Myrlie realized that she was now alone, an outcast.

She sat, still stunned at the words of accusation coming from Virginia Calloway, and her final command to return the book. After a few moments, Myrlie gathered herself and ran down the tunnel to the outer door. She hurried up the hill, slipping on the wet grass, her long cloak tangling around her legs. She regained her footing and tore off the cloak and gloves, leaving them behind. She ran around the old Calloway House, to the parking lot. Except for her car, the lot was empty. The cars that were there when she arrived were now gone, vanished in just a few minutes time. Opal, Tonya, and the others—everyone had abandoned her.

Myrlie fumbled for her keys, hands shaking. She got in the car and started the engine.

She had been loyal to Virginia since she joined the Sisterhood. She thought she had found a place where she belonged. And yes, she had kept the book from them. Especially from Virginia. It was her own secret, and her ticket out of a miserable life.

No, Myrlie would never relinquish the book to her. She would go forward with her plans to sell it, and the other books, and get on with her plans—without the burden of her invalid stepfather, without the failing bookstore, and without the Sisterhood, betrayers themselves.

Tomorrow, it would be over. The book would be sold, she would collect her money, and would soon be able to put the Closed sign on the door for good.

Virginia Calloway would not win this one. The other women may have been under her spell, but not Myrlie. Not anymore. She was finally free.

29

A COOL BREEZE RUFFLED THE CURTAINS at the open window of Kate's bedroom. It was nearing midnight, and she had slipped into a state of consciousness that was neither sleep nor wakefulness. Sounds of night birds clamoring in the gardens, the distant roll and splash of the brook, and the rustle of the wind in the trees seeped into the room, and her mind conjured images of those things. But in the midst of it, a new image came to her. There was someone in the garden—a young woman, her long dress trailing over the herbs as she walked slowly, almost floating, through the lavender and the sage. The woman turned and looked up at the window to Kate's bedroom. She raised her hand and motioned for Kate to come to her.

It was Arabella. Kate was suddenly alert and running to the window. But when she reached it, the garden was empty. No birds flew, and the breeze had stilled.

Kate let the curtain fall, and backed away to the bed. Her heart was pounding. She curled up under the covers, clutching at the bed sheets. She closed her eyes to erase the vision. It must have been a dream. Like the others, dreams of Arabella had followed her to Rye, and now she was manifesting herself here at the Calloway Manor.

Sleep was impossible now. Kate sat up on the edge of the bed and checked the time. It was now midnight. As startling as the dream had been, the vision had renewed her desire to know what secrets were held in this house. Maybe Arabella was trying to tell her to find those secret places.

She thought it couldn't hurt to take a look around the house—at least on the second floor. It wasn't as if she was a prisoner there. And no one else was staying on her floor.

Kate tiptoed to the door and peeked out. The moon shining in from a tall window at the end of the long hallway provided a faint light to the area. She closed her door quietly and padded down the hall. She cautiously turned the knobs on each of the doors, but they were all locked, until the last.

The door creaked at first, but as she opened it further, it pulled open easily. Behind the door was a set of stairs going up. Kate turned on her phone's flashlight and took a tentative step onto the first stair. The treads were dusty but solid. She doubted if anyone had used them for a very long time. She would worry about leaving tracks—evidence of her curiosity—later.

At the top of the stairs was another door, and she turned the handle. It was unlocked, and she pushed it open. Before her was a vast attic with massive beams arching overhead. She shone her light around the room, but the distance it reached was only a fraction of the entire space. She increased the brightness of her light and moved forward. Along one side of the attic, a row of crates was stacked three high. They were labeled KITCHEN, CHINA, CANDELABRAS—obviously, household items that were no longer in use.

On her left were trunks of all sizes and shapes and ages, and filing cabinets of both wood and metal. Furniture, probably enough to furnish another home the size of the manor, was scattered and stacked throughout the room. Kate knew she had to focus if she was to find anything here. And she wasn't even sure what she was looking for.

Kate stepped carefully but the floor was solid, and her steps made no noise. She tried the filing cabinets, but they were all locked, with no key in sight. Some of the trunks were locked. Some were open. But the opened ones were just full of old clothes and bolts of material. She moved past the crates since they all appeared to be nailed shut.

At the far end of the attic, she noticed a dress form covered with a white sheet. Kate walked to it and lifted up a corner of the covering, revealing what appeared to be a long dress with layers of lace at the hem. She unpinned the sheet from top to bottom and pulled it completely back to reveal a wedding dress. Kate first noticed the unusual design of the skirt, pleated and overlayed with a finely stitched lace. Small pearls covered the square neckline. She ran her fingers down the sheer sleeves, to rows of delicate lace trimming the wrists. She unpinned a floor-length train to let the diaphanous folds—also edged with pearls—fall to the floor, causing dust to rise in puffs around her. There were several noticeable tears along the hemline of the dress, possibly caused by curious rodents. In spite of its age, Kate was looking at a stunning designer wedding dress, specifically made for a society bride.

At the shoulder, a store tag was still fastened to the dress. Kate read the date: 1 June 1971, with the name Calloway printed on it. This dress, yellowed from decades of neglect in the attic, must have been the dress for Virginia's wedding that had never happened. The dress that held so much promise had never been worn.

Kate replaced the sheet as she had found it, carefully inserting each of the rusting straight pins through the original holes. As she tucked the train back under the sheet, her toe nudged a box on the floor, and she knelt down beside it. Upon lifting the lid, she saw studio photos of the couple, wedding and engagement party announcements, and society articles announcing the wedding of the year—of Miss Virginia Marguerite Calloway, of London, to Mr. Terrance Helmsford Billings, also of London. As Kate had learned at the historical society, the wedding had been planned for January 1, 1972.

Kate continued to search through the yellowing newspaper clippings, and finally found what she was looking for: the obituary for Terrance Billings, born April 17, 1948, died December 25, 1971, after a short illness.

The formal studio photos of the couple were of two young people of a certain class who looked out at the world, unsmiling and stiffly posed. Those were for the public to see. But other snapshots captured a happy couple at the beach, in a boat, at an amusement park. It was Virginia as Kate had never imagined her. She was in love.

It was impossible to think that this tragedy, as a young woman, had not shaped the rest of her life. As a girl, Virginia had lived a rather secluded life with her grandparents, and suffered through a stint at a boarding school that she did not fit in with. She'd had a brief love affair with the man she was to marry, and then, after a devastating turn of events with his death, she had apparently never sought companionship again. Instead, she had buried herself in her work, and had depended on a legend to put meaning into her life.

The situation brought tears to Kate's eyes as she looked through the photos. Life doesn't always work out as we plan, as she well knew. But Virginia had made her own choices, too. Kate could only imagine how Virginia mourned for the life she was meant to live.

Kate checked the time. An entire hour had passed since she first discovered the attic. And nothing seemed promising to help her answer questions about Arabella.

What had Winnie mentioned? *They are secreted away in personal collections, tucked away in boxes in attics or in dusty basements, often because they are the parts of people's lives that should never see the light of day.*

But what she'd learned about Virginia from searching the attic was even more telling. The woman did keep important things close. The wedding dress, even though it was hidden away in the attic, was not far from the box of mementos. Kate had a strong feeling that Virginia kept any information about Arabella even closer.

Kate heard a noise. She slipped her phone into her pocket to conceal the light, and listened. She heard something scurry across the floor and she let out a breath. A mouse, she could deal with. The butler, the guard, or Virginia—she would not want to face.

She retrieved her phone and took one last look around the room. It would take days to look through all of this, even if she had permission, or time, which she didn't. And everything stored in this attic were things that were no longer wanted or needed.

No, Kate was certain that anything related to Arabella would be somewhere else in this house, safe and secure, but held much closer to Virginia Calloway.

Kate tiptoed across the attic and down the stairs, carefully closing the door behind her as she reached the second floor of the house. She shut off her light and went back to her room.

30

IT HAD TAKEN HOURS for Kate to fall asleep after her furtive exploration of the attic. She was beginning to feel guilty for the invasion of Virginia's privacy after the discovery of the wedding dress that had never been worn, and then the box with mementos of both a happy and sad time in her life. But she could not take it back now.

She guessed she had only slept for a couple hours, but she remembered she was having breakfast at eight o'clock with Virginia, and hurried to get ready.

Virginia was at her usual place at the table, and had already started her breakfast when Kate arrived in the dining room. Kate filled a plate of food from warmers laid out on the sideboard, and sat down.

"Good morning, Kate. I trust you slept well?"

Kate hesitated. She decided a half-truth was better than a lie. Between her vision of Arabella in the garden, and her search through the attic, she had not slept well at all.

She took a bite, chewed and swallowed, then answered as casually as she could.

"I did have some trouble falling asleep. Just trying to take everything in from yesterday, I guess." She focused on her plate of food.

Kate was a terrible liar, and she knew it. Even the half-truth didn't help.

"Yes, of course," Virginia said. "I have difficulty falling asleep, too, sometimes. I tend to wander about the house when that happens."

Kate quickly—perhaps too quickly—replied, "Yes, I do the same at Howard's Walk. Or I walk in the garden if the night is nice." She let out a nervous laugh. "I would certainly get lost if I did that here."

"I'm sure you would find your way," Virginia said.

Kate could not make herself meet Virginia's piercing gaze. She could not decide whether Virginia knew about her midnight ramblings or not. But she was not ready to make a confession—yet.

"What is on the agenda today?"

"Well, that is up to you, Kate. Your time here seems limited, so what is your preference? It will—would—take years to teach you everything I have learned."

Kate caught the slip of the tongue—another disturbing reference to how long Virginia imagined Kate might be staying there. But she let it pass.

"It's going to be a beautiful morning," Kate said. "Could you show me the herb gardens? As you said, a novice needs to learn how and where herbs grow, the soil they thrive in, and when to harvest. I would like to be able to incorporate herb gardens into my plans at Howard's Walk, so I guess I should start at the beginning."

"Very well, then," Virginia said. "We shall start at the beginning."

After eating, they walked down a terraced slope to the larger herb garden, beyond where Kate had spent her time the day before. Her first impression of this garden was one of random plantings, without any of the order of the smaller herb garden, or what might be expected in a vegetable garden. She asked Virginia why.

"The herbs near the house are ones I use the most often," Virginia replied. "I keep that garden more organized— much easier to harvest. But keeping a large herb garden well-manicured is quite labor-intensive. I prefer to keep this one more loosely planted. But there is still a method and logic to it." She went on to explain the benefits of grouping herbs that have the same needs for sunlight and water. "It is essential to have a plan first. What kind of space are you planning your herb garden to be in?"

"It's a wooded section now," Kate said, "so we'll need to clear some trees. The current plantings at Howard's Walk have filled up most of the open space."

"Well, you would be looking at several years to complete it, then," Virginia said. "But here, it is already in place, as you can see. If you are clearing trees, it will look quite empty at first. Patience is required when dealing with herbs."

Virginia walked on, explaining ways to assess the soil, plan for the shady and sunny spots, map out the natural contours of the land, and pointing out the various herbs that were growing there. Her knowledge seemed inexhaustible. She delved into specific plantings and what they were used for medicinally, for teas and for food. But in spite of the animation in her voice, Kate could tell she was tiring. The property was hillier here, and the path not as easy to navigate.

"We could stop now, if you like, Virginia."

"Yes, I suppose we should," she replied, in a faint voice. "There is just so much to share, and so little time. If only there were more time."

She suddenly turned, and without another word, began walking back to the house. Kate followed her on the narrow path.

At the gate, Mr. McGregor and Alfie were waiting.

"Mister McGregor, I am glad you are here," Virginia said. "Would you mind taking over? I have some things to attend to in the house."

Mr. McGregor nodded. "Of course, ma'am."

She turned to Kate. "We will meet at four o'clock, for tea. In the sunroom."

Kate watched her until she reached the house and stepped inside. This morning, and at other moments, Virginia was sharp, firm, and at times, even cantankerous and intimidating. But at that moment, she seemed frail and wistful.

"Mister McGregor," Kate said, as they walked, "I'm curious about some of the Calloway family history. You've worked for them a long time, right?"

"Aye, miss. Almost thirty-five years. I came right after they opened the gardens to the public."

"I'm guessing Virginia was never married. But does she have any other family?"

"No, not ever married. And no brothers or sisters. She has a cousin, though. He and his wife run the day-to-day operations here."

"I would love to meet them," Kate said.

"Well, you would have to arrange that with Miss C."

Just then, she heard the sound of a bus braking in the parking lot, and the voices of tourists. She shaded her eyes and looked toward the sounds.

"I got the impression that Virginia is not too fond of the house and gardens being opened to the public," Kate said.

"Aye, well, it was an adjustment for her. When it's been your home for generations, and suddenly it's not just yours anymore—it can take a toll."

Kate could relate very well. Being surrounded by the Calloway Gardens, she found herself missing Howard's Walk, and remembering the day they opened it to the public. She had publicized the grand opening well, and there had been a line waiting at the entrance that day. It was exciting and exhilarating...and exhausting. Every waking minute was spent on more improvements to the house, and enhancements to the gardens. Was that what had started her on this journey to Rye, and to start thinking about the life she was meant to live? Was this trip just a temporary respite, or a time of more serious life decisions?

That was one thing she and Arabella had in common, Kate thought. They were both conflicted about similar things across the centuries, and now. And she had this same feeling in common with Virginia, of all people. Each day, the threads of the mystery came together more and more, slowly weaving themselves into a pattern. It was not clear yet, but somehow Kate felt that it would be completed soon.

Over the murmur of the tourists in the distance, Kate heard the sound of birds. She looked up and saw ravens swarming above her. They began to swoop and dive, closer and closer to the garden where they stood. Kate instinctively covered her head.

"Don't worry, miss," Mr. McGregor said. "They won't hurt you."

She ducked again. "I've never seen them that close before, or that many of them."

"Oh, they are here most of the time. They do like Miss C's gardens. Let's just move away from them, and they'll settle down."

The birds soon stopped their cawing and alighted in the treetops. But one flew closer and perched on a fence bordering the garden nearby. It made a clicking noise and tipped its head to look at Kate. The eyes, round and black, reminded her of the brooch, and of her talk with Madame Zaytsev in Rye.

This can be a symbol of a new phase in your life, a time to leave the past behind. There is magic and mystery all around us. Our dreams and the ravens are manifestations of so much that is hidden to us.

It resonated with Kate that Madame Zaytsev's words could have two meanings. For the first time, Kate wondered whether she could actually stay in Rye. Could this be that new phase in her life where she would leave her old life in Eden Springs behind? Or should she walk away from the past that had been revealed to her here—the past that included Arabella and the mysterious legend—and start a new phase of her life back at Howard's Walk, with Ben?

The raven flew off. Kate knew instantly which possibility was the one she truly hoped for, and at that moment, she desperately wanted to go home.

The morning had grown unusually warm, and she wished that she had brought a hat. She raised her face to catch a breeze, and as she wiped the damp tendrils of hair from her face, she glanced up at her bedroom window. There was a movement, and the person disappeared.

But someone had been watching her from her bedroom.

31

MYRLIE DROVE TO THE FLEA MARKET and finally found a parking spot. It was further from the entrance than she had hoped, but she wedged her Fiat into a small space and twisted her body out of the car. It was a struggle to pull the large box out of the small backseat. But once retrieved, she adjusted her handbag, hefted the box onto her hip, and walked to the flea market.

She had dressed in white pants, a sweater, and an overcoat, and wore sunglasses and a scarf over her head. The outfit was too warm and uncomfortable for the weather, but it seemed to be the only thing she had in her closet that would give her at least some disguise. She had avoided using her signature red lipstick, too, which somehow made her feel naked and exposed rather than disguised, but she thought it was necessary. Myrlie could not risk being recognized.

She had prepared for this after the disastrous meeting with the Sisterhood, Virginia's accusations echoing in her mind throughout a sleepless night. But as morning came, she pushed them aside. Edward was still in hospital, and she had no idea of what might become of him. Actually, she thought the timing could not have been better. Perhaps it was only a matter of days before she was packed and headed off into her new life.

Myrlie jostled through the crowd of people. She could have found a smaller box to carry the books in, but it was too late now. She would just have to manage.

She had rehearsed what to say to the man, then rejected it and rehearsed again. She was out of her element, and nothing felt right except her excitement of finally moving on in her life. When she reached Booth 25D, she still had no idea how to initiate the conversation.

The owner of the booth was with a customer, and she waited nervously, balancing the box on the corner of a table near the entrance. A man was looking over items in the booth to her right, and a woman was doing the same on her left.

Finally, her contact was free, and she was able to approach him.

"Excuse me. I'm here with the items you asked about." It was the only thing that came to her mind.

The man looked her over. "I don't know what you are talking about. Who are you, again?"

Myrlie realized that perhaps her disguise was too good. He didn't seem to recognize her.

She stepped closer and removed her sunglasses.

"I was here on Sunday," she whispered. "I have the *items*." She held the box out to him, feeling proud that she was using his own terms for the stolen goods.

A glimmer of recognition passed across his face. He looked around, nodded, and motioned her to come to the room behind his booth.

He put his finger to his lips to let her know she needed to be quiet, and motioned for her to set the box on the table, which she gladly did. He pulled a pocketknife from his jacket and quietly sliced the seal on the box, then opened it up.

There were five books in the box, and he took each one out and laid it on the table, until the last one, which he held in his hands. A smile crept across his face.

Myrlie said, "Yes, that's the one—"

Again, he hushed her.

He laid the book back in the box and peeked out to the front of the booth. Not seeing anyone, he returned to the table and retrieved the book once again, then scanned the rest of the books.

"I only asked for a list of your other items," he whispered. "What are these?"

"Well, I thought since I was here—"

He waved his hand to silence her, and returned all but one of the books to the box.

"Well?" Myrlie said.

He pulled the stub of a pencil and a small notepad out of his pocket, wrote on it, and handed it to Myrlie.

"This is not what we agreed. These books are valuable, too—"

"Listen," he hissed. "You are starting to be more trouble than you're worth. I'll give you that amount for the one book by Mallard, and you can take the others back. I can't do anything with them."

"But where—"

"Where can you get rid of them? That's your problem now. This is my final offer for the one book. Take it or leave it."

Myrlie simply nodded her agreement.

He pulled a locked box out of a drawer in the table, and counted out the money.

"We're done. Understand? Don't come back here." He grabbed the book and put it into a cloth bag. "Now, take your things and go."

A man and a woman burst through the door.

"Rye Police." One flashed his badge. "Gilbert Marlin and Myrlie Shaw-Windham, you are both under arrest for possession and sale of stolen goods."

He read them their rights as the second officer approached to handcuff them.

Marlin cursed under his breath as the handcuffs clicked around his wrists. Myrlie backed up into a corner as she recognized Miles Pixley standing behind the two officers.

"But Detective Sergeant Pixley, I—"

"Oh, just shut up, will you?" Marlin said, as they were taken away.

The second officer held up the book that she had taken from the cloth bag, and read the title.

"*Ancient Tales of an Ancient Town.* Is this the one you have been looking for, sir?"

"That's the one. I'll take it from here." Miles put the book into an evidence bag.

He did the same with the other books, and followed the officers as they weaved through a stunned crowd in the flea market.

32

KATE TOOK THE BACK STAIRWAY to her room to avoid tracking dirt from the garden and fields, in through the main hallway. Tea was at four o'clock sharp, and she was running late.

After Virginia had left them, Mr. McGregor had taken Kate on a tour of the entire property, a total of seventy acres—some planted, some fallow—through the barns and outbuildings, the fishpond, and along the length of Stalton Brook, from one end of the property to the other. Bouncing along in Mr. McGregor's ancient pickup truck, Kate saw a different landscape, as if it were the behind-the-scenes backdrop for the beautiful, immaculately cultivated gardens near the house. As they drove, Mr. McGregor reminisced about the way the management of the farm had been done in the past, and how it had all changed over the years.

"Some ways for the better. Some not. But that's progress, I guess," he said, as they navigated along the rutted lanes at the distant end of the estate, with Alfie laying between them, his head in Kate's lap.

She could picture it all as it was, just as she had been able to envision the old Calloway House as it might have been centuries ago. She saw in her mind the hired hands and the servants, teams of massive draft horses in the fields, planting and harvesting. She saw women in the kitchens, tending the children, and imagined them teaching the secret ways of herbalism to their daughters and granddaughters.

Kate reached her room. The door was closed, as she had left it, but she opened it tentatively, in case the person she had seen in the window earlier was still there. But there was no one in the room, and it didn't appear that anything had been disturbed, when she did a cursory search.

She quickly showered, put on an embroidered peasant blouse and a floral-printed skirt, brushed and twisted her hair into a braid, and added gold hoop earrings.

Kate went down to the sunroom, where a traditional cream tea had already been laid out, with homemade scones and butter, a small dish of strawberry jam, and one of cream. Virginia noted her arrival with a nod, and began to pour the tea. Kate sat in a wicker chair across from her, facing the windows. The room was still warm from the lowering afternoon sun, just now reaching the tops of the weeping willows along Stalton Brook.

Kate lifted the cup of tea that had been poured for her, and furtively took in the aroma rising from it. It was different than what she had remembered from her first visit to the house, and she hoped that it would not have the same effect. She couldn't think of a reason why Virginia would want her to repeat that experience. And Kate had survived the tea blend that she herself had helped create in Virginia's workroom. Nevertheless, she took only one small sip.

"Are you feeling rested, Virginia?"

"Yes, I am. Thank you for asking." Virginia chose a scone and spread a small amount of jam on it, and signaled for Kate to do the same. "I thought perhaps you could tell me more about your gardens this afternoon. Howard's Walk?"

"I would be happy to, Virginia. But I hoped we might talk about the legend, if you don't mind. The legend of Arabella. I haven't been able to learn much about it yet."

Virginia's gaze was steady. She poured another cup of tea for herself.

"Of course," she replied. "What would you like to know?"

"Well, on my first visit," Kate said, "you asked me where I had heard about the legend, and I said it was from the book

Ancient Tales of an Ancient Town. You seemed surprised. But that is where I read the legend. And that is also where I saw the etching of Arabella. It was shocking, of course, to see my likeness in the etching. It was a coincidence, I'm sure."

She thought perhaps there would be a reaction from Virginia, but her face was unreadable.

"I remember you told me about the book," Virginia said.

"Yes. And I took it back to the bookstore the next day. I don't have it anymore."

"I see. And what would you like to know about the legend, then? Do you think that perhaps you have a connection to the legend?"

This seemed to be the crux of the matter, Kate thought. That she had some mysterious connection to a tale from over two centuries ago.

"I doubt it very much, Virginia. I mean, how could I possibly be connected? But Mister McGregor was the first to say that I should ask you about it. There must have been a reason for that."

"Yes, Kate, there is a reason for that. The Calloway family is very closely connected with Arabella and the legend. You see, Arabella's lover, and the father of her child, was Ewen Calloway. I am a direct descendent of his younger brother Devon Calloway who was my great-great-great-great-grandfather."

A significant gap in Kate's understanding of Virginia suddenly closed. The distance down through the generations was a long one, but direct: the lineage from Devon Calloway, captain of the customs cutter *The Courageous*, to Virginia Calloway, who sat across from Kate, eating a scone.

"I see," Kate replied. "And Ewen Calloway was a distant uncle, then."

"Yes."

Virginia stood and walked to the windows, her gaze lingering on the trees and brook in the distance, over land that had belonged to the Calloway family since the fifteenth century.

"Devon Calloway, my grandfather from six generations back, was the younger brother of Ewen Calloway. Devon walked this land, lived in the old house, nurtured and expanded the family holdings to preserve it for future generations. Arabella should have been part of that legacy. But she and her son, Richard, were never given that chance."

"But is Arabella's story—the one in the book—is it true? Or is it a legend?" Kate said, keeping the facts that she had learned from her research to herself for the moment.

"Arabella was very real," Virginia said. "As was Ewen Calloway, of course. Their child, named Richard, was not given the Calloway name. They never married. Arabella's aunt raised him, and he was given the surname of Courbain. We do know that much."

It occurred to Kate once again that the name Courbain was very similar to Corbyn, although she had never been told of any connection of the two names. She knew so little about her own biological family history that anything further back than a couple of generations seemed unimportant.

Was this the link? Did the similarity in the names indicate that she could also be a descendent through Bessie Corbyn Howard? What if she actually were related to Arabella and her son? The thought, which she had so far denied as being possible, stunned her.

Kate hesitated to ask, but went ahead. "You said that you were a direct descendent of Ewen's brother, Devon. Did Richard have any descendants?"

"We do not have record of this," Virginia said. "We are not sure that the story about Arabella's fate was ever passed down, as it was in the Calloway family. But you..." She finally turned to face Kate, and whispered, "You are her exact likeness—enough to make one wonder if she has indeed returned. And aren't we all destined to live the life we were meant to live, Kate? In one way or another, we are brought to a place in time where we must decide. We must all decide, isn't that right?"

"This is still all conjecture, Virginia. And very farfetched, I think."

Virginia seemed to be deliberating about something.

Finally, she said, "Please follow me."

They walked to Virginia's library, where she went to a drawer built into the center of the bookshelf, unlocked it, and carefully lifted out an elaborately carved wooden box. She set it on the table in front of the fireplace and opened it.

Virginia took out the topmost item—a handwritten document, old and yellowed with age, in a clear sleeve.

"This is the original letter written by Arabella." Virginia gingerly took it out of its protective cover.

She handed it to Kate, who noticed that the box held more than just the letter, but Virginia quickly closed it and put it back into the drawer.

Kate turned her attention to the letter. The paper was coarse to the touch, and the script difficult to read. A quill pen most likely had been used, and even the paper Arabella wrote on would have been a luxury for a young woman as destitute as she must have been. Perhaps the paper had been a gift from Ewen. Perhaps he had taught her how to read and write. Or perhaps it was her aunt who had educated her, hoping for a better future for her niece.

Kate began to read.

16 November 1766.

My name is Arabella Courbain, daughter of William Courbain. I have done all that I could. If this letter is found, it will mean that I am gone, by my own hand. It will mean that I was not able to live the life I was meant to live with my son, Richard. I have given him up for his own safety. I

have lost my true love, Ewen Calloway. My future
is in the hands of Devon Calloway, and subject
to the whims of fate on the high seas, and to the
hearts of brave men. I wish them Godspeed. If my
days should end now, I vow to return one day to
live the life I was meant to live.

Kate was mesmerized that she was holding the actual letter from Arabella. She felt a tingling in her hands. This paper was held by Arabella herself. She had written these words. The story told in the book *Ancient Tales of an Ancient Town* may have seemed to be a distant tale, but the letter itself was not. This was real.

"You see, it is true," Virginia said, when Kate had finished reading. "And Devon Calloway searched for the boy, but never found him. The history has been passed down through the Calloway family, to this day."

Kate hesitated. "Virginia, what about William Courbain, Arabella's father?"

Virginia frowned and spat out, "What about him? He was a sea smuggler, a criminal."

"But surely there would be stories about him as well? After all, according to the legend, Arabella was betrothed to someone he chose. Whatever happened to him?"

Virginia's replied, "No one knows, and no one cares, Kate. His fate was likely the same as all the other sea smugglers, as far as I know—drowned, or hung, or died in prison."

"And no one ever researched it or found out what happened to him?"

"No. As I said, no one cares. And it certainly doesn't have anything to do with Arabella."

Kate thought for a moment, debating if she should say anything more. Her research didn't prove anything, but the information she had found, along with her own dreams and her reaction at Beachy Head, made her think there was something more to the legend.

Kate knew that there had been a battle between Courbain and Calloway on November 17, 1766. Guilford had said that sometimes locals would tip off the customs officials about smugglers. Could Arabella have done such a thing? If her father had been captured, or killed, perhaps she would have been free of the obligation of marrying John Rogers. But Kate's own research had shown that Courbain had escaped from that battle, and that there had been a reward out for his capture. And yet there was no record of him being taken into custody.

Kate needed to see what else was in the box in the drawer in Virginia's library. She decided to keep the information and her questions to herself—for now.

There was an awkward silence, and Kate realized that Virginia was not open to any other version of what might have happened to Arabella, nor would she believe that Arabella's father had played any part in her fate.

As Kate was deciding what to say next, Virginia rose without saying a word, took the letter from Kate, and walked to the door of the library—a signal that their conversation was over.

"Well, thank you for the lovely tea, Virginia. And thank you so much for letting me read Arabella's letter. I think I'll go to my room now. I have a lot of work to do on my blog.

"Of course." Virginia appeared to have composed herself.

Kate stepped into the hallway and walked to the stairs.

"Kate," Virginia called out. "You will not share any of this with anyone. Do you understand?"

Kate turned back and nodded. "Of course."

"Good. Tomorrow, you and I will continue in the workroom. There is still so much for you to learn."

33

IN HER ROOM, and with her journal on her lap, Kate made another attempt to write about her experiences since arriving at the Calloway Manor. But her brain could focus neither on the pages in front of her, nor the sounds of the evening outside her window—branches clicking against the stone walls and leaded windows of the house, the distant bells and mooing of cows coming home to a nearby farm, the chattering songs of birds darting through the clouds, overseeing the comings and goings of life across the countryside. All she could think about was Arabella's letter.

Kate wondered if Virginia felt as she did, that handing the letter over to her, possibly the last remaining possession of Arabella Courbain, was a momentous thing that deserved thought and reflection. Truly, though, Kate had wanted to grab the entire box from her, run to her room and lay out the contents on her bed and inhale the writings that she knew to be there. She had only had a glimpse of what was inside, but it was enough to hope that there was more to learn there—more secrets to be revealed, and maybe the truth.

Kate had touched something that Arabella herself had touched. She could almost feel herself sitting at a rough-hewn table, quill pen in hand, dipping into an ink well to write the words, shaking with despair, confessing the losses that she felt. She must not have had anyone to share her pain with, but in a cramped and awkward script, she had written what would be her legacy—to live on in legend until it found its way into Kate's very hands.

Virginia made no apologies for the connection that she felt to this young woman. Kate knew that she had created her own world around the legend, and that Virginia herself was a direct descendant of Devon Calloway, Ewen's brother. Kate had no reason to disbelieve the woman's claims of ancestry. But she was still unsure about the link of the Corbyn name to Courbain. Yet the connection she felt with Arabella was visceral and visual. She now believed that things that come unbidden to some people in dreams are powerful, and the young woman who had come to Kate in her dreams had left her mark. Now, after reading Arabella's letter, she felt the link with the young woman was physically complete.

Kate's instincts had been right. Virginia kept the things that were truly important to her closest. She had to see what else was in the box.

Kate waited until darkness and silence had settled over the house. She slowly opened the door to her room and peeked out into the hall. A noise startled her, and she quickly retreated into the bedroom and closed the door.

"This is such a bad idea," Kate whispered to herself.

She had no idea if Virginia or her staff moved about the house in the evening. They could appear at any time and catch her in the act of snooping through Virginia's private things— something she would never have thought of doing before coming to the Calloway Manor. But she had come this far...

If they catch me in the halls or on the stairs, I'll make up some excuse. If they catch me in the library, I'll say that I was looking for something I thought I left there. If they catch me looking through the box...well, I guess I'll be finding a way to get back to Rye.

Kate took a deep breath and once again left her room. With her phone as her only source of light, she found her way down the hallway to the top of the stairs. She took each tread down the open curving staircase cautiously, peering into the hallway below for any signs of Virginia or her staff. It was quiet except for the rhythmic throb of a pendulum from the grandfather clock that stood in the main hall.

She kept the light low to her side and followed the sound of the clock. Soon, she reached the door to the library. The pocket door had been left partly open, but there was no light coming from inside. She opened the door slowly and went in, closing it behind her.

The curtains had been pulled back from the tall windows, and she stepped closer. She saw a movement outside and stepped away. But another furtive look showed a group of people walking toward the old Calloway House. Virginia appeared to be in the lead. Kate could not take the chance that Virginia might return, so she hurried to the bookshelf where she had seen her retrieve the box.

She reached for the handle on the second drawer from the right and pulled it slowly, but it did not open. She recalled Virginia using a key to unlock the door, but she had not relocked it—at least, not that Kate had seen—so she tugged harder. Finally, at one last attempt, the drawer opened.

The box was still inside, and Kate lifted it out and sat down on a nearby chair, constantly listening for sounds of anyone coming into the house or down the hallway. She opened the box.

Arabella's letter was still on top. She set it aside and leafed through the rest of the papers. There was what appeared to be a print of the original engraving of Arabella, and it was still a shock to see her own face looking back at her. A few small books lay at the bottom of the box, and at first look, Kate found them to be from the late 1700s. Interesting, but probably not directly related to her search, and she left them in the box exactly where she had found them.

She took photos of the letter and engraving, and the box itself. Before she returned Arabella's letter, she read it one more time, thinking about what else she might have been trying to say. The words quickly began to take on a much deeper meaning.

Arabella had clearly planned to take her own life, such was the hopelessness she felt. But the next sentences jumped out at Kate:

My future is in the hands of Devon Calloway
and subject to the whims of fate on the high
seas, and to the hearts of brave men. I wish them
Godspeed.

Nothing in the legend itself ever mentioned that Arabella knew that her fate was in Devon Calloway's hands. But in her own handwriting, it was clear that she had placed her trust in him, and to their fate on the high seas.

I have done all that I could, Kate whispered, as she read on.

Arabella had somehow taken some kind of action, which she believed was setting a course for her future. Kate thought through the possibilities of what had happened, murmuring to herself the scenario that might have taken place centuries ago.

"Arabella wrote the letter on November sixteenth, 1766. She said that she had done all that she could, which could mean that she informed Devon Calloway of when her father's ship was arriving, or perhaps told someone else that could pass the information along. It might be possible that she knew when it would land. And if she did, then she might have found a way to hear about the fate of the two ships.

"'If this letter is found, it will mean that I am gone...'

"So if she found out that her father was killed or captured, then she probably would have destroyed the letter. Only if the letter were found would it be believed that she took her own life. But I know that William Courbain was not killed or captured after that battle. And Arabella did not return to destroy the letter, because it is right here in my hands. And according to Guilford, the punishment for informants against the smugglers was swift and sure."

A shiver ran through her as she recalled how she had felt at Beachy Head. Something else had happened to Arabella at the edge of those high cliffs. She was sure of it.

Kate quickly returned the letter to the box and slid it back into the drawer. Two hundred fifty-four years had passed between Arabella writing the letter and Kate holding it in her hands. An entire legend had been built up and perpetuated over the last hundred years—at least, to the point where Virginia Calloway was obsessed with Arabella Courbain and her belief that she would someday return. The pieces of the puzzle were falling into place. But the final answer was still not quite within Kate's reach.

She quietly returned to her room. It was chillier than she remembered, and she noticed that the window was slightly open. Thinking she must have forgotten to close it before she left, Kate turned the handle to close it and pulled the curtains tight.

She crawled into bed and looked at the photos she had taken. There might have been another ending to the legend. But Virginia had chosen to believe a tale written by Sir Archibald Mallard instead of searching for the truth herself. And what about Mallard's *Ancient Tales of an Ancient Town*? What if it were proven that the story of Arabella really had ended differently? What would happen to the supposed value of the book, both monetarily and historically? It was admittedly only one legend out of many in the book, but there could be repercussions in the literary world. But then again, perhaps no one would give it a second thought.

Kate knew that her scenario could probably never be verified. But she thought it made as much sense as Virginia's version. Dreams are not evidence. A feeling is not proof. William

Courbain was never tried for any crimes, that she had found, and the thought that he might be responsible for Arabella's death was unthinkable. But still, it was a possibility. Maybe the legend just took over the truth and people believed what they chose to believe. Maybe Virginia was so blind to the possibilities of what might have happened that she did not read into the letter what Kate had. And what was the harm in an old woman believing what she wanted to, anyway? Kate didn't understand the need for Virginia to do it, but was it really that important?

Kate decided that it was. She was part of this, whether she liked it or not. Whether she had asked for it or not. Virginia was obsessed, and she had drawn Kate—although, Kate admitted, somewhat willingly—into her obsession.

Kate decided she would stay for one more day to try to reason with Virginia and get to the truth of the legend of Arabella before she left the Calloway House & Gardens behind forever.

34

SIX WOMEN, clothed again in red hooded robes and red gloves, slowly filed into the secret room. Wisps of their chilled breaths escaped from them into the cold, damp air. They each took their place in front of a chair, waiting for a signal from Virginia before they took their seats. As she approached the central candle, she motioned to them, and they sat as one.

Virginia surveyed the half-circle of women—loyal friends, some of whom she had known for decades. Women she had brought into the Sisterhood because of their shared reverence for legends and things past. Together, they held the belief that when desired and demanded, the past reaches into the future. And when it does, lives change, and in turn, the future is changed.

In this place and time, Virginia felt vindicated. The lore had been passed down to her from her grandmother, who believed that Arabella would return, somehow, some way, and Virginia grasped that belief as truth. Her grandmother had at first explained that no one knew exactly how it would happen, or when, but it was a belief hardened into their souls.

Virginia knew the pain of having to give up the life she was meant to live, just as Arabella had been forced to do. Virginia's life, the happy life she dreamed of as a young woman, had been shattered beyond repair when her fiancé died. It was not something she had willed. Like Arabella, the tragedy had been forced on her by fate. The loss of the only man she could ever love drove Virginia even deeper into the world of legends and the lore of herbalism. Why else would she be here in this time and place? Why else would she have taken to heart the skills that Grandmother Mathilde had taught her?

Virginia had been with her grandmother on the night she died. Virginia alone had sat with her in her last days, taking care of her every need. It was Mathilde's wish that her passing would be attended by Virginia and no one else.

In her last moments, she had drawn Virginia close to her. The dying woman's cold shriveled hand had clutched at her granddaughter's as she whispered her final wishes.

"My dear, there is power beyond our understanding in the world of legends. There are secrets that must be ferreted out and brought into the light. You have learned well. You have learned the power of the herbs and the séance. The Calloway family is privileged to have the legend of Arabella as our history. It belongs to us. This is what we have survived for. What I have survived for. And you must carry it forward."

Soon, the woman's voice was no more than a sigh as she struggled to give one final legacy to her granddaughter.

"The return of Arabella will happen in your lifetime, dear Virginia. I have seen it. The vision has been given to me. And you must be prepared for it. I am old. I will not live to see her return. I must leave this to you, my dear. You must bear it now."

Virginia carried the memory of those final moments with her grandmother throughout her life, dedicating herself to the promise she made that she would continue the legacy and prepare for the return of Arabella.

A breeze caught the flame of the candle in the cold room. It flickered, and Virginia was drawn back to the present. She had waited all day for Myrlie to bring her the book of legends, the *Ancient Tales of an Ancient Town*, but she had not come, and the betrayal would make her an outcast, banished from the Sisterhood.

The book would find its way back to where it belonged—of that, Virginia was sure. It was the heart of the legend, and she was confident that with Arabella close now, the book would soon be in her possession as well. She shook off her worry and disappointment and scanned around the women seated in front of her.

Myrlie was not present now, and Virginia soon noticed that Opal had not joined them either.

"We are missing two of our members tonight," she announced. "And our betrayer, Myrlie, has not come forth with the book, as she was ordered to do."

A woman stood, her head bowed. "Sister Virginia, I have something to report."

"Go ahead, then."

"Myrlie has been arrested for trying to sell stolen books. She is in jail right now."

Virginia stiffened. "I see. And what of the book of legends?"

"I have it on good authority that this was the book that was involved in the...well, the attempted sale, I guess you could say. My husband Joe, he works as a custodian at the police station, and the place was all abuzz today with the arrests. I'm sure that was the name of the book. It would have been taken into evidence, I would imagine. And..." The woman hesitated.

"Go on," Virginia said.

"There's something else. Sister Opal has also been taken in for questioning."

Virginia was silent for a moment. Could the book be entirely out of her reach now?

No, she still believed it would come back to her. Her plans were no longer focused on Kate. Her plans were now for Arabella.

"No matter, then," she said. "Myrlie and Opal are no longer in our circle. They are banned for life. But we will not be deterred by these events, will we? The book was important, but as you know, we have something even better. We have Arabella."

"Sister Virginia, when will we meet her?" a young woman said. "This is what we have all been waiting for."

"Soon. Very soon. There are...arrangements to be made. I will gather you all together when the time is right. For now, say nothing to anyone. Do not engage with Miss Shaw-Windham or Miss Godwin. I forbid it. They will suffer the consequences of their actions."

Virginia stepped to the candlestick and lit the taper candle she carried.

"This meeting is ended. I have much to attend to."

She extinguished the large candle and walked down the long hall to the entrance, the women following her.

35

AS KATE ROUNDED THE CURVE of the stairway to the first floor of the manor the next morning, she hesitated at the sound of loud voices in the library. One was Virginia's, she was sure of that. But the other, she did not recognize.

Kate went down the last few steps and stood hidden next to the grandfather clock in the hall, and listened.

"You had no right, Virginia! You cannot just close down the tours on a whim."

The man's voice was deep, slow, and seemed patient, but there was an underlying displeasure in his tone that might have cowed a lesser person than Virginia.

"Well, I can, and I did," she replied. "This is my home, and those are my gardens, and I am tired of people coming and going, marching through the flower beds, throwing trash in the brook. They've ruined the lavender along the walk, did you see? I go outside, and all I can smell is diesel fuel from those blasted buses! They have no consideration. None at all."

"I'm sorry," the man said. "Yes, there were a couple incidents recently—"

"A couple? Hardly a mere couple. No! I have other work to do here, and those people are ruining the peace and tranquility I need in order to do my research."

There was a moment of silence except for the sound of a book slamming, then another.

"I see," the man said, a bit more respectfully. "I didn't realize it was affecting you so much. But still, Virginia, you can't just cancel the tours. People have paid—"

"I don't care, Hubert. It is done."

He gave a loud sigh, clearly submitting to Virginia's will.

"Let's give it a day, then," he replied. "You are right. It can't be undone now. But we will have to refund the money for the tickets on the canceled tours. And it's not good for our reputation."

"Our reputation?" Virginia seemed to be on the attack once again. "Is that all you care about, Hubert? Our reputation is as old as that monstrosity of a building out there. For over five hundred years, we have lived on this land and worked it, suffered through countless wars and personal tragedies. We are Calloways. You are a Calloway. Act like it. If you have to refund the money, then just do it."

"Of course, Virginia," the man acquiesced.

"I have one day, Hubert. Just one day," she said quietly, her voice breaking.

Kate sensed a weakening in Virginia—the resignation of someone who's time was running out for something very important to her.

"What do you mean?" he said, more gently now. "You have one day for what?"

"Nothing that concerns you," she said dismissively, the determination returning to her voice. "I simply need one day of peace and quiet. One day to concentrate on what needs to be done. I have things to plan."

"Very well, then," he said. "Is there something Julia and I can help you with?"

"No. This is something I will be doing by myself. Don't bother yourself with it."

"We'll talk later, then," he said. "And we will be back open tomorrow. Do you hear me?"

Virginia did not acknowledge his words. Kate sensed that the conversation was coming to an end, and slipped into the dining room across the hall so Hubert wouldn't see her. It occurred to her that he might not even know that she had been invited to stay there. It would probably be a shock to him, as Virginia was known to be a recluse.

Kate heard the front door close. But now there were other voices in the hall, and she peeked out of the dining room.

Samuel was leading a new visitor to the library—a short, stocky man wearing an ill-fitting, rumpled brown suit, and bowler hat. His small face was half-covered with a large handlebar mustache. He was not the type of guest that Kate thought Virginia would welcome to her home, but there he was, being introduced to the lady of the house.

"Well, it's about time," she heard Virginia say, and then the library doors slid shut with a thud.

Kate retreated to the dining room once again, where breakfast had been laid out, as usual, on the sideboard. She quickly poured herself a glass of juice and selected a croissant and jam.

A few minutes later, she heard a rustle behind her, and Virginia took her seat at the head of the table. She seemed rumpled that morning, with wrinkled linen pants, an oversized blue cable-knit sweater buttoned up over a red plaid turtleneck—a style decidedly different than the time they had first met. At that time, Virginia appeared polished and stylish. But she was no longer dressing to impress.

"Good morning, Virginia," Kate said, trying to keep the mood light.

Virginia murmured a good morning and began to butter a scone on the plate in front of her. They sat in silence for a few moments, until Kate realized that Virginia was staring at her.

"We will be in the workroom again, Kate," she said, when Kate met her gaze. "And then this evening I have something special planned."

Kate looked down at the pants and T-shirt she was wearing. She was quickly running out of clothes, having packed for just enough days for her trip.

"I'm afraid I don't have anything dressy with me."

"No matter. It is not formal. Wear whatever you like." Virginia pushed her untouched plate of food away and stood. "When you are done with your breakfast, please come to the workroom." She hurried away.

Virginia had already prepared the workroom by the time Kate arrived. Small woven baskets of rose petals, bowls, and the necessary utensils, and the scale were set in order across one end of the table. A thick book lay open in front of her, the pages held down with a stone pestle. The matching mortar was nearby, waiting to receive the herbs for grinding.

Virginia seemed both animated and distracted. There was a change in her demeanor, and Kate wondered if it was the result of the disagreement with her cousin. Or maybe there was some bad news from the visitor.

Kate shut the door behind her, and Virginia raised her head.

"Your apron is on the hook. Please put it on."

Kate was surprised at Virginia's demanding tone, but did as she was told. She was in agreement with Virginia on one thing: she, too, only had one day to accomplish what she had come there to do. And she was determined to do it.

Kate washed and dried her hands, then stepped up to the table to watch Virginia as she worked.

Virginia was a very talented herbalist, and a fount of knowledge. She had already proven that to Kate. She had spent her entire life learning, exploring, and writing about herbs. In that way, she was a true scientist, and Kate did admire her for that. But perhaps her solitary lifestyle was partly the result of people not accepting her role in this area of science. At least, not officially.

But in reality, it was likely more complicated than that. According to Winnie, Virginia had grown up in what appeared to be a troubled household. Her rock had been her Grandmother Mathilde, and Kate had already determined that the woman must have been in her seventies when Virginia was a young girl. Mathilde's influence had obviously been very important—critical to her development. That was the world Virginia grew up in, and it continued to be her lifestyle still today. Quiet seclusion, gardening, study, and research. The promise of a marriage, and possibly a family, had been torn from her, and she had retreated to the only thing she knew. The Calloway House & Gardens, and her work in herbalism, became her life.

Virginia had no one to pass her birthright to. It didn't seem that her cousin was interested except for the income that the Calloway House & Gardens provided—the public part of their legacy. Perhaps there were other cousins or children of cousins, but Kate hadn't seen or been introduced to anyone else during her visit. What would happen then to all of these journals and books, and Virginia's research? Would her cousin inherit them, along with the house and gardens?

Suddenly, Virginia's shrill voice cut through her thoughts.

"Kate! I need one teaspoon of ashwagandha powder. Please measure it out."

She pointed to a packet of powder, and Kate measured it, as she had been taught. Virginia hurriedly brought other packets and jars from other cabinets and drawers—dried lemon balm, tulsi, and linden flower. Soon, they were all together in a small bowl. And finally, Virginia measured out a cup of honey.

She made a motion to Kate, without speaking, to mix them with her hands. From the bowl, the mixture was poured through a funnel into a jar, and then the honey was poured in over the top of the colorful bits of herbs.

"This is very different," Kate said. "What is this called?"

She realized now that while Virginia was brilliant in all things herbal, and had a desire to pass on her knowledge, she was not the best teacher.

"It has many uses," Virginia replied brusquely. "The honey mixture can be added to tea or eaten on its own."

"And what is it used for?"

"To relieve anxiety, to help you relax. Anything affecting the nervous system." Virginia screwed a lid on the jar and set it aside. "This will need to sit for two to four weeks. Then it will be ready."

Virginia picked up the pestle to grind another small handful of dried herbs, and closed the book. She put it back in its place on the shelf and resumed her work crushing and grinding the herbs. Once again, her plan for teaching Kate what she needed to know apparently was lost in her concentration on the task at hand. And she appeared to be taking out her frustrations from the morning on the herbs.

"Virginia, could I try that?"

She stopped what she was doing and seemed to consider it for a moment.

"Yes, of course," Virginia said. "Perhaps I assume too much. I thought you must already know how to properly use a mortar and pestle."

"I can't say that I do," Kate replied. "I do have an electric spice grinder at home. It was given to me as a gift, but I admit, I haven't used it much."

"That will not do here," Virginia said.

She moved aside, and Kate took her place in front of the small bowl. It sat on a small base and was the size of a cereal bowl, but with thick sides.

"This mortar is made of stone, as is the pestle," Virginia said. "It was my grandmother's, and her mother's before her."

Kate liked the feel of the antique pestle in her hand. It fit well, and she tried to copy Virginia's motions. She held the mortar in place with her left hand, and gripped the pestle in her right. Virginia had placed various sizes of ingredients in the bowl, and Kate could see that it would take quite a bit of effort to reduce it all to even a coarse consistency.

For the next several minutes, Virginia seemed to calm herself as she shared various techniques of preparing herbs, peppercorns, salt, and coriander with the mortar and pestle, which Kate imitated, using the right pressure and movements to create the required texture for each of the ingredients.

"Yes, very good!" Virginia actually seemed pleased with Kate's progress.

But it was short lived, and her face once again lost the bit of pleasantness that Kate had glimpsed.

"Well..." Virginia moved to the sink to rinse her hands.

Her back was to Kate, and she couldn't see her expression, but her words were brusque.

"That's enough of that."

Kate was puzzled. For a woman whose desire seemed to be to pass along everything she knew to Kate, to another generation, her methods were unusual. Perhaps Kate's presence, despite that Virginia had initiated it, was something she did not know how to handle.

Virginia was a complex person, to say the least.

"This has been nice, Virginia. Thank you for showing me how to do these things."

Virginia wiped her hands on a towel, still with her back to Kate.

"Of course," she replied.

They spent the next few hours in the workroom, Virginia instructing Kate in methods and techniques of handling and preparing various herbs, the differences in tonics and tinctures, and simple remedies for various maladies. Small bags and jars filled with curious plants and roots and leaves appeared and disappeared into drawers and cabinets as Virginia continued to tutor Kate. Books and journals were pulled from the shelf and returned to their place in an order that Kate could not make sense of, but one that Virginia knew.

Kate began to feel a rhythm of the things that Virginia was trying to pass on to her. There were similarities in her recipes, yet differences in the use of roots versus leaves. The time and season to harvest medicinal plants was as crucial to their optimal use as their preparation.

Kate was determined to absorb it all, but soon understood that she could not possibly retain the volumes of information that Virginia was trying to pass along to her. She decided to simply listen carefully, do what Virginia asked of her, and remember what she could.

Virginia finally seemed to be slowing in her hurried outpouring of knowledge. When she went to the sink to rinse her hands. Kate took the opportunity to try to step away for a few minutes.

"I wonder if I could make a couple phone calls? I want to make sure my plans for tomorrow are in place for my return to Rye."

"I can have Mister McGregor drive you to Rye," Virginia replied, her back still turned.

"Thank you. But I have a ride arranged."

"Very well. I have a few things to attend to myself this afternoon. We'll meet for full tea at five o'clock."

As Kate hung up her apron, she noticed Virginia reach into the pocket of her skirt and pull out a small piece of paper. Kate left without another word.

36

AFTER KATE LEFT, Virginia locked the door behind her and unfolded the piece of paper. She read over the list of ingredients for the tea she was preparing for Kate that afternoon. It would be a sweet tea—flavorful, colorful, and of course, iced, as Kate was no doubt used to.

Reading the ingredients was simply habit. They were well-known to her, but to see them written in her grandmother's hand brought back a resolve that had momentarily wavered as she considered the consequences of what she was about to do.

Virginia tucked the paper back into her pocket. She measured out water into a pot and set it to boil, then hesitated for a moment, trying to recall where she had stored the hibiscus petals called for in the recipe. She soon found them in a jar pushed back into the corner of a cabinet. She struggled to open the tightly sealed jar, but finally the cover loosened. She picked out a few pieces of the dried flower and crushed them between her fingers. The motion released a soft floral fragrance into the air, and she breathed it in.

The pot of water was steaming now, small bubbles rising and popping when they reached the surface. She took it off the heat, measured out the dried petals, and sprinkled them into the water, marveling at the ancient and humble ritual of tea making. She would never tire of it.

Virginia's hands began to tremble as she took a sealed black pouch, the size of a teabag, out of the one locked drawer in the room. She held it up and ran her fingers over the lightly embossed design of silver threads depicting ravens and the moon and stars. She gingerly broke the seal and grasped two pinches of a finely ground herb the consistency of dust, and dropped them into one of two empty jars on the workbench, then brushed every single particle of the herb off her fingers and into the jar. She quickly resealed the bag and locked it back into the drawer.

The tea had steeped long enough. She strained the red liquid then, half into one jar, and then the remainder into the other. She covered each with a lid and watched with satisfaction as the tea in one of the jars turned slightly darker, almost the color of blood.

37

BACK IN HER ROOM, Kate punched Miles's number into her phone, and he answered after the first ring.

"Hi, Miles. I just wanted to let you know I'll be ready to leave here tomorrow, if your offer of a ride is still an option?"

"Sure, Kate. Just let me know what time. And, oh, I have some news."

"What's that?"

"Miss Shaw-Windham was arrested yesterday. She was trying to sell the *Ancient Tales of an Ancient Town*. And we took Opal Godwin in for questioning. No arrest there yet, but I'm pretty sure she was a part of it all."

Kate sat down on the edge of the bed. "Then she did have the book. And Opal was a part of this? Maybe that's what they were arguing about when I heard them?"

"I don't know," Miles said, "but she definitely played a role."

"What will happen to Edward, then?"

"He'll be placed somewhere where it is safe for him, and he'll get good care. So what's been happening there?"

Kate didn't know where to begin. "I've been immersed in herbalism. I can say that much. But honestly, it would take years for me to learn everything that Virginia knows. She pulled a fast one on her cousin this morning. I guess he runs the place, and she shut down the bus tours without asking him. He was here, and they were arguing. Miles, I don't even know if he knows I am visiting. I overheard them, but he didn't see me. And Mister

McGregor, the head gardener, he said that Virginia never invites overnight guests. But here I am. It's been an interesting couple days."

"Do you have anything planned for the rest of today?" Miles said. "I could come and get you now, if you want."

"I appreciate it, but let's wait until tomorrow. Virginia said she had something special planned for tonight. How about you pick me up tomorrow, after breakfast? Say, about nine? I'll let Virginia know."

"Okay. But be careful, Kate. I just have a feeling that things are not all quite sorted out yet."

"I will, Miles, and thanks again. I'll call you later, okay?"

"Remember, Kate. If I can't reach you, or don't hear from you—"

"I know, I know. You'll send in the troops. I'm fine, Miles. See you tomorrow."

The grandfather clock in the downstairs hall chimed the five o'clock hour three times, sonorous, then two sounding out a dull clunk. Kate wrestled her curls back into a loose bun, checked herself in the mirror, then went downstairs. She found Virginia in the sunroom, where full tea was set. A three-tiered tray of finger sandwiches, quiche, cheese and crackers, small cakes and fruit stood like a tower of goodness, and it was a welcomed sight.

"Please help yourself," Virginia said, and Kate made her selections, heaping her plate to compensate for missing lunch that day.

She noticed that Virginia had not prepared a plate for herself, but the woman had never had much of an appetite in any of the meals that Kate had shared with her.

"I thought we should have iced tea today," Virginia said. "I know that it is quite well-liked in the States, especially in the South. It will quench your thirst."

She poured the red liquid over a tumbler of ice and handed it to Kate.

"The color is lovely," Kate said, after taking a sip.

It was not as sweet as she was accustomed to, but nicely flavored.

"This is so refreshing. Thank you for thinking of it."

"My pleasure, of course."

Kate drank more of the icy cold tea and set the tumbler down, creating a ring of moisture on the glass tabletop.

"I want to thank you again for your hospitality, Virginia. I have learned so much over the past two days. And working in the gardens has reminded me of home."

Virginia merely nodded, not taking her eyes off Kate, who felt as if she were under a curious scrutiny once again as the conversation came to a halt. She wondered for a moment if Virginia was uncomfortable with silence, but her unruffled demeanor convinced her that she was not.

Miles had told her that the book was now in his possession. Kate wondered if Virginia knew, or would be surprised or have any emotion at all about that fact if she shared it with her.

But it occurred to her that Miles might not have wanted her to be the one to tell Virginia. There was still more she needed to know about the thing that had started this whole journey.

She decided to proceed cautiously.

"I wonder if you could answer a question for me, Virginia?"

"I will try."

"I once mentioned to you that I had seen the book *Ancient Tales of an Ancient Town*. I know you didn't believe me, but it's true. And I can't help but wonder how the legend came to be in the book in the first place. Do you know?"

"Of course," Virginia said. "My grandmother Mathilde Calloway knew Sir Archibald Mallard."

She stood and walked to the windows. A low rumble of thunder rolled over the hills in the distance—an unexpected sound in what had been a sunny afternoon. The breeze stirring the treetops began to quicken, and steely-blue clouds sailed high overhead, advancing the storm.

"But I don't suppose you knew that," Virginia said.

"No, I had no idea."

"Yes. Grandmother Mathilde was married to my grandfather Quentin Calloway. She was the one Sir Mallard convinced to publish *The Legend of Arabella* in his book. The family wasn't in favor of it, of course, but she went ahead with it."

"But what made the book so special?" Kate said. "Was it just the legend of Arabella?"

"Mostly. Of course, publicly, there is an intrinsic value to the book. But when it was published, the country, especially the area of East Sussex, went mad over it. I guess it was because it was our very own legends, and we take them very seriously."

The sky had suddenly darkened to an inky-black ceiling. Virginia reached out to the windowpane as heavy rain droplets slapped against the glass, and she followed them with her finger as they slid downward to the sill.

"But legends are not always true, right?" Kate said. "Maybe there is a nugget of fact in them, but perhaps the whole story is never really told?"

Virginia looked back at her then, her black eyes narrowed. Kate felt a change in the room, as momentous as the shift in the air outside the window, feeling that perhaps truth and legend were now finally converging. She forged ahead.

"I mean, what if there is something more to the legend? Or what if it didn't happen exactly that way?"

Virginia was silent, but Kate felt as if she had struck a nerve.

"Virginia?"

Finally, she smiled—a thin, humorless expression.

"You are very intuitive, Kate, did you know that? Very intuitive, indeed. Finish your tea, dear. I told you I had something special planned for tonight. I think you will find it very interesting."

Kate did not do as Virginia ordered, and instead left the glass on the table without drinking. Virginia had turned to leave the room, and Kate followed. They stepped outside and into the edge of the coming storm.

Kate clutched her arms to herself and called out to Virginia, who seemed oblivious to the intensifying gusts of wind and rain.

"Virginia, we should go back! This is no weather to be out in."

But her words fell on deaf ears. The storm was on them, the wind screeched across the lawn, flattening the delicate plantings, propelling loose branches across their path. The tops of the trees high above them bowed to the power of the storm.

Kate looked back at the house and realized that the path they were on was the one she saw from the library window the night before. Virginia seemed to have the same urgency now, as then. Kate knew she should have turned around and left Virginia to whatever illusions she had about her and Arabella, but she had come too far now to turn back. She hurried to catch up.

Kate's sandals soon grew muddied on the slick, sandy path that led to the oldest section of the Calloway House. They arrived at an old wooden door, now blackened with the rain, and covered with wet ivy drooping under its own weight. Virginia pulled a key out of her pocket, turned it twice in the lock, and held back the greenery covering the door, motioning for Kate to enter. Kate hesitated, but was eager to get out of the rain. She was now drenched and shivering, and as soon as she went through the door, she reached out to the wall to steady herself. Virginia pulled the chain hanging from the ceiling and lit up the long hallway.

"Where are we going, Virginia? I'm not feeling very well, and we really shouldn't be out in this weather."

"You'll see. Everything will be all right."

Kate heard the sound of the heavy door creaking shut behind her. She warily followed Virginia down the damp hallway, and they passed through a second door. Kate entered the room slowly.

In the dim light from a single candle at the front of the room, Kate saw a group of women seated in a half-circle of chairs. Their red cloaks and red leather gloves gave the entire scene a sinister look, and Kate stopped. She wrapped her arms around her, still unable to control her shivering, and she began to feel lightheaded.

"I insist that you take me back to the house, Virginia." Kate now realized that she was finding it hard to move from where she stood. "I'm really not feeling well."

Virginia brought her to a chair in the center of the room and helped her sit.

"You will feel better soon. But of course, you can leave at any time."

Kate welcomed her words, but when she tried to stand, she could not. *The tea.* She remembered then, the layers of flavors as she sipped it. There was a sweetness to it, the taste of mint... and something that came across her tongue as bitter. Virginia had drank the same tea. But hers had already been poured when Kate arrived.

Virginia came to stand in front of Kate, now wearing the same cloak and gloves as the other women in the room.

"Kate, you are probably wondering what this gathering is. This is the Corvos Sisterhood. They have been eagerly awaiting your appearance here tonight. Your arrival here was in some ways expected, but none of us knew when you—when Arabella—would return."

"I'm not Arabella!" Kate said. "You need to let me leave, now."

"Soon, dear, soon."

Kate's legs were like lead. Her hands tingled, and the bitter cold in the room had seeped into her bones. She knew now that she could not physically do anything to help herself. But her mind was still sharp, and she fought back the only way she knew how.

"Is that what this has all been about, Virginia? All along, you have thought I was Arabella returned, isn't that right?"

"Yes, I can admit to you that is true."

"But what if there is something more to the legend? Or what if it didn't happen exactly the way you think?"

"What are you talking about? It all happened exactly the way the legend says. Arabella gave up her life and pledged to return one day!"

"Listen to me carefully, Virginia. My research has shown that William Courbain survived a battle with a customs ship at sea. His ship was called *The Grand Lady*. The ship was lost, but he and some others survived. This happened on November seventeenth, 1766, just one day after the date on Arabella's letter."

"Your research?" Virginia laughed. "Anyone could know that. It means nothing."

"But there is more, Virginia. I found that Devon Calloway was a customs officer at that time. They were clearly involved in a battle with *The Grand Lady,* and—"

Virginia seemed to try to regain control of herself. "I don't know where you found this nonsense, but what if they were? And what about you? Your grandmother was a Corbyn. The name Courbain was changed to Corbyn by Jessup Corbyn in the 1800s. Jessup Corbyn was your grandmother Bessie's great-grandfather...and the great-grandson of Richard Courbain himself."

"How do you know this?" Kate said. "How do you know who my grandmother was?"

Virginia shook her head, dismissing Kate's question.

"No matter. As far as I am concerned, you are a direct descendant of Richard Courbain, son of Arabella Courbain and Ewen Calloway. There is no other explanation for your looks, your presence here today, at this time. And you have had dreams, haven't you?"

Kate was startled at this. "How did you know about my dreams?"

Virginia stepped closer to Kate, her tall, cloaked form throwing long shadows against the wall.

"Arabella comes to us all in dreams," she whispered. "Are you denying this?"

"No. I don't deny it," Kate said. "But what you don't know is that I have had visions about another ending to the legend. Another possibility of what happened to Arabella. I think her father survived the sinking of *The Grand Lady*. He knew that Devon Calloway was responsible for the attack. And I think her father blamed Arabella for tipping them off. If she was the only one who knew when he was returning, maybe she passed what she knew along to the authorities, or even Devon Calloway himself, and her father took out his revenge on her. She didn't throw herself off that cliff, did she? He found her, and he, or his men, pushed her."

"No, you are wrong!" Virginia rejected Kate's claims with a wave of her hand. "You are making it all up."

Kate knew she had to make Virginia believe that there was another ending, and hopefully that would convince her that, without the version of the legend that Virginia believed, Kate could not be Arabella returned.

"You know I am not making it up, Virginia. And that means the legend isn't true, doesn't it? What you have believed all these years is just that—it's a legend, not based on the truth of what really happened. It's not even a legend anymore. It's just a lie that you have perpetuated. And you've brought all these women into the lie, too. Arabella is not coming back. Not ever!"

The women sitting in the circle began to murmur to each other.

"Stop! Stop, now!" Virginia shouted. "You're ruining everything. You are not taking your rightful place as Arabella. And the book is gone from us forever because of a traitorous sister." She came close to Kate, her face contorted with anger. "And the ancients don't like it. No, not at all," she hissed.

Kate's head began to throb, and she pressed her hand to it, but her fingers felt distant and unconnected. She had little time.

"It's not the ancients you need to worry about, Virginia. It's the present. Now. What you are doing right now is wrong, because you have believed in a lie. The tragedy is that by alerting the authorities of when her father was planning to return, Arabella sealed her fate. By trying to do the right thing and give herself the chance to be able to live the life she truly was meant to live, in her own lifetime, I believe that instead she died at the hands of her own father."

Virginia was now pacing the room. "But you were brought here—by your dreams. You know this to be true."

"There are a lot of reasons that I came to Rye. The legend of Arabella was never one of them. But maybe I was brought here to uncover a truth. Yes, I have had dreams. And now that I know the truth, my dreams will finally stop. What about yours, Virginia? Can you live with this lie any longer? When will your dreams stop?"

One of the women stood. "Virginia, is she telling the truth?"

Virginia's eyes narrowed as she scanned the women seated around her.

"Each of you joined the Sisterhood because you believed as I do, that the past reaches into the present. We are not alone here in this time. We have the weight of the ages on us. Our ancestors cannot—they will not—leave us alone. We are at their mercy. Arabella was real. Her story was real. You've seen the letter in her own handwriting. We have reached out to her and spoken to her."

She turned, her gaze once again boring into Kate.

"And finally, she brought you to us, Kate Tyler, her identical image. Here is a direct descendent of Richard Courbain, Arabella's own son. What more proof do you need? The legend is true because what it promised has come to pass."

Kate rubbed her arms and her legs, trying to get the chill and numbness to subside, but it was no use.

"You can't keep me here, Virginia. I don't know what you've had me drink—again—but this is kidnapping and assault. These women are witnesses." She looked across the group of cloaked women. "And if you don't help me, you will be accomplices."

A murmur passed among the women in the room.

"Silence!" Virginia ordered. "Sisters, you are not to believe her. She is putting on an act." She took a deep breath to collect herself. "Now, this gathering is over," she said more calmly. "Kate and I have some things to discuss. You will all leave now."

The women seemed hesitant to leave, but once the first one left, the others quickly followed. Kate was left alone in the room with Virginia. Again, she tried to stand, but could not.

"People will be looking for me," Kate whispered. "You can't keep me here."

Her vision was blurred now, and she blinked to try to restore it. The candle was flickering and dancing across the room, but distorted and seemed to be moving on its own.

"You will not be here for long," Virginia said. "Once you have come to your senses and realize who you really are, and why you are here, we will go back to the house and begin to get you settled in. I have a much nicer room for you. We barely touched the surface of what you need to learn, you know. You were right about one thing. It will take years for me to teach you all that I know."

"Virginia, you have completely lost touch with reality. I am *not* Arabella returned! The legend that Sir Mallard concocted for the book is not what finally happened. And you know it."

"How can you be so sure, Kate? You have no proof."

Kate didn't want to reveal how she knew, but she was running out of options and time. Maybe a confession would bring Virginia to her senses.

"In the box...you have been keeping her letter in for all these years. What else is in there, Virginia? Pictures, journals..." Kate was struggling to get the words out.

"How would you know this? I never showed you—" She stopped. "I see, then. You have been sneaking around my house. I should have destroyed it all a long time ago. But I never envisioned such a betrayal as this. Especially from the very one who has returned—"

"I have not returned from anything! I am not Arabella. Virginia, I have my own life to live, and so do you. Forget all this, please. You have a full life here at the manor, and an amazing knowledge of herbal medicine. You need to share it with the world, not sink into fantasy and legends. Why not share the real experience that you have. Maybe that is the life you were meant to live, Virginia. Not a made-up one, but a real one."

Virginia's shoulders slumped. "But this is all I know," she whispered. "I have lost...everything else. My life, my future were determined so long ago. Except for this, I am truly alone."

Kate was fading fast, but still alert enough to take advantage of what might be a moment of clarity for Virginia.

"I know about loss, too. Believe me, I know loss. But look around you! Look what you have. You have your family here. You have Mister McGregor and all the people that work here, your beautiful home and gardens. You can't live in the past, Virginia. It's the present, the here and now, that is important. Don't let the past...and these fantasies... continue to hold you...back."

Words were slow in forming now. Her mouth was parched, and her head pounded out the beat of her heart, throbbing and painful.

Virginia wagged her finger, her voice now strong again.

"No, no, I have waited my whole life for this day. And now that it is finally here, I will not let it go. You will see—I will bring you proof. You will wait here." She turned and left the room.

The last thing Kate heard was the sound of the key in the lock.

38

VIRGINIA FOUGHT HER WAY BACK through the storm, to the manor. Now that she knew Kate had rifled through the rest of the items in the box, and had actually had her hands on it, Virginia needed to make sure it was still there, and that she still had the rest of the important documents. Kate was safe enough where she was. It was unfortunate that Virginia had to employ certain tactics to put her plan into motion, but it was necessary.

The women of the Sisterhood, when dismissed, followed each other like sheep out of the tunnel and into the storm, with not an original thought among them. Virginia knew it was partly her doing. Most of them had started out with her as impressionable young women, and she had been able to mold them over the years. She had chosen each of them for that very reason: they had minds that would be open to her teachings. Open to the lure and mystery of the séance and what lay beyond their own world, to lives from the past that reached out to those who would seek them.

But soon, Virginia would be done with them all. The Sisterhood was of no use to her any longer. Not since Kate—Arabella—had arrived. The Corvos Sisterhood would never be gathered again.

Myrlie and Opal had been the biggest disappointments. Their betrayal cut her to the quick. Who knew how things might have been different if Virginia had the book in her own hands—the original legend. What strength that might have given her? But she knew that the book was only one conduit to the past and to Arabella. Even though it was the original writing of the legend by Sir Mallard, given directly to him by Virginia's own grandmother, Virginia had the most important link—Arabella's letter in her own handwriting, and the etching created by Ewen Calloway himself.

She threw her wet cloak and gloves on the chair in the library and went directly to the drawer in the bookshelf. She lifted out the box. Something Kate said came to her mind. It was nonsense, of course, to think that there might be some other ending to Arabella's story. To think that Arabella had not thrown herself off of the cliff was ridiculous. The legend was clear. Sir Mallard clearly wrote that:

> *One moonless night, with only black ravens as winged witnesses, she stood on the edge of the cliffs overlooking the ocean, and stepped off onto the jagged rocks and wild surf below.*

The legend said that Arabella would return one day to finally live the life she was meant to live. And Virginia's own visions, and what she had witnessed in the séances, all proved that there was truth to the legend.

But was the real proof in the letter?

She put on her glasses and took out the letter once again. She had read it so many times before, but now, as she traced the inked lines with her finger, murmuring to herself, it was as if the words had shifted. As if someone had come into her library and replaced the letter with another one, a different one.

"My future is in the hands of Devon Calloway..."

Virginia muttered, "Of course her future might have been in Devon Calloway's hands. He was the head of the Calloway family. What other meaning could there be?

"I have done all that I could...

"Yes, she gave up her son for his safety."

Kate had seemed so sure that there was some other ending to Arabella's story. What research had she done that would tell something different? And the dreams that she spoke of? Arabella had clearly come to Kate in her dreams.

By alerting Devon Calloway, Virginia thought. If that were true...no, it was impossible.

Or was it possible, after all, that William Courbain was a missing piece, as Kate had hinted? Virginia had dismissed him as a thief, a criminal. He had deserved no further consideration from her, nor from history. Or so she thought.

Virginia slumped in her chair. She had waited so long for this day to come, and now, just when she should be rejoicing, she simply felt tired and confused. She had been betrayed, not only from members of her own Sisterhood, but now Kate herself, who was trying to change everything, calling her beliefs fantasies, putting into question everything she had ever believed.

It should not have surprised her that Kate took it upon herself to find out about Arabella. And perhaps showing Kate the letter was foolish on her part, but it was necessary. Kate had to see it for herself.

Virginia felt she was being tested, of course. The past had inexorably been reaching out to her. It had brought Arabella back by placing Kate Tyler here at the Calloway House & Gardens.

"Well, let the legend come to pass, then. Let it come."

The ancients had finally gained their foothold and set Virginia's life on a new path. A decision had been made.

Virginia left the library and went through the kitchen door to the outside, stepping into a chilly mist and fog that enveloped her and blotted out the debris in her path, left behind from the violent storm. Wet leaves lay plastered against the stone walkway. Twigs tumbled and spun along the path, caught by random remnants of the wind. Uprooted plants, their flower stems stripped of their blossoms, lay silent, ensnared in the bushes. But Virginia saw none of what surrounded her. Felt nothing beneath her feet.

With the soft cry of rattling noises and caws into the darkness, she lured her raven to her. He came, as she knew he would. He hopped behind her as she walked heedlessly through the wreckage of the storm until they arrived at the door to her workroom.

"Come in, my dear. Come in," she whispered, and the bird flew up to the workbench and settled there. "I must tell you what I am going to do," she said to the raven, as she pulled the light cord, bathing the room in a bright light. "I have decided to reclaim the old house."

The bird tipped his head.

"Yes, all of it, my dear. And we will close the gardens." She pulled small bags of herbs out of the drawers and scattered their contents across the bench. "No more strangers parading through the plantings and the woods. No birdwatchers, no curiosity seekers. And then, when I bring Arabella here to the old house, we will devote every minute to her. We will show her the ways of our ancestors. She will study my own research. And she will go beyond everything I have done, you can be sure, because we know that this is the life that Arabella was meant to live. There it is, my friend. I will not let Arabella go. I simply will not."

The drug and the cold and numbness had finally overtaken Kate, still imprisoned in the damp cellar. She could still see what surrounded her—the candle, the fireplace, the empty ring of chairs. The images made sense in her brain and evoked emotions, helpless as she was. But the drug had made it all dull. The sharp edges of conviction she felt earlier when confronting Virginia were now worn down, rounded and smooth.

Of course she could leave, couldn't she? Couldn't she pry the lid off of this prison with the strength she had left, and fly away? But there would be no answers there. The puzzle would still be carried along with her on her flight, the pieces floating delicately in her brain. Then one at a time, she might lose the pieces and lose all of the knowledge. All of the curiosity about what had happened to her. And she would forever regret leaving. At some deep level, she knew she could never let that happen.

She blinked as the images of the room swam around her. She knew that the tea Virginia had given her earlier had made her pass out, as before, but this time it was much worse. This time, she had been paralyzed, putting her into a dreamlike state. But she was determined to find her way out.

With a tremendous effort, Kate began to move her feet, then her hands. The tingling she had felt earlier was now replaced with pain, but it was a sensation she welcomed since it came with increasing movement. Her vision began to clear as she blinked away the vestiges of the drug and shook the cloudiness from her brain.

She called out for help, but knew that the walls in this part of the cellar were thick stone, and no one would be about this time of night to hear her weak cries. Her only hope was that Miles would try to reach her somehow. It had been foolish not to bring her phone with her, but she had no idea of what the night was going to bring. And she had just reassured Miles that everything was fine. She simply had to trust that he would do whatever he could to find her.

The tall candle in the center of the room had not burned down much, so Kate guessed that she had not been unconscious for very long. She at least had light—for now. But she was still alone. She called out again, but it was of no use.

As feeling slowly returned to her limbs, she was able to turn in her chair to get a better look around the room. At one end of it, opposite the entrance, there were heavy curtains hanging from the ceiling. She noticed a slight movement in the fabric and wondered if they could be covering a door or window or some other exit. If the room actually extended under the rest of the house, maybe there was a chance for escape.

She was still weak, but was finally able to stand. She grabbed on to the back of the chair and inched along the distance to the wall of curtains. She reached out and pulled them back at an opening and discovered that the heavy fabric covered a rough wooden door which, when she turned the handle, proved to be unlocked. She opened the door as far as she could. The area ahead of her was completely dark, and even the candle in the large room behind her was not enough to light her way.

Kate had to make a decision. She was still unsteady, but she didn't feel at all safe where she was since she had no idea of Virginia's intentions. She didn't plan on waiting to find out. If this were not a way out, she would return and face Virginia head-on.

With one hand on the wall, she shuffled along, running her hand along the cold, damp stone, letting her eyes slowly adjust to the dark. As she did, she sensed a light in the distance, and finally felt a sense of relief. There must be a way out ahead of her. She took another step forward. Suddenly, the floor disappeared beneath her, and she tumbled down a steep incline, landing hard on the stone floor below.

39

MILES DIALED KATE'S NUMBER AGAIN, but only reached her voicemail. She had said she would call him later, but the call never came. This was enough. He knew something must have happened. He had promised her he would come to her if she needed him, and he intended to keep his promise.

He called into the precinct and asked for backup to go to the Calloway House & Gardens in East Stalton, and then got into his car and headed in that direction. A strong storm had just passed through the area, and he swerved around broken branches and leaves scattered across the road.

A few minutes later, he pulled into the parking lot of the Calloway House, with two police cars following close. As he was explaining the situation to Officers Compton and Bullard, a car pulled into the parking lot. A young woman got out and tentatively approached them.

"Miss, you will need to leave," Miles said. "The grounds are closed now."

"I know, but are you looking for Kate Tyler?" she asked timidly.

"Yes. What do you know about her? Do you know where she is?"

"I didn't do anything! I won't get into trouble, will I?"

Miles was reaching his limits with the young woman.

"That depends," he hissed. "But if you don't tell me where she is right now, I can guarantee you there will be consequences."

"Okay, okay. Just follow me, then." She led them around to the back of the old house and down the path to a door that had been well-hidden behind a curtain of ivy. "In there," she said. "That's where I last saw her, anyway."

Miles pushed aside the ivy and tried the door, but it was locked. He pulled at the long vines until they were ripped away, and rammed the door with his shoulder, but it was too solid to break through.

He called out to the officers. "Someone get a ram down here!" He turned back to the door. "Kate! Kate, can you hear me?"

There was no answer, and he slammed his fist against the door, worried that he might be too late. He should have insisted that she stay in Rye instead of coming here to face Virginia and whatever insane plans she had for her.

He turned to the young woman, his face dark with worry. "Why was she in here? Tell me what happened."

"I don't know if I should..." The woman fidgeted with her jewelry.

"Tell me, now," Miles said. "She could be in trouble."

"Well, Miss Calloway called a meeting of the Sisterhood—"

"The Sisterhood? What is that?"

"Just a group of us ladies that like to get together for... well, seances, and the like.

"Wait, did you say séances?"

"Yes, sir. It's all harmless, really."

Miles fought to control his anger. "If it was harmless, then we wouldn't be standing here, would we? Now tell me. Were you meeting here tonight?"

"Yes, sir. And Kate Tyler was there. I couldn't believe the resemblance. She's the spittin' image of Arabella. But you probably don't know about that."

"I know enough," he said, becoming even more impatient with her story. "We need that ram. Now!" he shouted out to Compton, who had been sent to retrieve it.

"Oh...well, she couldn't walk for some reason," the woman continued. "Miss Calloway had sat her down in the chair, and they were arguing about the legend and—"

"What do you mean she couldn't walk?" Miles was getting more worried by the minute.

"She was rubbing her legs, and she didn't get up out of the chair, so I thought maybe she couldn't walk. Then Miss Calloway dismissed us."

"And why did you come back?"

"Well, I was on my way home, and I saw the police coming here fast, and I thought maybe it had something to do with her. She never did anything wrong to deserve being hurt or anything. So I came back. I'm only trying to help."

Compton returned with the ram, and after two tries against the door, broke it open. Miles and the others rushed down the hallway to a second locked door which was also easily smashed in, and he hurried into a large room. There was no one there.

"Is this where you last saw her?"

"Yes, sir," the young woman said. "She was sitting in that chair there, but it was in the center of the room then. Not over there." She pointed at the curtains.

"Compton, keep an eye on her," Miles said. "She's not to leave. Bullard, come with me."

Miles approached the curtain, pulled it back, revealing an open door. He shone his light into the darkness.

"Kate!" he called out again, but only an echo of his own voice came back to him.

He inched forward, and after a few feet, came to a large hole in the floor. He directed his light into the hole and saw Kate collapsed on the stone floor.

"Kate, can you hear me?" he called down to her.

No answer.

He turned to Bullard. "Call for an ambulance and get some rope. I'm going down."

The slope appeared steep and rocky, but as soon as the rope was brought to him, Miles was able to control his descent to the bottom.

He rushed to her and quickly assessed her condition. Her pulse was strong. She was conscious, but cold and wet. Except for a few scrapes and bruises, nothing seemed obviously broken.

"Kate, can you hear me? Come on, say something."

She opened her eyes.

"Miles? Where am I?" she said groggily.

"Don't try to talk. You must have fallen down into this hole. Did you hit your head?"

"I don't think so."

"Can you move?" he said.

"Yes. I can now." She sat up with a look of panic on her face. "It was Virginia, Miles! You were right. She's really lost it. How could I be so stupid."

"We'll figure it out later. Just sit still."

Compton called down to him. "Sir, the gardener's here. He says he knows another way in. There should be a door. Can you see it?"

Miles confirmed that there was a door across from them. He hoped it would be a better option than trying to take Kate back up the steep, rocky slope.

"Check it out and get a blanket down here," he said.

A few moments later, Miles heard voices at the door. The ram was used once again, and soon the door broke open and the light of several flashlights brightened the cavern where Kate had fallen. EMS personnel came in first and began to check on Kate's condition. They agreed with Miles that nothing seemed broken, and she was now able to move her arms and legs. With Miles's help, she was able to stand and walk up a stone stairway to the outside. He took her to the waiting ambulance. As soon as Kate was safe, Miles gave orders to find Virginia Calloway, her guard, and her butler.

"And I need to speak to the gardener," he said. "Bring him here."

"I'm here, sir." Mr. McGregor approached from the shadows. "How can I help?"

"We need to find Virginia Calloway. Do you know where she is?"

"I have a good idea of where she might be, sir, yes. I'll take you there."

They followed him to the entrance of Virginia's workroom, hidden in the shadows of the manor. The door was ajar, and Miles pushed it open. Virginia was standing at the table in the brightly lit room. A large raven, the color of midnight, sat on the table, pecking at the herbs that had been scattered there.

She looked up. "Detective Pixley. How lovely to see you again."

"Miss Calloway." He nodded to her and motioned for the others to stay back, and then approached her slowly.

"More questions about Arabella perhaps?" she said.

Miles realized that Kate's assessment of Virginia was accurate. She had now lost touch with reality.

"No. Not this time," he replied. "We have found her. But I guess you know where she's been?"

"Well, of course." She smiled. "Did she come along with you, then? I must get her settled in now. It's getting late, and we have so much to tend to. She will be moving in here, with me. Did she tell you?"

Miles nodded to an officer, who came around behind the table to take Virginia into custody.

"Virginia Calloway, you are under arrest for kidnapping and assault," Miles said. "You do not have to say anything, but it may harm your defense if you do not mention when questioned, something which you later rely on in court. Anything you do or say may be given in evidence."

Virginia appeared befuddled at what was happening.

"Young man, I cannot possibly leave. I have things to do. Kate—I mean, Arabella—and I...we have things to do. I have so much to teach her." She shook off the hand of the officer. "What is this about? I demand to know," she cried out, her voice shaking.

Miles signaled to the officer, who walked Virginia, still protesting, out of the shed. Miles hurried back to the ambulance. He hopped into the back and sat down next to Kate.

"Are you feeling better?" he said.

"Yes, but still a little strange."

"They'll check you out at hospital. I'll be there with you."

"My things, Miles—my laptop, my phone, my passport... everything. I left it all in my bedroom on the second floor. Can you get them for me?"

"Don't worry about it. We'll get them."

"Sir, we have to go now," the ambulance driver said. "You can meet us at Saint George's Hospital if you like."

"Good enough." Miles turned back to her as he stood. "I'll see you there, Kate."

"Miles." She took his hand. "I don't know how to thank you. You were right to be suspicious. I feel like a fool."

He just shook his head. "No worries. We'll get it all sorted out later."

40

KATE WAS EXAMINED at St. George's Hospital in Rye, and released after tests had returned satisfactorily without any side effects from the unidentified drug she had been given by Virginia Calloway. A few scrapes and bruises were the only visible signs of her tumble down into the pit at the Calloway House. She was told the signs and symptoms to watch for in a concussion, and was instructed to return for follow-up visit to be cleared for her flight home.

Miles took her to a B&B near Rye for the night. After she was settled in, he left, promising to be back first thing in the morning. Kate's clothes were ripped and dirty, and she rolled them up and stuffed them in the bottom of her suitcase. She pulled a T-shirt and shorts out of her bag and laid them on the bed. After a long, hot shower, she dressed and dialed Ben's number.

"Hey, Kate, I'm glad you called. I have a question about—"

"Ben," was all that she could say, before breaking down in tears.

She had held it together during the ordeal, through the tests and examinations at the hospital, through settling in at the B&B. But she could no longer hold back her emotions. The decisions she had made, the reasons she came to Rye in the first place, her gullibility with Virginia, all came flooding back to her.

"Kate, what's wrong? Are you okay?"

Kate curled up on the bed, trying to catch her breath between sobs. She could hear Ben's soothing voice trying to calm her.

"Kate, what's going on. Where are you? Tell me you are okay, please."

She was finally able to talk. "I'm...I'm okay, Ben. I just need to lie here for a while. Just keep talking to me, please."

"You are scaring me, Kate. Just tell me where you are."

"I'm at a B and B in Rye."

"Have you been hurt? Was there an accident? What happened?"

"No accident. It's such a long story."

"Just take your time. Tell me what you can."

She began, in halting breaths, to tell him what had happened to her since going to the Calloway Manor. And as expected, he said he would come to England immediately to make sure she got home safely.

"No, Ben, you don't need to do that. Just stay there. I can't leave until I'm cleared by the doctor tomorrow, anyway. I've learned a lot on this trip, Ben. I know I left you behind pretty suddenly, and I wish I hadn't done that, and I'm so sorry. But even with the way things ended up, this trip has opened my eyes. We'll talk more when I get home."

"I'll be at the airport, Kate. Listen, maybe we should take some time off from Howard's Walk and get away. This last year has been crazy, and I know there was a lot of pressure and demands on you here. Maybe a few days at Ocracoke? How does that sound?"

Kate smiled as she remembered her conversation with Miles and his pirate friends at the pub. She would have to remember to share that evening with Ben, too.

"That sounds perfect," she said. "I would love that."

She realized then that she desperately wanted to have that time alone with Ben. She hoped he would still be there for her, no matter what. She couldn't wait to be at home again at Howard's Walk.

⋙

Kate slept until noon the day after her rescue from the Calloway House. After her conversation with Ben, her sleep was deep and dreamless. And while she awoke stiff and sore from her ordeal, she felt as though a weight had been lifted off of her. The mystery of Arabella had not been completely resolved, and the truth of what had really happened to the young woman might never be known, but Kate felt a closure in her dealings with Virginia, and was happy to leave the memories of the Calloway House & Gardens, and the manor, behind.

Miles met her at the B&B, and after a quiet lunch, drove her to the police station to give her statement. She was reassured that nothing regarding the case would prevent her from leaving the country.

Before her follow-up appointment with the doctor, they walked the beach at Camber Sands. The waves slapping on the shore were gentle that afternoon as they strolled along the hard, flat sand, and Kate finally knew it was time to leave England behind and go home.

41

FRIDAY MORNING CAME, and since Kate had been cleared by the doctor to catch her flight, Miles picked her up at the B&B to take her to the train station. As she approached his Jeep, she noticed a dark-haired toddler tucked into a car seat in the back, peeking shyly out at her.

Miles said, "This is Josh. Josh, say hello to Kate."

The little boy set aside a well-loved teddy bear, held out his hand to Kate, and shook it like a proper gentleman. His dark, curly hair and blue eyes were unmistakably the image of his father. A dimpled smile came over his face as Kate tousled his hair.

"He is going to be a heartbreaker, Miles. You know that, don't you?" Kate smiled.

A blush rose up Miles's neck. "I don't know about that."

"Oh, I do. He's beautiful. And I'm glad I got to meet him. Does this mean..."

"Yes." He released a sigh of relief. "At least, we are working on custody. And it's all because of you, Kate. I can't tell you how much that means to me."

He loaded her luggage in the back, and they pulled out into the street. The train station wasn't far, and in a few minutes, he pulled into a parking spot. They found a bench on the platform and waited there for the train to arrive.

"I hope you accomplished something for your blog while you were here, Kate. I know things went kind of sideways for you."

She smiled. "That's an understatement. But I was able to get enough—with your picture-taking help, of course."

"Do you think you'll ever find out what really happened to Arabella?"

Kate shook her head. "I don't know. But I don't think it even matters to me anymore. That was a mystery that will stay here in England, I think. I do hope that Edward will be taken care of. And I know that Virginia needs to pay for what she did to me, but she is a disturbed woman. Do you think they will take that into consideration?"

"The family has gotten her a good solicitor, so I am sure it will be. And your testimony will be counted as well. I don't know if I would be as generous about it as you have been, though. It could have turned out much worse."

"I want to put it all behind me," Kate said. "But I will take home some wonderful memories, too. The gardens at the Calloway Manor are beautiful. Mister McGregor was so helpful. I met some wonderful new friends at the Mermaid Inn. And," she nudged him, "I met a real swashbuckler who rescued me from unspeakable dangers in the caverns deep beneath the ancient Calloway House." She shrugged. "What more could I ask for in a trip to England?"

Her train was announced. They stood, and Kate reached out to Miles, holding on more tightly than she had expected to.

"Thank you," she whispered in his ear. "Thank you for everything."

He nodded. "You've done more for me than you know, Kate. Safe travels."

She boarded the train and found a window seat facing the platform. Miles was still there, waving to her, Josh's arms wrapped around his father's neck.

The train soon pulled away from the station on its northwesterly journey to London. Her arrival in Rye seemed only a vague memory now.

She pulled her journal out of her backpack and looked back through the pages of notes and sketches and questions she had written over the past two weeks. She knew she would share everything with Ben. She wanted no secrets between them. And Kate knew he would listen, and hoped that he would understand why she had taken the road she did.

As the train gathered speed, racing over the bridges on the Thames, Kate understood that small movements in time, as on the river, can gather in strength and become waves that disturb the future. From Arabella Courbain to Virginia Calloway, and finally to Kate, down through the centuries, the legend gathered strength until its inevitable climax.

Kate had no regrets. In spite of everything that had happened, she was content knowing that she had played her part in the legend of Arabella Courbain.

Epilogue

One month later
Howard's Walk, Eden Springs, NC

THE FULL SUMMER HEAT hadn't reached the gardens yet, although Kate could feel it creeping in that morning, dampness gathering on her shirt, sunlight scattering through the leaves of the trees as it moved upward into the sky.

Early morning was her favorite time to garden. A quick yogurt and coffee, loose shorts and T-shirt thrown on with sneakers that never lost the reddish-brown color of southern soil, and she was ready to start her day.

She began a deep watering of the plantings since there had not been a good rain for several days, starting with the container gardens on the patio, and several that were scattered along the walkways. Then on to the shrubs and vegetable garden.

Ben had been up for hours already, clearing land for the new herb gardens by the light of two large lamps that had lit the area before sunrise. Kate could see him surveying the work he had been able to accomplish, leaning on his shovel and wiping his brow.

At first, he had not been sure that Kate's plan for the herb garden was a good idea. He thought it might be too much of a reminder of her experiences at the Calloway Manor. But Kate had assured him that it was exactly the right thing to do. No matter how the experience in England had ended for her, it was the legacy that she cared about—the legacy of herbalism, healing, and teaching that had been passed down through the generations to Virginia Calloway. Kate now wanted to recreate the best parts of that legacy, there at Howard's Walk.

She walked up to Ben with a chilled bottle of water.

"Thanks. Just what I needed." He smiled, pulled off a glove, and reached out to wipe a smudge of dirt off her cheek.

Kate scanned across their work in progress. She was getting better at visualizing the finished gardens, even at the early stage of tree stumps and piles of brush that needed to be hauled away. But she admired Ben's ability to make her vision a reality, from drawing the plans and deciding on what the plantings would be, to tending to the completed gardens that she admired. Kate admitted to herself that the gardens would never have been all that they could be, without Ben. And neither would she.

Kate thought back to something Virginia had said during one of their walks through the gardens: *Patience is required when dealing with herbs.*

Kate knew that this applied to most things in nature, and even to relationships.

She and Ben took that trip to Ocracoke when Kate got home from England, and it was a turning point for them. She had thought that she was the one who needed to be completely honest about their relationship and how she had been feeling. But she soon learned that there are two sides to every story. And Ben had finally admitted that he was afraid of losing her to her former life, and it had taken every bit of self-control he had to not stop her from going to Rye.

"I didn't want you to go, but I knew that you had to," he had told her, as they walked the beach late one night. "But you didn't tell me why, and that made it even harder. And not hearing from you...I know we made promises to talk as often as we could, and I know I could have called you, too, but the longer it went without us talking to each other...it wasn't good. I need us to be honest with each other, no matter what. I was starting to make plans about what I'd do if you decided not to come back, or decided to give up Howard's Walk. I was miserable. I don't want to go through that again."

Honesty can be painful. Opening up that place in your heart that wants to stay closed can be terrifying. Admitting to Ben that she didn't really understand why she had to go to England, either, was the first step. But then she took another step, and then another, even trying to explain that there must have been something outside herself that was drawing her to Rye, too.

Learning about Arabella and experiencing the frightening events with Virginia Calloway, in a way, had helped put together some other missing pieces in her life—pieces that she had not even known were missing. But Ben took those steps with her, and they discovered, in the end, that in spite of everything, they had confidence in their future together, and they both gained a peace in their hearts that they thought had been lost.

Later that morning, while loading brush into a wheelbarrow, Kate turned her head at the sound of two short beeps in the driveway.

"The mail's early today," she said.

"They're trying to beat the heat, like everybody, I guess." Ben leaned the shovel up against the wheelbarrow. "I could use a break."

He grabbed her hand, and they walked to the mailbox. A large, padded manila envelope was bent inside the mailbox, and Kate pulled it out with a few other pieces of mail. The return address on it surprised her.

The Rye Historical Society
300 B Cinque Ports Street
TN31 5 AF, Rye, England.

She leaned up against the side of Ben's truck and eagerly tore open the envelope. She pulled out a letter and another smaller envelope.

"This is from Winnie and Guilford," she said. "They are the couple I told you about from the historical society in Rye. They were such a big help to me when I was there."

She read the letter as Ben looked on over her shoulder.

❧

Dear Kate,

Guilford and I hope you are doing well at your home in North Carolina. We are keeping busy here, now that we have been named caretakers for some very special documents. I must update you on what has happened.

We recently received a large carton from Virginia Calloway's cousin, Hubert Calloway, along with a request to catalog and preserve the documents within it. He and his wife discovered them in Virginia's library, and indeed hidden throughout the Calloway Manor, shortly after you departed from England. We have been named as caretakers for the entirety of the Calloway family documents, and we expect many more cartons to arrive. It will keep us very busy for a long time! But we are excited to be a part of it.

The first delivery was a treasure trove of original papers from the 1700s, mostly Calloway family history written out in letters and journal pages and a few miscellaneous books.

But this particular document that I have copied and included in this mailing, I thought was very special. It is a journal entry, apparently torn out of the daily journal of Devon Calloway, from late November 1766. It was found folded between the pages of one of the books about the customs officers of the late 1700s. When we read it, we knew it was something we needed to pass along to you, and I have included the copy here.

You may also want to know that Virginia Calloway was declared unfit to plead and is still in hospital due to her mental state and other health concerns since you left. It is unclear what the future holds for her now. We were saddened to hear of this, and of what you endured at her hand, and we do hope that you are able to put it behind you and hold on to fond memories of your time here in Rye, and with us at the Rye Historical Society.

Perhaps this letter will give some measure of closure for you. We wish you all the best, and hope that someday we may visit with you again here in Rye.

Regards,

Guilford and Winnie

Kate opened the second envelope and pulled out the photocopy enclosed in it. As she grasped its contents, she read it out loud through her tears.

Journal entry: 30 November 1766

A man has come forth with a declaration and witness of an event on 18 November of this year. It is a tragic truth that he swears to on the

Bible. It is his word that he witnessed a young woman and two men struggling on the cliffs at Beachy Head on that day. The young woman was tormented by one of the men riding a horse, and then beaten by the other man. It was his testimony to the officials that the man on foot did push the young woman from the cliff and watched as she fell to a certain death on the rocks below. The offending man who committed the murder was recognized as the sea smuggler William Courbain, whose ship, The Grand Lady, was in battle with my own customs cutter, The Courageous, on 17 November 1766. The Grand Lady sunk to the bottom with its cargo, and it was believed at the time that some men did escape and swam to shore.

William Courbain was one of those men.

The man who came forth with this declaration described the young woman to me. He believed, as do I, that the young woman was Arabella Courbain.

My guilt is great. Miss Courbain came to me with word of her father's landing in Romney Marsh. Her word was true, and I did not protect her from the sure fate that she faced at the hands of her father. She was the mother of my nephew, who now seems lost to us forever. But I will continue to search for him.

May God forgive me.

Devon Robert Calloway

Kate began to sob, and Ben held her tight until her tears finally slowed, and her trembling stopped.

Kate could now acknowledge one final, profound truth. Arabella Courbain's journey and her fate were not simply the stuff of legends, woven into a folktale of half-truths and conjecture, and used to manipulate and control others, as Virginia Calloway had tried to do. Arabella was very real. She had lived in a time that was not kind to women. She had loved and lost and sacrificed her happiness for the good of her child. She had chosen the difficult path, and in the end, had suffered the consequences.

Perhaps it was that very strength that carried Arabella's story forward into the future. Perhaps it was that strength that had drawn Kate to the ancient town of Rye to uncover, once and for all, the truth about the legend of Arabella. And most importantly, to begin that journey of discovering the truth about herself.

THE END

ACKNOWLEDGMENTS

TO MY FAMILY, Dan, Michelle, and Tyler, thank you for your encouragement, advice, and support—it meant so much to me as I wrote this book!

To my editor, Anna Benn, whose advice in the continuation of Kate Tyler's journey was invaluable.

To the team at Light Messages Torchflame Books, thank you for your professionalism, encouragement, and advice in making this book a reality.

To my fellow writers in the NC Scribes Writers Circle, thank you for your encouragement, support, and feedback on this manuscript! I am honored to be included in this circle of amazing talent!

And finally, I can't imagine a more wonderful setting for this story than Rye, England. It is a place that will always be in my heart! The history and traditions of Rye and the surrounding area of East Sussex drew me in and made Kate's journey more wonderful than I could have ever imagined.

Two locations in the book deserve special mention: The Mermaid Inn and The Rye Harbour Nature Reserve.

The Mermaid Inn on Mermaid Street in Rye dates back to the 15th century and earlier. This magnificent inn, rich in history, balanced between the ancient and the modern, was the perfect setting for Kate to begin her journey. I invite you to visit the inn online and learn more about its fascinating history at www.mermaidinn.com.

The Rye Harbour Nature Reserve is home to thousands of species, some considered endangered in Britain. Kate's hike through the reserve gives her a view of a variety of habitats: saltmarsh, shingle ridges, sand, marsh, and woodland. The reserve is home to the Camber Castle and the Red Roofed Hut, two famous landmarks that capture Kate's imagination along her journey. The Sussex Wildlife Trust continues its important work to preserve and protect the wildlife and habitats in the reserve. Visit them online at rye.sussexwildlifetrust.org.uk for more information about the amazing Rye Harbour Nature Reserve.

ABOUT THE AUTHOR

AWARD-WINNING AUTHOR NANCY WAKELEY grew up in the New York State Finger Lakes region and now resides in Apex, North Carolina, with her husband. She completed her degree in health information management from Stephens College, Columbia, Missouri, and spent her career in the health information management and clinical research fields until the writing muse lured her into retirement.

Nancy belongs to the North Carolina Writer's Network, NC Scribes Writers Circle and the Military Writers Society of America and gives back to her community through volunteerism. She embraces all things fashioned out of musical notes and words as the ultimate reflection of life's exquisite journey.

The Legend is the second of the *Kate Tyler Mysteries* following Nancy's award winning debut novel, *Heirloom*.

Connect with Nancy:

Facebook @authornancywakeley
Twitter @nancywakeley
Instagram @nancywakeley2
www.nancywakeley.com

Heirloom

BY NANCY WAKELEY

KATE TYLER IS ALREADY IN A LIFE CRISIS when she inherits Howard's Walk in Eden Springs, North Carolina, after the sudden death of her twin sister, Rebecca. The last thing she wants is to be tied down to an abandoned estate and its neglected once-famous gardens. She vows to sell it as quickly as possible.

When secrets begin to surface within the old house, Kate questions the connection she feels with a mentally challenged young man from the farm next door. When she meets the owner of a local garden center, she begins to open her heart again to the possibility of love.

Kate learns that a powerful and vengeful man who was denied ownership of Howard's Walk in the past is determined to finally own it at any cost. She must decide.